Rise

Of The

Hell Fire

Storm

BOOK 1

Damian L. Johnson

ISBN 978-1-0980-7851-5 (paperback)
ISBN 978-1-0980-7852-2 (digital)

Christian Faith Publishing, Inc.
832 Park Avenue
Meadville, PA 16335
www.christianfaithpublishing.com

Printed in the United States of America

Elements of Peace Co.
Other books to come:

Book 2: *The 12 Elemental Keys*

Book 3: *The Universal Bind*

Book 4: *Rage of the Black Storm*

Book 5: *I Met a Female Dragon*

Book 6: *Cries of Mother Earth*

Book 7: *The Fall of the Dark Dragon*

To Grandma Georgia, aka GG, the one who believed in me
And to my firstborn, Damian Johnson Jr.,
a love that could never be broken

Contents

Time Line

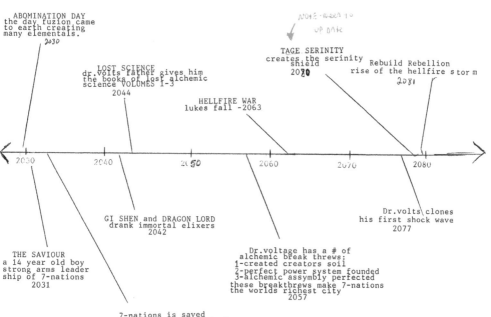

ABOMINATION DAY
the day fuzion came
to earth creating
many elementals.
2030

LOST SCIENCE
dr.volts father gives him
the books of lost alchemic
science VOLUMES 1-3
2044

NOTE-NEED TO
UP DATE

TAGE SERINITY
creates the serinity
shield
2070

Rebuild Rebellion
rise of the hellfire storm
2081

HELLFIRE WAR
lukes fall -2063

2030   2040   2050   2060   2070   2080

GI SHEN and DRAGON LORD
drank immortal elixers
2042

THE SAVIOUR
a 14 year old boy
strong arms leader
ship of 7-nations
2031

Dr.voltage has a # of
alchemic break threws:
1-created creators soil
2-perfect power system founded
3-alchemic assymbly perfected
these breakthrews make 7-nations
the worlds richest city
2057

Dr.volts clones
his first shock wave
2077

7-nations is saved
dragon lord has a war with the
grifflings for clearing the lands
of wild creatures surrounding
7-nations 2033

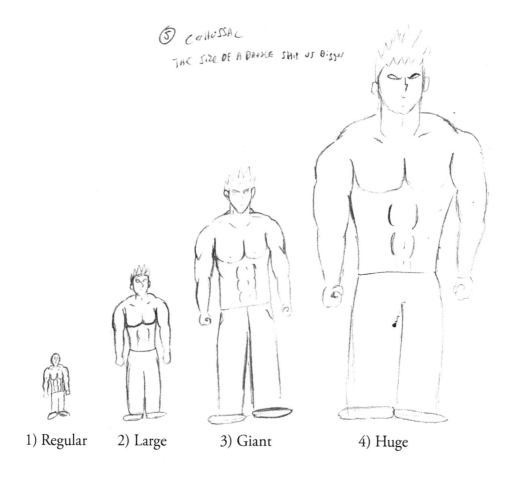

⑤ COllOSSAL

THE SIZE OF A BATTLE SHIP or Bigger

1) Regular   2) Large   3) Giant   4) Huge

Chapter Cipher

Elevation

In the year 2030, an astral diamond meteorite came to the planet earth. This meteorite dug and burrowed itself deep into the earth and linked an emerald beam of energy to the earth's core. This link of unknown energy destroyed most of earth's environment and almost left the human race extinct. The emerald energies link to the earth's core caused a chain reaction or blast-like wave that spread great amounts of emerald energy like a blanket over earth. Then the energy returned to the meteorite, but the wave of energy was now fused with violet hues of the fifth element. This glowing fifth element was the spirit energy from all of the lost life on earth. *(Keep in mind that energy cannot be created or destroyed).*

The people and the living creatures of earth that were too close to the meteorite when it came to earth met instant death. The farthest away from the meteorite was thought to be safe until…people and creatures on earth started becoming blind, sick, and paralyzed. In some cases, it was much worse… Life started mutating into things unknown to man. No place was safe.

Wild abomination mutated creatures suddenly stood bold looking into the face of humans. Every aspect of creation on earth had reached a greater level of intelligence. Many creatures (see mutated races) appeared all over earth after the wave of emerald energy returned back to its meteor shard source deep in the earth. These wildling humanoid races were created with deadly strength, and most creatures held a great amount of hatred for the human race. This threatened the survival of the human race even more. But the will of the human race was strong, and they fought for earth and their existence.

The remaining human survivors of the planet earth relocated to the farthest and most safe location. A rare place that was unaffected by the meteor shards wave. This place was the heart of Asia.

A few humans who came in contact with the wave of energy and lived to tell about it heard a voice in their heads.

Fuzion's Message to the Greater Essence 24

Hello, all... I am called Fuzion. I am the astral diamond of energy who has linked to Gaia's core. I am a supreme being, the highest form of energy which is thought. I am a great gathered amount of knowledge, wisdom, and understanding that came from the source. I am one with all life, nature, and energy.

I have come from the depths of all universe to elevate life on this planet. I have chosen...or more like you have chosen to be the first twenty-four human elementals in this realm of existence.

I have given each of you an elemental orb bound to your spirit so that now you can wield the elements with your spirit energy. This power must be used to sustain the universal balance...

I am the sixth element and the emerald light of elevation. The time is now for this planet's awakening.

Mutated Races

When the meteor shard fused to earth, fusions worldwide spread of energy created not only elemental orbs but also many different wild creatures that evolved into intelligent races and beings.

This day is known to all elementals as abomination day. The first elementals who became intelligent enough realized the true goal in existence was to seek out higher knowledge and rare power in preparation for ascending. Leaders of great nations and cities even set out on a quest where no elementals have gone.

These elemental races learned fast and grew just like humans but with rare abilities from their primal race such as changing shape to their animal form or sharp claws or deadly venom.

Not all results of abomination day came with great creations. Some mutations resulted in deadly nasty vile creatures whose sole purpose is to cause havoc and destruction on planet Gaia. Here are a few examples of mutated races one might encounter in the world.

For this very reason, the sharklings have an underground city under the desert of seven nations. This city is called understand city and very few elementals know about this city.

Ana-Cobra

A large humanoid mix of an anaconda and cobra. This creature's special abilities are spitting venom and changing shape to either snake.

Ape

Medium, giant, or large apes who are known for their brute arm strength. An elemental ape's fur is always the color of their primary element.

Dark bats

Creepy-looking, dark, leathery humanoid bats. Known for their night vision and demon-like wings, the dark bat's common size is giant, and their common primary element is shadow.

Cheetah

A rare race known for its deadly speed, a cheetah can also change back and forth to humanoid and cheetah form.

Drakes

Drakes, short for drako-
nians, are descendants of all rep-
tilian creatures. They are known
for their feared dragon breath
and their ability to change into
dragon form. A drake's skin color
is determined by their primary
elemental orb.

Griffling

Grifflings are tall skinny
muscular birdlike humanoids
with powerful wings. Grifflings
can change into a griffin, which
has an upper body of an eagle,
a lion's lower body, and a long
spiky tail.

Polar bear

The common element for this large creature is water and ice. Polar bears are rare strong humanoids found in cold regions.

Sharkling

The meteor shard gave the sharkling race the gift or curse to walk on land and burrow but at a deadly cost. This race lost the ability to breathe underwater for long periods of time. Ninety percent of the sharkling race's primary orb is earth. For this reason, the underground city under the desert of 7-Nations south that few know about.

Titans

This large human race is said to be a different form of evolved humans. Titans are known for their pride in physical strength and the ability to survive on the brink of death.

Fox-wolf

This abomination race is known for its ability to change back and forth from fox to wolf. Either form gives this creature the cunning fox-wolf speed, which allows this race to run at a high rate or speed.

Shape-shifting

Hawk

This humanoid's beautiful feathers shine and glow. The hawk is known for amazing air combat and its feared element ball shower power that rains down from its wings.

Liger

A liger is a mutation of a lion and tiger. Although this is an abomination of a race, ligers do not have the change-shape ability. But they are still strong creatures.

Pure elementals

When the meteor shard came to earth, Fuzion's energy manifested pure elemental energy into humanoid beings of free will and spirit.

Panthrainian

Wild panthers exposed to the energy of Fuzion changed these creatures into gray furred muscular humanoids that roam earth in packs.

force   EArth

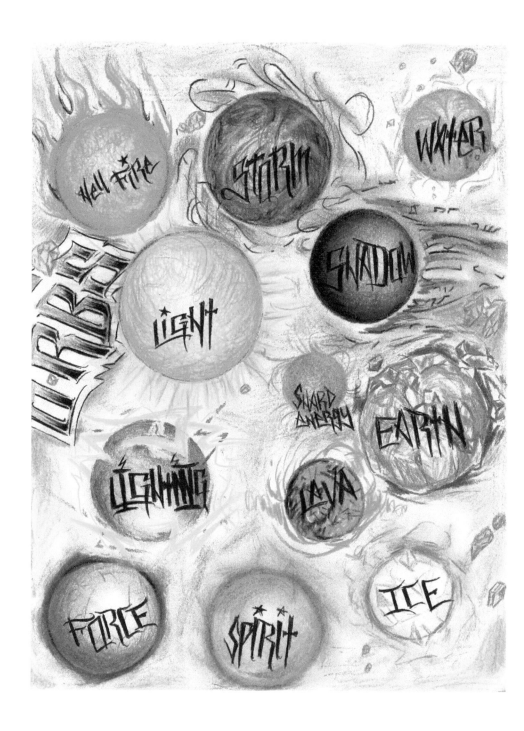

Chapter 1

Savior

The human race had lost everything before the arrival of Fuzion. Technology, the economy, and society fell to chaos. As an attempt to start over and rebuild their lives from nothing, the imperial king and current nation leader of China elected six other world leaders who survived the wave to help him govern a new-formed province known as 7-Nations. Each nation would have a job to help rebuild human civilization. All of the remaining human race came together to survive by using what was left of earth's natural resources and elements.

With the positivity and will of the human race to survive, things got a lot worse. There was barely enough food and water for one nation of people; and here stood seven groups of different people with different lifestyles, skin color, and minds. But they all had the same thing in their hearts, love and the will to survive. But the last nation of humans would soon fall from attacks from deadly creatures, bloody riots among themselves, and the gathered fear and greed. The Chinese leader called a meeting of world leaders.

Nation leaders

- United Sates president—a beautiful, wise, loving woman who had light-brown skin. She went by the name of Oprara.
- China imperial king—a man whose family's bloodline led Asia for the past decade. The imperial king's father named him Lee.
- African spiritual leader—a dark-skinned man who returned to Africa to the lost motherland. He was known as Zu Zane Cipher.

- Canadian prime minister—a half-Black-and-White male who went by the name of Quake.
- Soviet Russian Union leader—a sixty-year-old general who had strong-armed the position as czar.
- Australian president—a wildlife specialist who was forced into leadership because he was the oldest from Australia. His name was Crocodile Sundee.
- United Kingdom queen—a woman who had an angelic face and pale skin; her name was Angelina.

The meeting was held in the nation's largest dojo. The topic of discussion was survival. The nation leaders would brainstorm and vote on a solution to their problems. After hours of arguing and no solution, the Chinese leader stood up and said, "Have any of you heard of the spiritual elemental powers the meteorite can give?"

The imperial king stared into the fearful eyes of his fellow world leaders and said, "What if we can use these powers to save humanity, or even human evolution is possible?"

"How can we harness this power, Lee?" said Zu Zane.

Lee said, "From my understanding, a select few have been chosen to wield these gifts."

"A gift from whom?" asked Queen Angelina.

"From the universal heavens," said Lee.

"What proof do you have to believe that the meteorite gives gifts and is the answer to our problems?" said US President Oprara.

"Son, come!" yelled the imperial king.

Seconds later, a young Asian boy no more than the age of fourteen entered the dojo and said, "Yes, Father," in a calm voice.

"Show them," said the imperial king.

The boy placed his palm on his chest, closed his eyes, and concentrated for ten seconds. Then the boy pulled a white silvery orb from his chest. The energies in his palm whined and hummed. The orb first appeared small, and then it expanded to the size of a soccer ball. The boy looked down at the orb in his palm and said, "This is a power orb of force, all of my chi and life energy and spirit bound to the force element and compacted into an orb by thought. I am a human evolved to a human elemental." The boy smiled as his silvery light lit the dojo.

"H-h-h-how do you know this?" stuttered Sundee.

The boy's smile widened as he said, "Fuzion, the meteor shard, told me in my mind. Fuzion told me there are more human elementals like me, and when my will is strong enough, I'll realize the truth and be the first human elemental to ascend."

"That is enough! This is an outrage," shouted the Russian leader rudely cutting the boy off. The Russian leader stood up and shouted, "The human race is on the brink of extinction, and you bring a child to this committee with cheap tricks and silly talk of orbs and elementals! Lee, you are a fool!"

Spittle flew from the mouth of the Russian leader as his words made the world leaders uneasy. "Calm down, Czar. You will respect me and my son in our home," said the Chinese leader.

The boy looked up as he absorbed his force orb back into his chest. Then the boy stepped close enough to whisper to the Russian leader, "Do you not believe?"

"Mind your tongue, boy. Speak when spoken to—" said the Russian leader, but before the czar could finish his sentence, a deadly ball of force energy came from the boy's right hand and slammed the Russian leader into the wall, killing him instantly.

"Now...does anyone else have any doubts of my power?" said the boy, drunk with power as force energy filled his eyes in a silver glow. Then force energy formed an aura around him. No one said a word. All of the world leaders except Lee and Zu Zane looked down, not wanting to make eye contact with the boy.

"That's enough, Angel," said the imperial king.

"Very well, Father," said the boy as he powered down the lashing force aura around him. The boy looked around the dojo at the fearful nation leaders and said, "Do not fear me, Leaders. I am the chosen one, humanity's savior. I think I'll fill the open nation leader's seat, unless someone disagrees."

No one said a word.

The African spiritual leader said, "Tell me, Angel, can you sense these energies in a being?"

"Yes, I can," said the boy in an innocent tone.

The African spiritual leader said, "My son, he's about your age. He's been acting weird as of lately ever since we got separated on our way here. I had lost him. I was sure he was dead. Then in the impossible odds, he met us at the gate of this province. Now he leaves on missions and journeys to secret locations, and our father-son talks are rare nowadays. Perhaps, you should meet him. His name is Luke Saint."

Chapter 2

Orbs, the Story of Creation

I am Fate, a being of light. I read you this story from the book of balance. Most elementals on earth believe earth's destruction was caused by Fuzion when he linked to the core of the planet. The sad truth is, we the higher beings and wild creatures destroyed earth's surface by fighting over territory and faith, as well as control of the meteor shards power on what the humans call Abomination Day. The energy of Fuzion only dug a hole in the earth's crust in the center of what the humans call Brazil, which is now called the Land of Lost Orb Souls. The link of Fuzion's emerald energy to the earth's core caused a wave of energy that killed many, but all life and spirit that were taken are still stored at the Land of Lost Orb Souls today in the form of many different elemental orbs in the circular stream of mixed violet spirits and emerald shard energy above the meteor shard. When an elemental orb is created, the spirit must always be bound to an element because the spirit is the foundation of existence.

Spirit, essence, or energy always existed in some form or another. It only evolves, so in all truth, the lost life on earth is not truly lost, but the balance must be sustained.

The balance is the equal use of energy from all in existence. Those on earth and those in the universal heavens all draw power from the same source and all. As long as this balance is sustained and Fuzion is well the earth and all creatures on this planet will live forever. My job as the noble god of light is to make sure this balance is never broken.

Twelve Elements

Fire, water, air, earth, ice, lightning, and *force.* Some would say that force is not an element, but it is force and the will of all that hold the universe together. *Light, shadow,* and *shard energies* are advanced elements. Then you have the lava and spirit elements which are outlawed elements because they draw too much power from the source. Shard energy is an outlawed element also.

NATION
CLOTHING
LINE

DANTE SAINT

Chapter 3

Absorb the Truth

Fifty years later in 7-Nations

Dante lay on his back in the Lotus Forest, which was surrounded by a beautiful glowing lake. The lake was made from daily offerings of lotus monks' healing and energizing waters from their special amulets. One drink of these mystical waters cured wounds and rid one of fatigue, and Dante really loved the soothing taste of the waters.

Dante was eighteen years old with wavy light-brown hair and red eyes. He's six feet tall and weighed two hundred pounds. He, however, was exhausted from a series of brutal training sessions from Lou Shen, his mentor and grandfather. Dante's body ached, and too much consumption of the lotus waters in a day lessened the water's healing results on the body. Dante pushed himself to his limits multiple times today, and the waters stopped healing him.

Lou Shen, a fearless lotus monk, was forty years old and had an orb level 2. Dante and his grandfather met up at the Lotus Forest every morning before work to learn new elemental attacks and fighting five styles and ways to better control and manipulate orb chi. But most importantly, Lou Shen trained Dante with a goal to see if Dante was ready to absorb the next elemental power orb to obtain the next level of power. Secret lessons based on absorbing orbs and also having orbs in 7-Nations could get them both killed if Dragon Lord where to find out. This was against the law in 7-Nations.

"Grandson, do you remember the lesson about the relationships between the chakras and elements?" said Lou Shen in a calm voice as he stood with his hands behind his back.

"Yes, my generation calls the chakra's hypermodes. The first hypermode is earth, which is the personal seat of power, connection, and charisma." Dante grunted, sat up, and then said, "The second hypermode is the water element and also ice, connection intelligence and vital life force. Then the third hypermode is fire connection, which is strength. The fourth hypermode is wind, based on speed and breath. The heart chakra's connection is wisdom," said Dante.

"Very good, grandson. There are more chakras that we have not discussed in great detail, but we will eventually. Some say that if you can raise your energies to the highest chakra or reach orb level 7, you can tap into the power of the gods or, simply put, ascend. By absorbing elemental orbs, you naturally raise the energies within your being," said Lou Shen as he grabbed a power orb carrier from his bag by a tree. The orb carrier glowed with an orb of grayish-blue energy inside. Lou Shen walked over to Dante and said, "This orb belonged to a good friend of your mother's. He was killed by Dragon Lord fifteen or sixteen years ago for fighting Dragon Lord over your mother. I don't know the story in great detail, but before he died, he sent me his seeker orb. It has the special speed ability which will make you faster."

Dante asked, "How did you know that the seeker orb was coming to you?"

Lou Shen said, "I had a feeling, and I sensed the energies coming. Plus with my position secretly aiding the rebellion of Dragon Lord, it's always good to keep an orb carrier in arm's reach."

Dante said, "Can I ask you a serious question, Grampa?"

"Absolutely, grandson," said Lou Shen as he sat next to Dante holding the orb carrier.

Dante paused, looking at the orb, and then he took a deep breath and said, "Did my parents really lead the rebellion all those years ago? It seem like no one knows or talks about it."

Lou Shen said, "Your parents were great leaders, but you must understand something, grandson. Your parents and your hellfire clan were strong warriors, but the hellfire war came too soon, and your father was not prepared. Your father was kindhearted and a noble, orb level 5. He trained his mind, body, and spirit to balance the elemental powers within so he would not become evil and crazy with power. At a young age, Dragon Lord strong-armed leadership of 7-Nations by killing anyone who stood in his way. Then when Dragon Lord would fight off a deadly creature that attacked 7-Nations on the brink of death, Dragon Lord would fearlessly absorb an orb to be victorious. The killings and the lack of will to control so much power drove Dragon Lord crazy. So when your father and Dragon Lord fought, Luke barely lost even though Dragon Lord had one more orb than your father. Your father is an honored hellfire clan leader, and many hellfire warriors died with your parents that night, almost leaving your clan and hellfire human race extinct. Now I can only count twenty-five hellfire humans alive today—eleven and you in this city and fourteen in the world."

"When I absorbed my father's orb a few months ago, it almost killed me. The power was too much for me to handle. If it wasn't for the light being there guiding me through, I wouldn't have made it."

"Your father's orb is a greater essence orb. Only twenty-four exist. These orbs have great power and give natural ability and were only given to a select few on Abomination Day."

"I'm not ready." Dante looked at the orb in his grandfather's hands.

Lou Shen looked into Dante's eyes and said, "Nonsense. I have trained you all this time for this very moment. You just have to believe in yourself. You are an orb level 3 hellfire human elemental. You have inherited a water orb from your mother and a powerful energy fire orb from your father. This combination of power makes you very strong. Your chi is so great it's hard for you to hide. I can sense your massive aura from far away. You can't see it, but I know you are ready."

"Each time you try to absorb an orb on top of your own power, it gets harder to advance orb levels. I have seen elementals get obliterated at dragon tournaments for being too weak while trying to absorb orbs. We will both be killed if I can't contain the power."

"Listen, grandson, Dragon Lord must be defeated. The world nations are tired of Dragon Lord's evil ways. You must surpass him in strength and avenge your parents and fallen clan's deaths. Use that anger, hurt, and loss to fuel your orb absorption."

Dante touched the orb carrier and said, "May the being of light guide me once again." Then Dante stood up and got into ready position.

"I won't let you die, son. If it becomes too much, I'll take it out if you can't absorb it."

"Right," said Dante in an unsure tone.

"Now clear your mind of doubt, and let your energy run freely," said Lou Shen as he stood up and lifted the top of the orb carrier.

The storm power orb shot out of the orb carrier and zipped up and straight. The quick old monk caught the orb with his right hand while holding his right wrist with his left hand. In the same split second, Lou Shen dropped the orb carrier to get a better grip on the orb. Lou Shen held his wrist so that the orb wouldn't attempt to travel into his body. The winds around the orb started lashing out deadly spasms of grayish-blue storm energy. In a few seconds, Lou Shen got the orb completely under his control. Then he raced toward Dante and shoved the beautiful glowing orb into Dante's chest. Dante staggered back a few steps from the impact, letting his body take in the orb. Then Dante clenched his fist and screamed for what seemed like eternity. His legs grew weak, and he fell forward on his hands and knees.

"You must let all your power out. Do it now, son!" shouted Lou Shen.

"I c-can'tt... Tooo m-muchhh!" yelled Dante between breaths and throat-burning screams.

"Very well, son. Give it back then," said Lou Shen in disappointment as he kicked Dante's right shoulder. Dante fell on his back in unbearable pain. Lou Shen leaned over Dante and put his hand over Dante's chest and summoned orb. The orb came out of Dante's chest halfway, making humming sounds.

Dante grabbed the orb and absorbed it back into his chest while rolling around screaming, "I... I...won't...give...up!"

"I won't let you die, son. You have a purpose," screamed Lou Shen as he approached Dante to take the orb out once more.

"Get...baack!" snarled Dante. Lou Shen froze in his tracks when he looked into his grandson's eyes and saw a storm of red fire and bluish-gray storm fight for control. Dante got back on his hands and knees, punched the ground with a powerful blow, and yelled, "Ahhh!" as the crater formed from a fiery blow from Dante's fist. Lou Shen teleported in glowing mist gaining some distance from Dante, as the young hellfire warrior let off another ground-rattling, chaotic fiery punch. Dante slowly stood up as blue-gray waves of wind energy started to form around his body. The storm formed a colossal sphere around Dante, and elemental wind energy started forming all around the sphere in a tornado like fashion. Then the sphere of storm energy lifted Dante thirty-five feet into the air while destroying the trees around.

Lou Shen shouted, "That's it, my boy. Let it all out. Then use your fire element to contain the wind element."

The energy sphere surrounding Dante got bigger and bigger until finally a vicious fire energy covered the sphere from bottom to top. Then the sphere shrank until just Dante remained outlined in a red aura of power. Dante's body build was slightly larger and more muscular. A hellfire aura surrounded Dante as he started to fall out of the sky. The fiery aura slowly eased him to the ground ten feet away from Lou Shen. Dante turned off his fiery aura and said, "The wind orb belonged to someone named Johnathan Swift. His spirit showed me him and my mother living a happy life in storm nation with a baby boy." Dante let silence settle in, and then he asked, "Did you know?" Lou Shen just smiled remaining silent. Dante hugged his grandfather and said, "Why didn't you tell me I have a brother?"

Chapter 4

Life in 7-Nations

The great lotus lake and river shone and glowed turquoise in the bright summer day. Inside White Lotus Compound 1, Gi Shen, who was the leader of the lotus clan, taught a group of kids about how things were run in 7-Nations today. Gi Shen lectured every day at his dojo to anyone who would listen. The wise monk's audience were mostly children from his water clan and a few from the orphanage. The children listen eagerly seated in Indian style on a padded mat in the center of the dojo.

Gi Shen spoke. "All of 7-Nations work together to sustain life in this great province. Each nation has its own elemental clan, as well as a very important job which fuels 7-Nations' economy and dominates the world trade market. First, we have the hellfire clan. They are a small group of strong fearless fire elementals who mostly work in the mines or at the slaughter house. Some highly skilled fire humans work as weapon masons," said the monk, pausing for questions.

"My daddy said a lot of fire people are dead. What happened to them?" asked a little girl.

Gi Shen said, "Most of them were killed in a deadly war seventeen years ago for defying Dragon Lord's rule. Less than thirty fire humans live today. Mostly rogue ninjas or soldiers live in the wilderness. It is rumored there is a secret city somewhere in the tainted lands, but it is very dangerous outside of the 7-Nations gates. One would find mutated creatures, unsafe environments, very little safe natural resources, death at every step. Now hellfire nation is mostly ran by anyone who chooses to stay there. Second, we have subzero, the clan of ice which is located near Blizzard Mountain. In Ice Nation, it stays cold all year round because of the icy mountain and a few minor alchemic climate modifications from the thunderbolt clan. Athena Frost is the clan leader of the ice element. This cold nation has three great warehouses that hold great amounts of frozen fish."

"Where do they get all of the fish from?" asked a little boy.

Gi Shen said, "The fish comes from the ocean, and some meat comes from the slaughterhouse in Fire Nation. There is also a large market and small city inside Blizzard Mountain. In the icy market, one could find thick fur coats, large quantities of fish at low prices, and rare weapons of ice. The ocean squad's job is the most dangerous job in 7-Nations, brave elementals of the ice clan, group into squads of five or less. The squads travel deep into the ocean on an iceberg created by one of the members of the squad. A rope is tied to the iceberg, and the net is thrown into the ocean to catch fish, but this also attracts deadly abomination sea creatures. Dragon Lord does not allow the ocean squad to take ships into the ocean, because they get destroyed very quickly.

"Third, we have the thunderbolt clan of the lightning element. These great minds are the inventors and the holders of technology. Thunder Kingdom is an electric-gated nation that powers 7-Nations. Dr. Voltage is a brilliant alchemist and scientist who leads the thunderbolt clan and provides 7-Nations with new and better technology. Some would say that Dr. Volts is crazy, but he has earned his respect as a scientist because he has successfully created a bioengineered elemental human years ago, and now Dr. Volts is the founder of the bioengineered race as alchemist all over the world copy Dr. Volts's work. Thunder Kingdom is mostly a massive factory and assembly line with all sorts of alchemic experiments. Dr. Volts oversees these experiments that are sometimes forced by Dragon Lord. The thunderbolt clan also built 7-Nations' only two trains," said the monk.

"How come 7-Nations only has two trains?" shouted someone in great excitement.

Gi Shen said, "The gated 7-Nations are cluttered enough. I don't think our great province could manage to fit another train."

"Aawww!" whined the group of children in a playful manner.

"Also the thunderbolt clan is famous for the alchemic invention known as the serenity shield. The alchemist Tage Serenity just created the serenity shield days ago. The serenity shield is a war machine and suit of armor fused with orbs capable of great power. Oh, and Dr. Volts has three volumes of lost science from long ago. These books are priceless, and they are the foundation of Dr. Volts's many alchemic experiments."

"I want to be an alchemist," said a little girl from the Earth Nation named Alora.

"Well, you can't. Only lightning elementals can," said a little boy.

Then the little girl said, "Yes, I can. My daddy says I can be whatever I want to be in life."

Monk Gi Shen said, "I agree, young Alora. Anyone can be an alchemist or whatever they want to be as long as they put their mind to it. Earth is the fourth nation and clan of 7-Nations. Earth Nation's city is the biggest city in 7-Nations. On top of a cliff, an earth building called Earth Nation Center splits Earth Nation and Force Nation. Elizabeth Granite is the clan leader of Earth Nation. She is a beautiful queen. The earth clan's main job is to build and repair homes. If an earth elemental cannot build, then they work in landscaping. Elizabeth wants to expand 7-Nations and clear the ruined land outside of the city's gates and over time return to earth its mothers and fathers of civilization. Elizabeth's ancestors were some of the architects who rebuilt 7-Nations after the arrival of the meteor shards.

"Our fifth nation is called Windmill City. This is home to the clan of wind clouds and storm, these elementals call themselves the Merciful Storm. Windmill City is led by a wise man known as Lee Windol, who takes pride in training wind elementals in his spare time at the wind arena high in the sky. Lee Windol is in charge of 7-Nations agriculture and also operates the train with thunderbolt elementals. The two trains are 7-Nations' main source transportation. 7-Nations' population rides one train to get from nation to nation, and the second train is used to transport goods. Lee Windol also runs the produce market in the wind nation.

"The sixth clan is called the White Lotus Monks. These elementals wield the healing waters of life. Thanks to Fuzion, the fountain of life in our souls is amplified. We are peaceful selfless monks and the healers of 7-Nations. We are the backbone and the main reason we have made it this far as the human elemental race. I am the leader of the lotus monk clan. I teach mastery of self, chi control, as well as meditation. I teach my clan to help and heal others. Selfless acts are rewarded in the life after death or interlife of the infinite. There are three lotus compound dojos in 7-Nations, where monks provide healing and martial arts training and teach knowledge and understanding to all clans."

Chapter 5

Fearless and Foolish

"Brother, you left your post. Something must have happened… Is everything all right?" said Monk Gi Shen.

"Everything is fine at my post, brother," said Lou Shen with annoyance in his voice.

"Then what brings you to my acquaintance, my younger brother? You know Dragon Lord does not like order broken in his province," said Gi Shen.

"You know I'd never cower before. What makes this visit any different?" said Lou Shen.

"It's just that our lord has been on edge lately," said Gi Shen.

"When is he not?" said Lou Shen.

"It's Dante, isn't it?" said Gi Shen.

"Wow, you may be the next chosen scion of the prophecy." Lou Shen laughed.

"Enough of your games, brother. I sensed a massive power in the forest yesterday morning. Was it him?" asked Monk Gi Shen in a serious tone.

"Yes, brother, I've been training Dante for a while now. He has advanced to orb level 4, and I need—"

Before Lou Shen could finish his sentence, Monk Gi Shen shouted, "Silence, children!" An uncomfortable quiet filled the dojo. Startled kids stopped playing and laughing amongst themselves. The children stared at the White Lotus brothers with open mouths. *Awws* and *shhushes* echoed through the dojo from surprised children seeing their teacher out of character.

"That is all for today, children. Come back tomorrow morning, and we will continue where we stopped today's lessons," said Gi Shen.

Children gathered their belongings moaning, "Aww, man," and disappointments for the day's lesson ending early. Once the last child walked out of the dojo doors, the lotus brothers stared at each other in silence… Then Lou Shen said, "Brother, you must understand my reasons for—"

"Foolish, have you learned nothing in all these years?" said monk Gi Shen, cutting his brother off in a low raspy angry voice.

"Brother, you are not the only one with visions from the first scion. Soon the prophecy told by the fifth scion (living wisdom) will be fulfilled. The rebellion still stands strong as ever," said Lou Shen in a calm pleading voice.

"Nonsense. The fifth scion's time is short. Dragon Lord has her locked away in his personal quarters. She mumbles countless riddles day and day out. Just the other day, she foretold that the prophecy will not be possible for another five to six years, yet I sense strong auras in young elementals every day," said Gi Shen.

"The fifth scion's visions have come true before," said Lou Shen.

"Even so, it's only a matter of time before Dragon Lord tires of her games and decides to end her life," said Monk Gi Shen as he walked to his chair and sat down in the corner of the dojo.

"The fifth scion says what she says for a reason. You of all people should know that," said Lou Shen as he walked over to his older brother's chair and took a knee in front of him.

Gi Shen shook his head and said, "The rebellion stands with you now, but they will cower at the sight of Dragon Lord's power."

"All the rebellion needs is a strong and smart leader, and I intend to bring forth that leader whether it be Dante or his older brother," said Lou Shen.

"And what will happen if Dante's mind is not strong enough for all that power? He may be come just as evil as Dragon Lord or maybe even worse," said Gi Shen.

"That's what we train for, brother. Dante has a strong mind and a very pure heart and spirit. I truly believe he may be the chosen one," said Lou Shen.

Monk Gi Shen took a deep breath and said, "Young brother, haven't we lost enough life to a pointless cause? All you have done is put targets on my head, on your head, on our grandson's head. Dragon Lord is not stupid or blind."

"But, brother, Dante is so strong. In time, he will surpass Dragon Lord," said Lou Shen.

"Five orb level-seven elementals will only be a small test for Dragon Lord's power," said Gi Shen.

"I have dedicated my life to aiding Dante on his path. It will not be easy, but it must be done for change to come," said Lou Shen.

"What a great waste of lives. The rebellion's death list grows," said Gi Shen.

"You know the greatest thing about being an elemental is anything is possible. With your help, we could—"

"You must have lost your common sense, younger brother. I will not help you on this meaningless quest," said Gi Shen, cutting his younger brother off.

"No, brother, I'm positive you won't, but maybe you could point us the right direction," pleaded Lou Shen.

"How so?" said Gi Shen.

"Dante had a vision from the wind orb during his absorption confirming what I had speculated all these years," said Lou Shen.

"And what might that be, my fearless foolish brother?" said monk Gi Shen.

"My daughter Clara left a son in Windmill City," said Lou Shen.

"Interesting news," said Gi Shen.

"Yes, it is, brother. All those years ago when you told me and Clara of Dragon Lord's choice to force my child to wed the hellfire clan leader, Clara was heartbroken because she was already in love, so she ran away to Windmill City to enjoy that love while she could. His name was Johnathan Swift. She sent me messages from time to time letting me know she was okay, but she never mentioned anything about a child," said Lou Shen. Gi Shen remained silent while rubbing his beard in deep thought.

Lou Shen said, "Tell me, brother, do you know of anyone named Johnathan Swift?"

"I think I do," said Gi Shen, searching his long memory…

Fearless Fall
Story told by Gi Shen

Sixteen years ago, a young man named J. Swift stood outside of Dragon Lord's fortress yelling for Dragon Lord to come face him. J. Swift was a strong and fast trained storm ninja who worked on the cargo train as a guard, if I'm not mistaken... He had defeated over twenty Dragon Lord guards before Dragon Lord finally showed his face. J. Swift drank his last light-and-dark elixir and asked in calm voice, "Where is she?" Dragon Lord didn't say a word... "Give her back, Angel! You have no morals," said J. Swift in anger. Dragon Lord did not say a word as he stopped five feet away from J. Swift with his hands behind his back and no emotion on his face.

J. Swift and Dragon Lord stood in the courtyard outside of the bar in Force Nation. People started to gather around as the two elementals stood bold silently staring into each other's eyes, surrounded by unconscious bodies. Both fighters had no fear as they were evenly matched in orb levels.

"Treacherous coward," snarled Swift, and he grabbed the beautiful legendary wind katana blade from his back and screamed, "Wind scar!"

J. Swift swung the energized sword in a fast underhand swing, followed by an even faster second swing, sending two giant swords of razor storm energy straight to Dragon Lord. The wind scars slammed into each other, leaving a great explosion of grayish-blue energy where Dragon Lord stood. J. Swift began to deliver a third wave of wind scars until Dragon Lord tapped J. Swift on the shoulder standing behind him. Dragon Lord laughed in J. Swift's ear and said in a mocking tone, "You will never hit me that way. Your way too slow."

"Fight me, you coward," said J. Swift through gritted teeth while he attempted a backward slash with the sword. The sword left a deadly arc of bluish-gray energy in its path. Dragon Lord easily weaved J. Swift's attack by leaning to the right in a blur of speed. J. Swift followed the second failed attack with a backward helicopter slice, twirling the sword in circles over his head, sending multiple giant wind blades of energy toward Dragon Lord. In an even faster blur of speed, Dragon Lord dropped to the floor on his back and sent two lightning-fast kicks—one to the hilt of J. Swift's legendary sword, sending the powerful weapon flying over 7-Nations' skyscraper walls. The second kick went to J. Swift's back, sending him fifty feet into the air. Tornado winds formed around J. Swift, levitating him in midair.

In an instant, J. Swift turned around in the air and screamed, "Element tornado!" throwing several tornadoes of mixed wind, fire, and lightning energies from his closed fist down at Dragon Lord as if he was punching the air.

Dragon Lord put his hands together in the shape of a diamond. He closed his eyes and whispered, "Force shield," as a silvery-white dome of energy shimmered around him in a split second. The deadly sharp razor wind mixed element tornadoes hit the dome of force energy and then bounced off and hit the ground, slicing several 360 degree cuts in the ground. The force shield around Dragon Lord disappeared as Dragon Lord said, "That was your level 4 combined elements attack, correct? My defense was my simple force shield. Make your next move count. It will be your last."

J. Swift lifted both hands to the dark sky and closed his eyes, concentrating and gathering energy. Two zips of storm energy mixed with fire and lightning shot to each of Swift's hands from the sky, forming two compacted large orbs of energy that spasmed and electrified.

"I hope you're ready for this, Angel! This is my storm blitz ascended power!" shouted Swift as he threw one mixed storm orb at Dragon Lord. Then J. Swift flew directly behind the first orb with graceful speed-building momentum from the suddenly stormy sky. J. Swift let out all of his orb chi into the second storm orb he held in front of him as he sent the power of the storm to Dragon Lord.

In the exact same second, Dragon Lord moved at the speed of thought with unseen agility and said, "Dragon force blades," and twenty different daggers of mixed force and ice collided with J. Swift's storm, devouring them into nothingness. At the last second, J. Swift spun into a quick defense of tornado windshields as he fell to the ground, barely escaping death. J. Swift lay lifeless on the ground looking at Dragon Lord as he walked in his direction.

"Do it," said J. Swift as he lay there with various cuts, burns, and numb body parts, unable to move because of the intense pain.

"Now who is the coward?" said Dragon Lord, squatting and leaning over J. Swift's face.

J. Swift spat in Dragon Lord's face and said, "You will meet your end soon enough, Angel."

Dragon Lord wiped spittle from his face as he stood up and said, "I'll show you true power before you die." Dark force electrical power started to form in Dragon Lord's palm. Then a deadly force aura formed around Dragon Lord and lifted him into the sky. The combined power in Dragon Lord's hand grew bigger and bigger until it blotted out the full moon.

"Any last words?" said Dragon Lord as he began to launch the enormous power at Swift.

"Just two, seeker orb," whispered J. Swift as he searched for a life force to send the last of his power and spirit to before the deadly blast swallowed all in its path. J. Swift's orb zipped out of his left hand and flew north into the night.

✶✶✶✶✶

"And that's how the orb came to me, weak and dim but still full of power. When Swift searched for my spirit, I felt him, so I got a power orb carrier ready," said Lou Shen.

"Is that all you have come here to ask me, brother?" said Gi Shen in still in deep thought.

"I'm sorry to ask you this, but in two days' time, I will need you to help me steal several power orbs from Dragon Lord's orb vault. Dante and I are going on a journey into the wilderness to search for Hell Mountain and join the rebellion so we can train without worry."

"That is a very dangerous journey, brother. How do you know this rebellion even exists?"

"My dreams haunt me to the point where I must find truth and freedom."

"You will find truth for sure on your quest, truth in your strength or truth at death's door from all of the crazy creatures you will encounter," said Gi Shen, looking into his younger brother's eyes with great concern and love.

"I know the odds we are up against, but I have been planning this for some time now. Will you help us or not?" said Lou Shen, staring into his older brother's eyes with determination. Monk Gi Shen moved uncomfortably in his chair.

"Brother, I have had a vision that you will go on a dangerous journey and lose your life trying to accomplish an impossible task," said Monk Gi Shen sadly.

"Dante does not consider you family. He says cowardice does not run in our bloodline. Don't you see? We must overthrow Dragon Lord at all cost. Fear and death have run 7-Nations for far too long."

"Very well, brother," said Gi Shen after a few moments of silence.

"So you will help us?" said Lou Shen as he jumped up and tackled Gi Shen playfully.

"I will help you, but you must do this my way. I see you have made up your mind. I have a friend, the leader of Earth Nation. She will help you leave 7-Nations undetected," said monk Gi Shen as he stood up and wrestled back with Lou Shen.

"Head Monk," said General Kano as he entered the doors connecting the dojo to Dragon Lord's estate.

"Yes, General," said Gi Shen, a little startled.

"Dragon Lord wishes you and your guest to come to him in his special scouter division quarters," said the orb level 7 general of Dragon Lord's army. General Kano smiled and left the dojo.

"This cannot be good. Dragon Lord must just gotten his SSD online," said Monk Gi Shen.

"Foolish cocky force general. I would give him a run for his money in battle, and I only have two orbs," said Lou Shen in disgust.

"Don't underestimate the general, brother. He led the front line of force elementals in the hellfire war seventeen years ago. Now let's go," said Monk Gi Shen. And the lotus brothers entered the steel doors leading to Dragon Lord's fortress.

Chapter 6

The Monk's Decision

The lotus brothers entered Dragon Lord's fortress and walked down a hall in the direction where the special scouter division was located. They talked in low voices.

"The dark lord must suspect something. He will kill me at this level... I should leave 7-Nations now," said Lou Shen nervously.

"General Kano would have killed you on sight if Dragon Lord knew you know Dragon Lord's law *zero* tolerance for talk of rebellion. Just mind your manners, and follow my lead," said Gi Shen.

"I have told you many times, brother. I don't fear Dragon Lord," said Lou Shen as they reached the end of the hall.

Two Dragon Lord guards sat at a gray quartz crystal desk, focused on the touch hologram computer screen.

"Good day, noble elementals," said Gi Shen as the lotus brothers walked around the desk and turned left down the hall.

"We will see how good of a day it will be once you see Dragon Lord," said the Dragon Lord guard seated to the left known as Jimbo.

"Let's watch last week's dragon tournament," said Jimbo as he manipulated the holo screen.

"Cool with me," said the second Dragon Lord guard known as Ki-claw.

As the lotus brothers walked, they passed a door to the left that read *Prison*. They kept going for a few seconds to the right of the hall. Signs and doors read *Power Training Room*. Then they passed a door to the left that said *Orb Vault*.

Lou Shen stopped and looked closely at the vault door to see the lock's wheel turned, and the vault's door slightly cracked open.

"Brother, this may be my only chance," Lou Shen whispered, preparing to open the steel vault door. The Dragon Lord guards were in deep focus at the holo screen at the other end of the hall.

"Brother, I am very proud of the man you have become, and I honor your bravery," said Gi Shen as he took of his special greater healing amulet and gave it to Lou Shen.

"I cannot take this. How will you perform the healing ritual? Father's dying wish was for you to have this if you ever decided to leave 7-Nations," said Gi Shen as he hugged Lou Shen. Then he placed the glowing amulet in Lou Shen's hands and walked off in tears. A ten-second walk gave Gi Shen no time to think. He wiped his eyes. The hall turned right, and he saw a series of rooms reading *Elevator, Train Dock, Orb Absorption Room*. Straight ahead, a double door made of gray quartz crystal read *Special Scouter Division*.

"Good luck, brother," said Gi Shen as he stepped through the doors.

Dragon Lord's scouter division was a hive of supercomputer terminals that projected 3D hologram screens, that were placed in an octagon shape through the whole room surrounding Dragon Lord in his rotatable throne platform. The imperial king had on a shadow energy hooded cloak of power over a suit of fine green silk garments. A silvery white orb with a gray silhouette of a dragon surrounded the force orb on Dragon Lord's chest. In front of the great king glowed the largest 3D holo screen with two smaller screens on each side of the bigger screen. The middle screen showed a detailed map of all of 7-Nations, color coded by element. On the map, Windmill City and the Lotus Forest blinked rapidly. Displayed on the screen to the right showed a sky view zoomed in on the Windmill City sky arena. On the screen to the left of the middle screen showed a data pool of holo messages and conversations from the people of 7-Nations. A team of thirty human receptionists manipulated the holo computer screens at Dragon Lord's command.

"My lord, the SSD system located an unknown level-four power yesterday morning around 7:00 a.m. in the Lotus Forest. But the system lost the power signature. Would you like me to rescan a certain nation?" said a receptionist to Dragon Lord's right.

"Scan all nations, and find the power now!" shouted Dragon Lord.

"My lord, a new orb level-three power has been located in Earth Nation three hours ago!" said a human receptionist named Tina.

"Does the system know who the second power is and the power's current location?" said Dragon Lord.

"Yes, sir, Wind Nation, efficiency number one named Wind Burn," said Tina.

"Show me Wind Burn's profile," said Dragon Lord, clearing his throat. In seconds, a small file opened on the left screen over the data pool messages.

"Wind Burn's profile, screen three," said Tina. As Dragon Lord looked at Wind Burn's profile picture, he noticed that Wind Burn looked exactly like Swift, whom he had killed so long ago.

Orb Level 3: Essence Ability
Wind Burn's Profile
Primary element: Wind
Parental origins: Unknown
Power level: 80,900
Bank account: 987 platinum
Orb level 3 essence points: 48/50/45/38/56/35

A picture of Wind Burn and all of the information the system could come up with concerning Wind Burn's life appeared over the view of the Wind Nation screen on the right.

"My lord, you have a holo conference from Dr. Voltage," said a Dragon Lord guard in one of the cubicles to Dragon Lord's right.

"Put him on holo screen one," said the imperial king.

A tall man with short spiky hair, medium build, and surgically implanted computerized eyes that read orb levels and enhanced his vision and memory appeared on the largest middle holo screen. Dr. Voltage had on a doctor's coat, and he's standing next to a strange-looking human.

"Good morning, my lord," said Dr. Volts.

"If you bring good news, it will be a start," said Dragon Lord.

"I do bring good news. My orb level-five bioengineered human droid has finally stabilized and will be ready for any missions you request. With your consent, I will modify the fifth assembly line for the construction of your army, my lord," said Dr. Volts.

"I have a mission for you now," said Dragon Lord.

"Just send me the mission information, and I will send Shock Wave Number Thirty-Two. He is fully operational and equipped with the most advanced orb energy, tech, and weapon systems," said Dr. Volts.

"Very well, send the shock wave to Wind Nation. His mission—seek and destroy Wind Burn," said Dragon Lord.

"It is done, my lord," said Dr. Volts.

"And start the construction of my army as soon as possible," said Dragon Lord. A second later monk, Gi Shen walked through the doors. "I want a wind orb in my orb vault by nightfall. Do you hear me, scientist?" said Dragon Lord.

"Your will be done, my lord," said Dr. Volts, and the largest middle screen went back to the detailed sky view of 7-Nations.

Gi Shen stood there in silence a few feet away from Dragon Lord's throne and waited for Dragon Lord to speak to him.

Dragon Lord removed his hood and looked up to the sky and said, "Lord of darkness, Death, Shadow God, when will I join you and the ascended? I grow tired of this strain on Fuzion."

Orb vault

Lou Shen wiped his face with the back of his hand as he grabbed his older brother's lotus amulet and put it around his neck. As Lou Shen entered the orb vault, he could feel the rare amulets energy making his orb chi and life energy stronger. He also felt and sensed many strong elemental orbs as he walked. Lou Shen made his way around the room guided by dim glowing light from orb energy. Lou Shen reached the first set of orbs of the orb vault's chamber. He stopped to gather himself and looked around the room. There were rows and rows of orbs in locked orb carriers segregated by color. Lou Shen looked to his right to see a cart with a leather tarp inside. Lou Shen quickly grabbed the cart and rolled it along the first row of power orbs that shone bright red. He grabbed two and placed them into the cart. Then Lou Shen continued onto the next row of shining violet-and-yellow orbs of lightning element. He grabbed three, then placed them into the cart, and then turned left to a small row of silvery-white orbs, which were the smallest collection of orbs. He grabbed two and then placed them into the cart. Lou Shen passed up the lotus orbs... *No need*, he thought. He and Dante had lotus water orbs already. Lou Shen stopped at the grayish-blue orbs and grabbed two and stacked them in his cart with the others. Lou Shen turned the cart right and collected two earth orbs. Then he went out of the orb vault back to the Dragon Lord guards who were still watching the holo screen. Lou Shen pushed the cart up to Ki-claw and Jimbo and said, "Greetings, our savior wishes me to deliver these orbs to the thunder kingdom. I need a hover craft and 7-Nations air clearance as soon as possible. My lord does not like waiting!"

"Dragon Lord has not informed us of this," said Jimbo just as Ki-claw handed Jimbo a chopped chicken sandwich and a drink of OJ.

"What's in the cart?" said Ki-claw.

"Power orbs," said Jimbo with a worried look on this face while reaching for his food.

"What for?" asked Ki-claw.

Lou Shen leaned over the desk and whispered, "They're for Dr. Volts's experiments for Dragon Lord's new half-robot, half-human army. It's highly confidential. My lord could have our heads just for me telling you." Ki-claw and Jimbo stared at each other in silence until Lou Shen said with confidence, "Call my lord to clarify his orders."

"Shh... I ain't calling. Last time someone questioned Dragon Lord's orders, they ended up dead in the hellfire mines," said Jimbo.

Ki-claw scarfed down his sandwich, grabbed his drink, stood up, and said, "To the air hangar we go."

Special Scouter Division

Dragon Lord closed his eyes and rubbed his temples while enjoying the silence and computer chimes that indicated incoming messages.

"Lemons, water, and a shadow apple, Tina," demanded Dragon Lord.

"Right away, my lord," said a beautiful woman in the cubicle next to the bar. Tina nervously walked into the small bar room to a mini refreshment station to do Dragon Lord's request.

"What do you know about this unknown orb level-four power my scouter system has detected?" said Dragon Lord, looking at Gi Shen.

"I know nothing, my lord," said the head monk.

"You must know something. It happened on your clan grounds. You're a scion. Your orb is touched by the god of the water element. Scionic powers reach far beyond the boundaries of mere mortals," said Dragon Lord, trying to read the head monk's body language.

"I assure you, my lord, I don't have a clue about any unknown powers," said Monk Gi Shen.

"You anger me so with your games, Monk," said Dragon Lord as his eyes glowed with deadly dark force.

Monk Gi Shen dropped to his knees in prayer and pleaded, "I promise you, my lord, you are the savior, the first of our kind who will ascend. Why would I defy you, the imperial king?"

"I was told your brother was here. Where is he now?" questioned Dragon Lord.

Gi Shen laughed and said, "My foolish brother came to discuss our clan's annual healing ritual ceremonies. I sent him back to his compound. I knew him being out of place would anger you, sire."

"And yet you still anger me because I ordered you two here. How is your grandson? What is his name?" said Dragon Lord.

"Dante is well, my lord. My brother teaches him the art of spirituality," said Monk Gi Shen.

Tina pushed a small stand over to Dragon Lord's side that had a tray filled with one glass of ice, one glass of water, and a small bowl of sliced lemons and shadow apples. Dragon Lord grabbed some lemon slices, squeezed them into the cup of ice, and then dropped them in. Then he grabbed the glass of water and poured half of it into the glass of icy lemon and said, "Water, the divine substance of all life," as he ate a slice of shadow apple. "You obviously don't understand the seriousness of this situation," said Dragon Lord as he stood looking over the stand for something. "Tina, come over and taste this, and tell me what's missing," said Dragon Lord as he picked up the glass of iced water.

Tina stood frozen in fear by her cubicle. In a knotted tongue, Tina managed to get out, "Sugar," before Dragon Lord waved his hand around the cup of iced water until the water froze and rose out of the glass and formed a solid shard of ice. Silvery-white force surrounded the ice shard as Dragon Lord threw the combined elements at Tina with the flick of his wrist.

By the time the force ice shard entered Tina's skull, her body hit the ground, and Dragon Lord was already on his intercom on his chair "I need a cleanup crew for a regular human and a new receptionist for cubicle number eight, and for the sake of the gods, I need some sugar," said Dragon Lord calmly as if nothing happened. "Follow me, monk," said Dragon Lord as he and Monk Gi Shen exited the room.

"You don't look so good, Head Monk," said Dragon Lord. Monk Gi Shen said nothing as the entered the prison chambers.

Air hangar, third floor, Dragon Lord's fortress

Lou Shen pushed the cart of power orbs out of the elevator with Ki-claw right behind him. They walked in silence for a few seconds until they reached the entrance to the air hangar door. Ki-claw stepped to the door with his holo net wrist computer blinking "Access to Air Hangar: Yes/No." Ki-claw typed *yes* on his holo net, and then the holo screen turned from red to green as the two doors slid open.

"After you," said Ki-claw.

Lou Shen pushed the cart through and waited as Ki claw stepped beside him. Dim light on the floors and walls shone bright, revealing numbered eleven-by-six rows of aircrafts, tanks, and hovers in different shapes and sizes.

"Welcome, Dragon Lord Guard Ki-claw," said a female computerized voice as Ki-claw walked to the right side of the air hangar where an oval-shaped terminal glowed to life with 3D hologram screens. Ki-claw stepped up to one of the holo screens and started moving and rotating glowing screens aid objects in midair.

"You will be taking hc-2-model-60, row two, hangar three," said Ki-claw. Lou Shen located the hangar and row. Then once he found the hovercraft, he opened the craft's main door and started loading the orb carriers in the hovercraft's cargo space. Once Lou Shen finished, he sent two messages on his holo net, one to Dante and on to the storm clan leader, Lee Windol. Then Lou Shen returned to the air hangar terminal to find Ki-claw seated in one of the terminal chairs navigating through multiple screens on his holo net wrist computer.

"You left without giving me the quadrants to which Thunder Kingdom dock. You know, Dr. Volts is high on security. What are the quadrants?" asked Ki-claw.

"My mistake, I must have forgotten to get them from Tina," said Lou Shen in a joking manner.

"Tina is dead. I just got done speaking to SSD receptionist number five, and there has been no such orders given, you lying monk," said Ki-claw as the colorful holo 3D from Ki-claws wrist disappeared.

"I may not have been truthful, but I am leaving here in that craft," said Lou Shen confidently as he put his hands, palms facing Ki-claw with his knees bent in a lotus palm defensive fighting stance.

"Silly old water monk. You are no match for me. I am an orb level-three elemental. My lord will have your orb in a box." Ki-claw laughed as he stood up and stretched side to side, eyeing the monk.

"I teach this to my grandson: strength is only half of the battle, and you will learn it today when an orb level-two water monk beats you," said Lou Shen.

"Stop your bickering, monk!" shouted Ki-claw as he charged Lou Shen and threw two fast dragon fighting style punches, followed by a knee thrust aimed at Lou Shen's gut. Lou Shen sidestepped with grace and evaded the two punches and then palm blocking Ki-claw's knee thrust and countering Ki-claws attacks with a lotus palm to Ki-claw's chest.

"Give me more credit than that, young force warrior," said Lou Shen as he got back into his lotus palm stance.

Ki-claw stumbled back a few feet from the impact of Lou Shen's blow and said, "Lotus palm, the lost fighting style." Ki-claw rubbed his chest. Lou Shen nodded in approval.

Ki-claw's hands engulfed in a bright silvery force energy. Ki-claw put his hands together in the shape of a diamond and yelled, "Force fiery orb!" Fire and force energy circled one another into a combined compacted ball that beamed at Lou Shen at the speed of Ki-claw's thought. With great speed, Lou Shen formed a water shield of turquoise energy that seeped from his brother's amulet.

"Water mirror," said Lou Shen as the mirror shield swallowed the force/fire orb and shot it back at Ki-claw.

"You think you can outsmart me, old monk," said Ki-claw while he countered his own attack with a second force flame orb. The two balls of energy collided into each other as reddish-silvery-white energy exploded brightly lighting up the air hangar, and then the energy vanished.

"I hope that is not the depths of your power. So sad you don't have enough chi to break my water mirror," said Lou Shen.

"You have mocked me for the last time, monk," said Ki-claw as a body of force and then a deadly force aura surrounded Ki-claw. Ki-claw summoned force energy from deep within and yelled, "Ahhh!" as force grew brighter and more vicious. Waves of silvery force engulfed in hell flames, and the deadly energies compacted into razor elemental gloves around Ki-claw's hands.

Ki-claw said, "The Ki-claws are ascended powers founded by father and passed down through bloodline. Now you will feel the terror so many hellfire rebellion elementals felt when the elite force army and Dragon Lord slaughtered all who stood to face this powerful orb, the force element." Ki-claw charged Lou Shen with all he had, slashing violently, barely missing Lou Shen as the old monk evaded multiple attacks.

"You let your emotions control your actions in battle, not very wise," said Lou Shen as he barely dodged the last claw slash which burned and sliced his cheek from being too close. The wound and Lou Shen's brother's amulet glowed simultaneously as the cut healed in seconds.

"Your tricks will only prolong your death, monk," said Ki-claw with scorn in his voice.

"Paralyzing water palm," said Lou Shen as his new special amulet glowed to life, seeping turquoise energy from the amulet forming gloves of water energy around Lou Shen's hands. Lou Shen remained in his lotus defensive stance and said, "Now it's time to put out the fire."

"Tell me, monk, are all lotus elementals weak, or is it in the lakewater?" said Ki-claw.

Lou Shen said, "My defense is just as tough as my offense. This makes me excel in battle where you fall short. Look as you now tired and drained of chi from reckless attacks."

"Shut up, monk!" shouted Ki-claw as he charged Lou Shen once again, slashing with all his might and will. Lou Shen blocked the ascended Ki-claw slashes with his water palms. Mixed fire and force and water energy clashed, making sizzling sounds upon impact. Ki-claw attempted a wide slash at Lou Shen's face. Lou Shen evaded the slash by an inch, sidestepped, and countered Ki-claw's attack, paralyzing Ki-claw's neck. Glowing waters seeped into Ki-claw's pores. The force energy aura around Ki-claw's body slowly evaporated in thin air. By the time Ki-claw's knees hit the ground, his compacted force Ki-claw's had vanished meaning he had lost control of his body and power. Ki-claw looked fearlessly at Lou Shen and said, "Get it over with, monk. Kill me."

Lou Shen's face saddened, and he said, "I am no monk. I gave that path of life up long ago when Dragon Lord killed my twin daughters, but I'm not heartless. You pose no threat to me." Lou Shen pulled Ki-claw to a random hovercraft, opened the cargo hold hatch, pulled Ki-claw in, and said, "Tell the dark dragon his days are numbered. The rebellion is still alive."

Lou Shen shut the ship's cargo hatch and returned to the terminal and navigated through the computer's system. Lou Shen ended up with 7-Nations air clearance for hc-2-model-60 with no certain destination on the logs. Lou Shen opened the roof panel doors to the air hangar in Dragon Lord's fortress and prepared for a short journey to his small dojo for one last time.

LOU SHEN

Chapter 7

Mission: Return to Lost Loved Ones

Windmill City was the third largest city in 7-Nations and a very important nation at that. Seventy percent of 7-Nations' food supply came from Wind Nation's farms. A small amount of crops fed 7-Nations' large population with no hassle. Food grew quickly in Wind Nation, thanks to one of Dr. Volts's inventions known as creator's soil. This soil was priceless and only found in 7-Nations. It was said that only Dr. Volts can make this soil, and he obtained the knowledge to make this soil from one of the books of alchemic lost science—books that his father received from fate. Food grew so fast that crops could be harvested in weeks' time once planted. This allowed Dragon Lord to control one of the world's most profitable markets.

Wind Nation governed the two electric trains that were built by Dr. Volts's family when 7-Nations was first rebuilt. These trains were powered by pure electric energy.

The most important feature Wind Nation had was multiple windmill solar generators that acted as a second backup power system for the main power system in Thunder Kingdom. Without these two systems of power, life would be very hard in 7-Nations.

Lee Windol was the merciful storm clan leader who ran the train station and combined food market. Lee Windol was an old but strong orb level-5 human elemental. In his spare time, he trained his son Wind Burn and other storm elementals to perfect the mind, body, and spirit. Every now and then, a wind elemental would compete in Dragon Lord's weekly dragon tournaments.

Lately, Lee had been having a hard time keeping up with Wind Burn's strength and showing Wind Burn how to suppress his growing power and anger. Plus work had seemed to hold Lee more and more. Lee had no love life. He gained joy from watching his clan grow strong. Lee did not get involved with the rebellion, but he still had ties to the black market to keep certain illegal items in arm's reach for a stormy day. Lee and Wind Burn loved stormy days. But sometimes, the storm of life could blow the mightiest of elementals off their feet.

Wind Burn

Wind Burn woke at six in the morning with his holo net alarm going off. His father, Lee, was gone, and he hadn't woken him, which was strange because Wind Burn always helped his father with the major tasks of running Windmill City. What really angered Wind Burn was that his father had been neglecting their training time together. The father-son quality time was what Wind Burn valued the most.

"Come, Wind Burn, it's time!" said an unfamiliar voice.

Wind Burn sat up in his bed and said, "Lights on, alarm off." Then he looked around his room to find no one there. "I must be going crazy," Wind Burn said to himself as he got out of bed, walked to his closet, and put on his custom storm cloth armor and black boots. Wind Burn went to his restroom and brushed his teeth, and he heard the voice again. Wind Burn left his room and said, "Lights off." Then he walked down the hallway and stopped when he heard the voice again coming from his father's room. Wind Burn ran to his father's room door and yanked the door open and yelled, "Who's in here?"

No one was there. Wind Burn's stomach howled for food. He began to close his father's room door when he heard the voice again shout, "Windston!" so loud coming from his father's closet he almost jumped out of his skin.

Wind Burn raced to the closet and opened the door and said, "Lights on." He looked in to find an ordinary closet. He turned to leave, but he sensed strange energies he never felt before. Wind Burn searched the closet from top to bottom until he stumbled upon an indention. In the wall behind his father's clothes, Wind Burn could feel air coming from the edges of the indention. Wind Burn pushed at the wall, but nothing happened. Wind Burn sat there thinking for a few seconds until he got angry and then threw a weak wind punch at the wall. Like magic, the wall moved in and opened around the indention, revealing several custom foreign swords in cases and a small crystal cube with strange engraved violet-glowing hieroglyphic symbols and writing from an unknown language. This strange alchemy was all over the cube.

"Alchemy, the deadly science," said Wind Burn, amazed by the orb carrier. Wind Burn put the cube on the floor in his father's room and stared at the marvelous energies of the grayish-blue orb contained in the cube. It called to him. Wind Burn could not fight the urge to obtain this power. Without thinking or realizing his actions, Wind Burn grabbed the cube and one of his father's bags and headed for the door. Wind Burn raced to the train to get to Earth Nation with one thing on his mind—power.

WIND BURN

GOD
NATION
CLOTHING
LINE

Wind Burn returned home tired and beaten but successful at his task. Lee was seated in his chair in the living room in the dim light from the fireplace. The thin long case from the closet sat on the floor in front of Lee.

Wind Burn walked slowly toward his father and said, "I'm sorry, Father, I—"

Lee raised his hand and said, "I knew this day would come, my son. I have something to show you. Open the case."

Wind Burn opened the case and saw a stunning sword embedded in crushed gray velvet cushion. The sword had a slender razor edge. The blade gleamed with a mix of silvery blue. The sword's length was inscribed with hieroglyphic writings known only to those who practiced alchemy. The middle of the blades hilt was surrounded by a ball of opal-blue crystal and more strange writings. Inside the crystal ball was a storm orb that slept, dormant of energy. Wind Burn could feel the powerful aura coming from the sword, and he wanted to explore the depths of the weapon's power. Wind Burn reached for the sword but fell short when Lee closed the case. Wind Burn looked up at his father in annoyance and then stood and said, "Is that what I think it is?"

Lee nodded yes and then remained silent.

Wind Burn said, "I've been sensing these strange energies coming from your room. I had to see what it was. It kept calling me."

Lee stood up and grabbed Wind Burn by his shoulders, looked his only son in the eye, and said, "They belong to you. Your father left them to you."

"What…? I don't understand," said Wind Burn.

"You will in time," said Lee as he picked up the sword and backpack Wind Burn had. Lee searched the bag to find an empty orb carrier. "Where is it?" said Lee with worry in his voice. Wind Burn touched his chest and said nothing while looking at the ground. "Where did you do it?" said Lee.

"The secret passage under Earth Nation," said Wind Burn.

"Good," said Lee, calming down. Lee took a deep breath and went to gather some of Wind Burn's things from Wind Burn's room.

Then Lee went to his rooms' closet, also gathering things and putting them in the backpack.

Wind Burn followed behind Lee and shouted, "Where are we going father?" Lee found what he was looking for—a custom pouch full of red crystals, a polished beautiful katana blade, a war utility belt, camouflage cloth armor, elemental damage-resistant boots, and a double back sheath for two swords.

Lee gave all of the items to Wind Burn and said, "I'm not going anywhere."

"What? I'm not leaving you by yourself, and I can't make it on my own in the wilderness." Wind Burn and his father met in the living room over the case of the sword.

Lee grabbed Wind Burn by his shoulders. Wind Burn could see tears falling down his father's face that flickered in flames from the fireplace. "There is a secret bounty on your head, a death bounty from Dragon Lord," said Lee.

"I'll kill them first. I've done nothing to violate Dragon Lord's laws," said Wind Burn in anger and disgust.

"My son, you must listen to me and calm down. Dragon Lord issues this bounty on strong human elementals, with 3 orbs, or who are not in his good graces. Those news come from the platinum assassins who are Dragon Lord's trained killers from Death City, Shadow Empire," said Lee.

"But no one knows I have three orbs but you," said Wind Burn.

"Dragon Lord has a new computer system that ranges all over 7-Nations that gives him information on anyone he chooses. You must have alerted his system by absorbing that orb. Plus, this week's dragon tournament is a highly anticipated contest, and you and Frost Bite are expected to show awesome power, and you have gotten much stronger. By the gods, you will need it," said Lee.

Lee's holo net started beeping, indicating that he had a message, but it wasn't the small slick silver holo net on Lee's wrist that was beeping. Lee reached into his pocket of his grayish-blue nation leader suit and pulled out a black thicker model of a holo net. Lee removed Wind Burn's silver holo net and replaced it with the black older model.

"Send me a message through Elizabeth when you can. Go to White Lotus Compound 2 and find Lou Shen. You will leave 7-Nations with him as soon as possible," said Lee.

"Let me get this straight. You're sending me to the deadly unknown wilderness with a monk. You might as well kill me now, Father," said Wind Burn as he readied all of the equipment his father had gathered for his journey. Lee hugged Wind Burn for a few seconds, but time seemed to stop.

Lee said, "I remember when your mother brought you to me. You were still a baby, and you barely could stand. Now here you are, setting off on a life-and-death adventure." Lee let go of Wind Burn, and they slowly walked to the front door.

"Oh, I almost forgot," said Lee as he grabbed Wind Burn's wrist and pressed two buttons on the holo screen. A small black chip popped out of the side of the device.

"This is for you to read when you get safely outside 7-Nations," said Lee as he took the chip out of the black holo net and placed it in Wind Burn's hand.

"Will I ever see you again?" said Wind Burn sadly.

"That is up to you. You control your own destiny by the choices you make. I want you to know something. No matter what happens from this point on, you will always be my son, and I love you."

"What's that supposed to mean?" said Wind Burn in confusion.

"In time, all will be clear. You must go. Time is short," said Lee as he opened the doors.

Wind Burn stepped outside of his home for twenty years and said, "I love you, Father. I will see you again," as the winds seemed to come out of nowhere around Wind Burn, lifting him into the air.

"At times, the storm may be merciful," shouted Lee.

"And I am the swift wind that burns, and I will not be merciful," shouted Wind Burn as he disappeared into the gray sky...

Dante

Dante sat on his bed in his cubicle at Inferno Village with Elisha, his girlfriend and childhood friend, next to him. Dante and Elisha were in a heated conversation about Dante not staying under Dragon Lord's radar. Dante stared at Elisha in amazement at the sight of her beauty as she yelled at him.

Elisha was nineteen years old, with light-brown skin, tan eyes, long black straight hair, and the face of an angel. Dante could remember the first time he met Elisha ten years ago.

Dante learned fast. By the time Dante was eight, Monk Alia Weddens school of mandatory general knowledge of math, reading, writing, and god theology taught at White Lotus Compound Dojo 3 had been completed by Dante. The following month, Lou Shen enrolled Dante in the basic fighting/chi control class for the youth taught at White Lotus Compound 2. The first day of class would be the day that Dante would never forget. It was 7:45, fifteen minutes before class would start. Dante's teacher and grandfather Lou Shen had not showed up yet. In the dojo, kids were seated in groups talking about Dr. Volts's latest invention and who would win the next dragon tournament when Fredrick Bold walked into class. Someone yelled, "Hey, look it's Freddy, the king of the melted ice sickles," and everyone started laughing.

Fredrick just stood there with his head down as more insults came his way. That's when Dante saw her for the first time. She had on Earth Nation brown clothing with her long down hair. Most of the kids stopped laughing when they saw Elisha's serious face. Elisha walked into the middle of the dojo and yelled, "His name is Frost Bite, and anyone who has a problem with my brother has a problem with me."

An eleven-year-old girl named Halie Vice walked to Elisha and snickered in a sarcastic tone "Just because your mother runs the orphanage does not mean he is your brother, dumb rock girl!"

"Force tomboy, wanna make somethin' of it?" said Elisha getting in Halie's face.

All of the kids surrounded the two girls, chanting, "Fight, fight, fight!"

Halie's joking manner quickly turned to anger as she got in Elisha's face yelling, "Get out of my face, and shut your mouth before I shut it for you!"

A ten-year-old boy named Mark stepped in the circle of kids behind Elisha. Fredrick stepped up and grabbed Mark's left arm and said, "It's one on one, bro." Mark turned around and shoved Fredrick's chest with his full strength. Fredrick flew straight into Dante's arms.

"Frost Bite, are you okay?" said Dante.

Fredrick was holding his chest, dazed and dizzy. "Get off reject," said Fredrick as he crouched to the floor in pain. Dante stepped into the circle of kids behind Mark. He could see Elisha and Halie still yelling and name-calling at each other's necks.

"I don't know who you think you are. My father will have your head and your mother's position as Earth Nation leader," said Halie.

Elisha balled her fist and said, "Don't talk about my mother."

"Hey, guys, calm down. Fighting won't solve anything," said Dante, standing behind mark.

Mark turned around and threw a mean right hook at Dante's jaw and said, "Mind your business." Dante easily weaved the punch and then sidestepped, attempting to restrain Mark by wrapping his arms around Mark, which turned into a wrestling match. Elisha cocked her fist back and launched a wild punch at Halie. Lou Shen appeared out of nowhere in a water energy mist teleportation and caught Elisha's fist.

"Enough nonsense!" shouted Lou Shen, and the dojo went quiet. Mark and Dante stopped wrestling and got to their feet. From that day on, Elisha and Dante had been friends ever since.

Current time...

That was nothing compared to how mad Elisha was at Dante right now. Dante had never seen the love of his life so angry. Her eyes were watery and red, and she wouldn't let Dante talk. She just let him have it. But that's why he loved her so much. She always spoke her mind. To her, what's right is right and what's wrong is wrong, and Elisha had no problem letting you know how she felt.

"Dante! Hellooo? Earth to Dante. See, that's what I'm talking about. You just drift off. Where do you go?" yelled Elisha in Dante's face.

Dante kissed Elisha's soft lips and said, "I was just living in the past."

"Well, in the present time, you now have four orbs, which in reality make you a target for Dragon Lord," said Elisha, annoyed by Dante's lack of seriousness, as she wiped off Dante's kiss.

"Elisha, you worry too much. You know my role in this," said Dante as he checked his holo net.

Elisha said, "I know, but I've seen this too many times. When human elementals get too strong, they seem to disappear. Promise me you won't compete in this weeks' dragon tournament."

"You don't understand—"

"Promise!" yelled Elisha, cutting Dante off midsentence. Dante looked into Elisha's eyes! And he could see them watering.

"I promise."

Elisha wrapped her arms around Dante's neck and hugged him. Tears ran down her cheeks. Dante and Elisha lay back in the bed and held each other in silence. Dante dried Elisha's tears with his shirt.

"Thank you," said Elisha between sniffles.

"It's okay. I'll get a new shirt, beautiful."

Elisha laughed and said, "Not that, silly. Thank you for promising me."

"Anything for the love of my life."

"What were you thinking about a minute ago?"

"About the day we first met, you almost got yourself killed by hitting Dragon Lord's daughter," said Dante as his holo net started beeping and flashing message.

Dante raised his arm so he and Elisha could see his holo net.

"It's a message from your grandfather," said Elisha, and she opened Dante's message.

> Message from Grampa
> Pack your most valued belongings, only what you can carry. Meet me at the White Lotus Compound 2.
> Grab the two bags in the dojo's closet.
> I'll be in the sky.

*****

Shock Wave Model 35 arrived at Lee Windol's home to see Wind Burn flying toward the Lotus Forest. The Shock Wave's eye scouter cams linked directly to Dr. Volts and Dragon Lord's supercomputers. The Shock Wave's right arm had many component modifications. One feature was a holo pad computer that glowed to life in a 3D picture of Dr. Volts.

"Follow the target. Stay out of sight," said Dr. Volts. Then the message ended as the hologram picture disappeared.

*****

It was maybe six or seven in the evening when Wind Burn got to Lou Shen's dojo. The doors were open so Wind Burn peeked in. The dojo was empty and lit from glowing monk's waters in wells along the walls.

"Monk," yelled Wind Burn as he stepped inside. Wind Burn stopped to use his holo net and remembered his father had his. "I guess I'll wait," said Wind Burn.

*****

Elisha stood up, crossed her arms, and gave Dante the evil eye. Dante quickly got on his hands and knees under his bed looking for something. Dante came up from under his bed with a small black safe. Dante pressed a series of numbers on the safe's screen and opened the safe. Dante made sure his platinum marks and crystals and information chips from his parents were there. Dante closed the box and then stood to face Elisha.

"What's going on, Dante? Where are you going with all that currency? Why is your grandfather in the sky? That's illegal," questioned Elisha in a heartbroken tone.

Dante walked over to Elisha with the safe under his right arm and said, "I love you. You mean the world to me, so I'm going to tell you. My grandfather has been secretly training me to surpass Dragon Lord to dethrone him as the imperial king of 7-Nations. Grampa told me he would ask my coward grandfather Gi Shen to help us get out of the city undetected."

"Which all of that just landed a bounty on your head," said Elisha.

"I don't have a bounty on my head yet, to prevent that we are 7-Nations now. I need more intense training," said Dante.

"Where are you going to?" asked Elisha with tears building up.

"Somewhere in the wilderness. Honestly, I don't know, but I have to do this for us, for 7-Nations and our race," said Dante as he tried to hug and kiss Elisha, who moved out of the way to wipe her face to keep the tears from falling.

"Why didn't you tell me? I could have helped you using my mother's secret underground passage," said Elisha.

"I didn't want to worry you. And the passage is not so secret. Dragon Lord suspects. Tell your mom to be careful, and I'll be in touch," said Dante as he tried to move close to Elisha again.

"*No!* No goodbyes. I'll see you when you defeat Dragon Lord. Then you can meet your son. I'm pregnant," said Elisha as she stormed past Dante and out of his cubicle in an emotional wreck…

* * * * *

Wind Burn waited in the corner of the White Lotus Compound 2. Dante walked in and rushed to the back of the dojo. He went to a closet, opened the closet door, grabbed two bags, and turned around to leave when Dante and Wind Burn locked eyes with each other.

Dante put the travel packs down and walked toward Wind Burn.

"Thief," shouted Dante as he got into a dragon fighting-style stance.

Wind Burn met Dante in the middle of the dojo and attacked Dante with vicious tai chi fist that was surrounded by storm. The punch only hit air as Dante evaded and teleported behind Wind Burn in a blur of fiery speed. Dante appeared in the air above Wind Burn's head spinning, putting all of his momentum into a deadly fiery kick. Dante's kick left an arc of flame in its path. In a split second, a vicious storm aura surrounded Wind Burn as he evaded the attack and went into a backward handstand, followed by a windmill dance attack of deadly storm and energized winds coming off Wind Burn's body. Wind Burn's spinning dance movements sent multiple sharp winds in every direction around him. Still in the air, Dante formed an inferno shield around himself. The winds and fire clashed and pushed Dante farther up into the air of the dojo where Wind Burn's winds could not reach. Dante started to fall, but a hellish-looking aura of flames came around Dante and guided him to the ground. Dante's flames disappeared. "I don't have time for this," said Dante, calmly taking a quick glance at his holo net. Then Dante got back into his dragon fighting-style stance.

Wind Burn's aura of winds levitated him slightly off the ground as he yelled, "You will die before I let you take me to Dragon Lord!"

"And why would I want to do that?" said Dante calmly.

Wind Burn eased to the ground as his storm aura faded away and said, "I'm here to see the monk Lou Shen. Where is he?"

"He should be here any second. Why do you seek the monk, and whose things are you stealing?" said Dante.

"These are my things, so I'm not stealing anything. And I can't tell you why I'm looking for the monk," said Wind Burn in an angry tone.

"Still always angry for no reason, I see," said Dante as he stood straight with his hands behind his back in deep thought.

Dante and Wind Burn stood there in silence for several seconds until Wind Burn asked, "Why are you here? There are no classes this late."

"I'm going on a secret mission with my grandfather, and I think you're coming with us," said Dante, looking over at Wind Burn's travel gear.

"Great, just great. I'm going to the deadliest unknown parts of the world with hundreds of strong mutated creatures, with a monk and a hellfire elemental who both have two orbs," said Wind Burn as he walked over to his travel gear picked up his exotic sword case and sat down next to his backpack.

"I have four orbs," said Dante as he gathered the two bags he had and his safe and sat a few feet away from Wind Burn.

"What's in the case?" asked Dante.

"Nunya," replied Wind Burn as he strapped the case around his back.

"What's nunya?" asked Dante, confused.

"Nunya beeswax, fool. I can't believe you fell for that," said Wind Burn. Just then Dante's halo net lit up with message. Dante opened the message and read it, and then a frown came across his face.

"What's wrong?" asked Wind Burn, worried and paranoid.

"My grampa says I can't take my holo net," said Dante sadly as he left his holo net on the floor.

"Everybody knows that this thirteenth version holo net has a tracker," said Wind Burn.

"Let's go," said Dante. The boys gathered their things and went outside to see a silver hovercraft in the sky over Lotus Forest.

Chapter 8

Shocking Escape

To Lou Shen's surprise, he flew the hovercraft right over 7-Nations skyscraper black steel fortress walls. A few Dragon Lord guards on top of the fortress wall most likely saw them leaving, so why hadn't Dragon Lord sent his destroyer ships to blow them out of the sky? Unless they were being followed, Lou Shen activated the craft's radar system and then programed the craft to autopilot. A hovercraft is the smallest ship Dragon Lord's air hangar stationed. This model was a sleek slender craft with five seats including the seats in the pilot pit, a small cargo space, and a bathroom. This craft was not made for arsenal or speed. It was made to carry goods and passenger transportation. *Looks like Ki-claw got the last laugh after all,* Lou Shen thought.

Lou Shen spun around in his chair to look at Dante and Wind Burn, and before he could say anything, Dante said, "Elisha's pregnant. It's a boy."

Lou Shen almost fell out of his seat as he said, "Is it yours?"

"Yea… About six months ago, we, uh, kinda got curious, and, uh, lost our virginity together," said Dante uncomfortably.

Lou Shen cleared his throat and said, "Wow, okay…we will talk more about that later. Okay, fellas, stay strapped in your seats. We need to put as much ground as we can between us and 7-Nations before we lose this craft.

"Why would we lose this craft, and where are we going anyway?" said Wind Burn disrespectfully.

"First, you will show your grandfather some respect," said Lou Shen.

"Big bro, I knew it," whispered Dante.

"You have no proof, Monk," said Wind Burn.

"If the ships shields fail, we will be automatically ejected out of the craft by the emergency safety program installed into the Craft's computer software. So keep your belongings in your lap," said Lou Shen as he grabbed a bag from Dante's side and checked the food and supplies. "I hope you boys are well rested because we are in for a long journey. Dry City is located at the end of the great chasm and some unknown mountains. At this speed, we will get there in a day and a half. On foot, maybe three days. It really depends on how fast you two move through the hot desert. Whatever you do, conserve your energy. Both of you like to show off. Brothers are alike in so many ways."

"What proof do you got, Monk?" said Wind Burn on the verge of exploding. Lou Shen spun around in his pilot seat back to flying the ship and said, "I see I'm going to have to teach you some manners, grandson. Have you looked at your information chip yet?"

Wind Burn dug in his pocket and pulled out the small black chip like disk his father had given him. Then Wind Burn inserted the chip into his black holo net.

"Dante, some of this may pertain to you, so pay attention," said Lou Shen. Both boys sat quietly as the 3D holographic image and recording shone to life…

*****

Shock wave and two shadow assassins flew and trailed just out of sight of the hovercraft's computer system's radar range. A 3D holographic map on Shock Wave's holo pad on his arm showed him that the ship traveled southeast toward the deepness of the desert and approached Death Chamber. A 3D holo picture of Dr. Volts appeared over the world map.

"Kill them all, and destroy the craft," said Dr. Volts.

"Affirmative," said the Shock Wave as his rocket boots and jet-powered wing component mods activated. The Shock Wave blasted off in full speed, leaving the shadow assassins.

Recorded holo message (1 of 3); 2 minutes, 32 seconds; date: December 15, 2061

A 3D holographic image of a man in grayish-blue clothing, with long black curly hair that was tied in a gray string. The man had very light skin and facial features the same as Wind Burn's. The holo image perfected itself as the man spoke.

"Windstin Burnum Swift, odd name, I know your mother named you. She was the most beautiful, loving person I've ever known, a true goddess on earth. Anyway, my name is Johnathan Swift. I'm making you this recording to clear some things up.

"First, the wind orb belonged to a childhood friend of mine. I left it for you. The legendary weapon was mine. Also I paid a great amount of currency for it at the black market. I hope it does you more good than bad.

"Second, I'm your biological father. Dragon Lord took your mother from me because I would not join his army and also because your mother had special scionic powers. So I had to leave you with my teacher and father figure Lee. I know he will raise you well. I must challenge Angel no matter the cost to show the nations we must stand up for what we believe in. It's strange how love makes you do crazy things.

"Third, the legendary weapon. It enhances your attack and powers, but it's a drain on your energy. The weapon has a mind of its own. Don't let it control you. Look where it got me. If you have any questions, ask your grandfather Lou Shen. He will train you and help you master the weapon. I love you, son. I just want you to know I wish things would have turned out differently.

Please forgive me and your mother for our faults, for we only played the cards that life dealt us."

The image of Wind Burn's father disappeared.

"So it's true—fools fall in love," said Wind Burn, fighting back tears as he loaded the next holo recording.

Recorded holo message (2 of 3); 2 minutes, 24 seconds; date: August 5, 2063

A 3D holographic image of a beautiful brown-skinned Asian woman in a tight fancy red dress that was draped with dark-red crystals holding an infant wrapped in a red blanket shone from Wind Burn's holo net as the woman spoke.

"My name is Clara Shen… Well, now it's Clara Saint Cipher. This is Dante, your younger brother. Windstin, my firstborn son, how are you, love…? Um, this is hard for me to explain in this short amount of time, so know this, I love you and Dante with all my heart. My actions were always made to protect you both and better your futures. If you're reading this, that could only mean one thing: you have I gotten too strong and you're on the run from Dragon Lord. There is a secret rebellion city in the tainted lands in a mountain. Here are the quadrants: 27645573. My sons, you both have inherited a lotus orb from me. I am one of Fuzion's first chosen twenty-four elemental humans. This is all the proof you need. Search deep in your souls, and feel my spirit with you both. You two will need a strong bond to get through this. I had a scionic vision that my sons will restore balance to the earth. Certain sacrifices had to be made. I love you, boys. You are the suns and foundation of a new beginning—*rise of the hellfire storm.*

Wind Burn quickly started the next recording.

Recorded holo message (3 of 3); 3 minutes, 37 seconds; date: 2060??

A 3D holographic image of Johnathan Swift stood in a cave lit by a small fire in the cave's canter. Swift held the legendary weapon in front of him as it glowed and amplified a large razor sword made of storm…

As soon as Wind Burn saw the sword, he ended the message.

"You knew all along," said Wind Burn to no one in particular.

"When your father challenged Dragon Lord, the evil lord searched out all your family on your family's side and killed them, so Lee Windol changed your name to Wind Burn and hid you until the heat died down," said Lou Shen.

"Warning. Warning. An unidentified object is approaching fast," said a female computerized voice. By the time Lou Shen looked at the radar screen—*zip, zip, zip*—lightning sounds came from outside. The craft's computers lights and navigation systems and engine systems all started to malfunction from loss of power.

"Nooo!" shouted Lou Shen as he failed a second time trying to stabilize the hovercraft.

Dante looked out of the craft's window next to him and said, "A new Shock Wave with more robotic parts."

Shock Wave was slightly above Dante's window. With lightning coming from the sky to his hands, Shock Wave controlled the lightning that drilled at the ship's shield of energy until the ship's shield broke. The craft's speed is decreasing, and we're losing altitude," said Lou Shen.

"Two on one, we could take him," shouted Dante.

As soon as Dante finished his sentence, everything went dark inside the craft as the ship lost all power.

"Grab all of our things, and teleport outside!" shouted Lou Shen as he unbuckled himself and bolted to the back of the craft. Wind Burn and Dante did as they were told and teleported through the pilot window. All that the two brothers could do was fly to the ground as they watched Shock Wave manipulate enormous amounts of electricity from the sky and destroy the ship. Dante and Wind Burn landed at a ruined fortress known as shadow tower in the desert.

"Grampa!" yelled Dante as he fell to his knees. Wind Burn stood behind Dante an opened the case to the beautiful sword. As soon as Wind Burn made contact with the sword, he felt a great drain on his orb chi. The blue crystal orb at the hilt of the sword absorbed Wind Burn's energy but still remained dormant and lifeless. Wind Burn tried to channel his wind element through the sword, and immediately he felt even more large amounts of his energy and orb chi being drained by the sword.

"Ahhh!" yelled Wind Burn as he fell to the floor on his knees and dropped the legendary weapon. Dante got up and turned around and rushed over to Wind Burn.

"Bro, are you okay?" said Dante as he reached to grab the sword.

"Don't touch it. It will drain you. Something's wrong with it," said Wind Burn and stood up slowly, regaining his balance.

Kaboom! Dante and Wind Burn looked into the darkening sky to see the ship blowing up in a rainbow of elemental colors as Shock Wave used lightning to guide the exploding ship into the chasm.

"So much obliterated orb energy," said Wind Burn in amazement.

"Where is Grampa?" said Dante in a low voice. Wind Burn picked up the sword and placed it back in the case, closed the case, and looked up to see Shock Wave and two hooded shadow assassins flying to them.

* * * * *

Lou Shen barely had time to think as he rushed to the back of the ship guided by touch in the dark ship. Lou Shen grabbed two orb carriers and teleported out of the ship's side window before the ship exploded. When Lou Shen appeared outside, he could see dark earth on one side and the remains of the energy explosion above him and the never-ending darkness of the chasm below him. All Lou Shen could do was teleport to a sturdy group of branches hanging from the dark earth wall of the chasm. Lou Shen stuffed the two orb carriers into the sleeves of his monk robe and began to slowly climb up the bottomless chasm. Lou Shen tried his best not to make noise that would attract deadly chasm worms to his hidden location. Lou Shen glanced over at the explosion to see five ancient chasm worms appear by the lingering ship's energy explosion and eat and drink the deadly energies. The wise monk quickened his climbing pace before he became next on the abomination chasm worms' dinner list. Lou Shen slipped on some loose earth and fell five feet. The quick monk created a giant hand of glowing lotus water that regained hold of the chasm. Then Lou Shen rode the water hand to the top of the chasm with great speed.

* * * * *

"We got company," said Wind Burn as he gathered their things in one pile. Wind Burn walked over to Dante to see a worried look on his face.

"Look, I'm sure the old man is okay. Now I need your head in the game," said Wind Burn as he looked into Dante's eyes in a serious manner. Dante nodded as the shadow assassins and Shock Wave clone surrounded them from the air. Dante and Wind Burn got back to back. Wind Burn stood in a tai chi fighting stance, Dante in a dragon fighting stance.

Shock Wave's gloves lit with electricity as they controlled lightning from the sky. Shock Wave sent bolts of violet lightning energy at the two brothers. Wind Burn teleported in a gust of wind behind Shock Wave and countered with an orb level 3 combined tai chi attack.

"Storm fist," yelled Wind Burn as wind and water energy formed a storm around his fist. The blow hit Shock Wave in the back of Shock Wave's neck. Shock Wave absorbed Wind Burn's attack, smiled wickedly, and then said, "Weakling target acquired." Shock Wave turned to face Wind Burn.

Dante dashed to his left with graceful speed and threw two small compacted orbs of hellfire rain at each shadow assassin. The orbs flew over the shadow elementals' heads and exploded into shards of hellfire. The shadow assassins put up shields made of black and gray flames, but Dante's fiery shards burned through the shadow shields like hot raindrops. The hellfire rain poured down on the assassins until they hit the ground.

Wind Burn stood there in shock looking up at Shock Wave with his freaky bioengineered robotic eyes and component mod body parts mixed with his humanly features. Wind Burn could sense Shock Wave's high-power level.

"Lightning sword," said Shock Wave as lightning formed in his right hand in the shape of an oversized bastard sword. Force energy surrounded the electric energy sword and compacted the two. Shock Wave connected an upward slash to Wind Burn's chest. The blow threw Wind Burn back twenty feet and knocked him to the ground as the energies burned his body. By the time Wind Burn got on his and knees, Shock Wave was already next to him about to deliver another combined sword attack at Wind Burn's neck.

"Brother!" yelled Dante as he raised his hands over his head and summoned a giant hellfire orb and threw it at Shock Wave. In the blink of an eye, Shock Wave teleported in a beam of lightning and appeared on the rooftop of shadow tower. Before the giant hellfire orb could hit Wind Burn, a light-blue liquid mirror swallowed the fiery orb and disappeared. Wind Burn looked behind him to see Lou Shen approaching covered in dirt, holding two orb carriers, one glowed red and one glowed silver. Time seemed to stop as they all remained quiet and still for the moment.

"Well, stand up, grandson," said Lou Shen as he placed the two orbs in the sand by Wind Burn's feet.

"The Shock Wave is orb level 5. We're going to die," said Wind Burn as he slowly got to his feet. Dante walked up and picked up the orbs and handed the red one to Wind Burn.

"Should we run?" asked Dante.

"We cannot outrun an orb level 5 elemental," said Lou Shen.

"This is our only option," said Wind Burn, looking at the power orb he held. Out of nowhere, a violet lightning grenade landed on the floor in the middle of Lou Shen and the two brothers.

"Look out!" screamed Dante before he barely evaded Shock Wave's attack by teleporting out of the blast range. Lou Shen and Wind Burn were not fast enough to evade the blast.

"Ahhh!" they both yelled and were thrown twenty feet in the opposite direction and knocked to the ground.

Lou Shen stood to see Wind Burn in the distance unconscious as he held the power orb. In a watery mist, Lou Shen teleported to Wind Burn and then summoned some monk's healing waters from his amulet into his palm and touched Wind Burn's chest. The liquid energy glowed as Wind Burn's body absorbed the healing energy. Wind Burn woke angry. He sat up and yelled, "Screw it. Live or die!" as he grabbed the orb carrier and opened it. The red orb zipped to Wind Burn's chest as Lou Shen teleported next to Dante. Lou Shen and Dante stood next to their travel gear. Dante thought about if he should absorb his fifth orb or not.

Lou Shen said, "Your brother is right, live or die."

Dante said, "I'm not ready, but I have a plan. Let's just hope Wind Burn makes it to the next level."

Chapter 9

The Next Level

Shock Wave's computer systems told him that the lotus monk was the weakest target. But he was out of range. Shock Wave's systems didn't have much information on the hellfire elemental, but his eye scouters told him that the fire human was the strongest. Shock Wave activated his lightning aura and jet wings and began to approach.

Dr. Volts appeared on the holo screen on his right arm and said, "Stop. Keep your distance. My lord wants a full recording of this absorption," and then the holo screen went blank.

*****

Wind Burn wasted no time releasing all of the orb chi from the hellfire orb. A huge glowing sphere of red energy came around Wind Burn and levitated him high into the sky. Wind Burn's screams shook the earth as the red sphere grew until it lit the dark sky like a red sun. Small amounts of grayish-blue wind energy started to seep from the bottom of the sphere and attempt to engulf the fiery power.

Dante, Lou Shen, and the Shock Wave all watched a colorful battle of tug-a-war as red and grayish-blue energy fought for control of the sphere.

"Wow, I've never seen it so close, so real, so big," said Dante, looking to the sky in awe.

Lou Shen said, "If Wind Burn succeeds, he and you will be evenly matched in orb levels, but your chi and ability essence is much greater than his because of your father's greater essence orb."

"How do you know if Wind Burn is winning?" asked Dante.

"His born element or primary element is wind, which is the grayish-blue energy. So if the wind energy can surround the red energy, Wind Burn can absorb the hellfire power. But with each failed attempt, every ten seconds, Wind Burn loses life energy. If Wind Burn does not absorb the orb before all of his life energy is gone, he will be obliterated," said Lou Shen.

"I know he can do it," said Dante.

"I hold high hopes that he can because we cannot make it in the wilderness with only two of us," said Lou Shen.

Wind Burn could not be seen through the sphere of energy, but from the looks of the sphere's energy battle, it was evenly in the middle.

"I think Wind Burn is having trouble with the mental stage of controlling all of the elemental power," said Lou Shen.

"He can do it, Grampa. I know he can," said Dante with full confidence in his older brother...

Wind Burn's mind

Windstin walked hand in hand with his mother and father to the market on a bright sunny day. Windstin wondered what his mother would cook or if his father would buy a live animal and let him gut it. For some strange reason, he loved causing things pain and death. It freed him from that moment of existence to have power over something. He embraced the feeling of darkness in his heart. Wind Burn started to ask his father if he would buy him a pet, but his mother's head was on fire. He tried to let go of his mother's hand, but he could not pull free. Then Windstin looked at his father's head to see it change to Dragon Lord's head and face. Hate and anger in Windstin's heart started to overflow. Dragon Lord cut his mother's head smooth off her shoulders. As Windstin's mother's body hit the ground, the sunny day turned dark. Dragon Lord was disappearing while saying, "You are a mistake. No one loves you but death's darkness."

Windstin dropped to his knees and grabbed his mother's hand and cried, "Mother, Father, why did you leave me...? No hope, only death… I will kill Dragon Lord at all cost… Nothing else matters." Then everything got clouded in a grayish-blue storm…of darkness.

* * * * *

"He's doing it," said Dante as they watched the grayish-blue energy swallow the red energy in a wind tornado motion from bottom to top. Then the huge sphere of wind got smaller and smaller until only a small aura of blue energy remained around Wind Burn.

In the blink of an eye, Wind Burn teleported and stood over their pile of belongings and searched through the pile until he found the sheath and katana blade. Wind Burn looked at Dante and said, "Don't interfere." Then Wind Burn moved in a deadly storm toward the Shock Wave. Wind Burn had a point to prove, and he wanted to test his new powers. But most of all, Wind Burn wanted to show Dante…

Shock Wave's systems were locked on Wind Burn's energy signal. Shock Wave watched Wind Burn appear next to some bags. His wings and lightning aura glowed to life as he began to approach his targets. Shock Wave's computer systems told him that he had a 70 percent chance to win a one-on-one fight against an orb level 4 elemental. A 60 percent chance to win a fight against two level 4 elementals. By the time Shock Wave's computer screen cleared, Wind Burn was already ten feet away. Wind Burn pulled out a beautiful custom-made razor-sharp katana blade from its sheath. Shock Wave stopped his approach, deactivated his wings and lightning aura, and said, "Nice blade." Shock Wave touched a circle of alchemy on his right hand, and a small amount of violet energy brought the spell to life. The circle in Shock Wave's right hand glowed and transformed his hand into a large great sword that was made of crystal. Inside of the sword's crystal blade was compacted lightning.

"Orb energy concentrated weapons created by alchemic scripture," said Wind Burn, a little surprised.

"Yes, anything you can do, I can do better," said Shock Wave mockingly.

"Such a big blade, you won't hit me with it," said Wind Burn as a storm aura came around his katana blade. All at once, Shock Wave's body began to change three laser disk mines glowing red appeared on Shock Wave's left forearm. A cannon appeared on Shock Wave's right shoulder with a scope and an infrared beam, and a ball of lightning formed in Shock Wave's chest. The red beam shined on Wind Burn's head.

"Gotcha," said Shock Wave as a massive blast of lightning energy and laser energy shot from Shock Wave's body.

Wind Burn dashed to the left, easily evading the attack while slicing at the air toward Shock Wave in a side-to-side helicopter motion. Three medium-sized helicopter blades of wind shot toward Shock Wave, who created a shield of force and lightning around himself, blocking the wind blades. The wind blades exploded in multiple clouds of storm energy, By the time the clouds of energy evaporated, Wind Burn had already teleported behind Shock Wave, savagely slashing Shock Wave's back with the power of 300-mph winds. He yelled, "Wind scar!"

The scar of winds hit Shock Wave and swallowed him. In the same second, Wind Burn sheathed his katana blade and said, "Storms of flame." More 300-mph winds mixed with shards of hellfire rain hit Shock Wave with so much force he had no time to react. The blow of storm blew Shock Wave thirty feet into the air. In seconds, Shock Wave's wings stabilized his flight.

"I'll turn you into scrap metal," yelled Wind Burn as a vicious wind aura came to life around him.

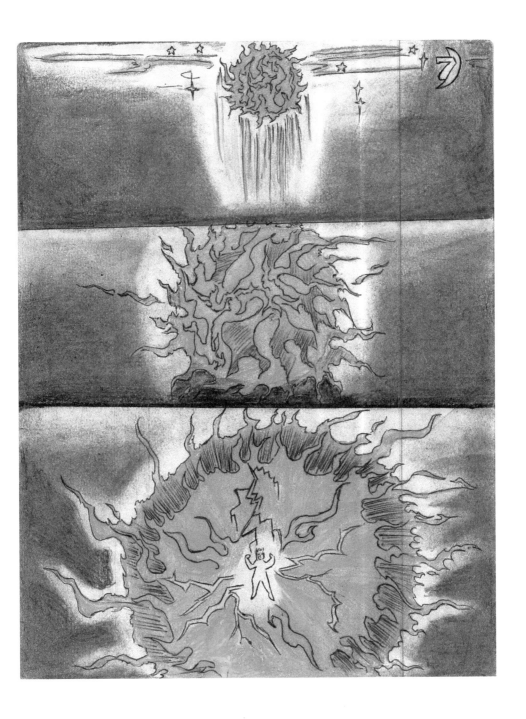

"You anger me, Wind Boy," said Shock Wave as a buzzing sound of energy hummed. Shock Wave's shoulder cannon came forward a few inches as energy began to form into an enormous ball.

"Level four shock ball," said Shock Wave as the energy zipped lots of lightning and two other elements toward Wind Burn with speed and accuracy. The magnificence of the energies stunned Wind Burn for a slight second. Red and silvery-white energy glowed and circled in a giant ball surrounded by violet electricity, leaving a color-ful glow in its path. At the last second, Wind Burn barely managed to put up a shield of winds and two other elements before the shock ball devoured him. Shock Wave's giant ball of energy met Wind Burn's combined shield in a clash of energies.

The element shock ball contained so much energy that it broke Wind Burn's shield and dug a huge hole in the earth before it disappeared.

The shock ball burned Wind Burn's body as it cratered him into the earth. Wind Burn shook of the pain and got to his feet and then flew into the air in a vicious storm. Wind Burn stopped fifteen feet away from Shock Wave and shouted in an angry tone, "Burning storm wind scar!"

Wind Burn created a large circle of wind that twirled with shards of fiery rain and acid rain, then shot the wind at Shock Wave.

With the help of Shock Wave's force-powered jet wings, Shock Wave teleported behind Wind Burn and tried to slice Wind Burn with his energy sword. Wind Burn teleported Shock Wave's attack and appeared behind Shock Wave and said confidently, "Burning storm wind scar!" An upward wave of winds, water, and flames hit Shock Wave dead in the back. Shock Wave turned around in a swift air dash perfected by his wings and said, "Lion maw!" A furious beast's mouth made of water, force, fire, and mostly lightning bit Wind Burn. Wind Burn tried to put up a level 4 shield but fell short.

"Ahhh!" yelled Wind Burn as the lion maw bit Wind Burn all the way down to the ground, crashing Wind Burn into the earth once again. A bleeding Wind Burn stumbled to his feet and looked up at Shock Wave to see another element shock ball coming his way.

Wind Burn's shield barely blocked the attack, and then Wind Burn teleported to the roof of shadow tower.

"So this is the game you want to play, huh? Burning storm wind scar!" yelled Wind Burn as a storm of winds, fire, and water energy shot toward Shock Wave.

"All my chi is in this attack. I hope you are ready. Death awaits one of us," said Wind Burn. With computerized calculated speed and grace, Shock Wave's wing component mod glided Shock Wave back ten feet as he formed and combined another element shock ball and quickly countered Wind Burn's attack. The energies met diagonally in the middle of Wind Burn and Shock Wave in an explosive energy war of will…

* * * * *

Dante and Lou Shen watched the battle eagerly from afar. Every time Wind Burn got hit, Dante asked his grandfather the same question, "Should I help him?" while moving closer to the battle.

"Your brother wishes to prove a point," said Lou Shen, placing his hand on Dante's shoulder to calm him.

"What point?" asked Dante with the orb carrier in his hands. The battle moved higher and at faster speeds that were hard for the normal eye to keep up with, but still Dante stayed in reach, ready to help his brother at any given moment.

"His point to be proven is that he is equal to you in strength and power," said Lou Shen.

"I don't care about that. I'm just happy to have a brother," said Dante.

"I know, grandson," said Lou Shen.

"It doesn't feel right standing here watching him die so he can prove a meaningless point," said Dante.

"It's the code of an elemental—" said Lou Shen.

"Elemental ninja's strengths are power and leadership, which are the foundation of a great warrior. I know, I know you've said it a thousand times, but what is the point in being reckless and suicidal?" said Dante, finishing his grandfather's famous quote.

"That is something you and him need to settle at some point," said Lou Shen. Just then Wind Burn appeared on the rooftop of shadow tower and launched an unbelievable amount of energy in the form of a deadly storm at Shock Wave. Then Shock Wave countered the storm of energy with an energy attack of his own. Now Shock Wave and Wind Burn were in a war of ability and vital life force, pushing the ball of energies toward each other. One slip or miscalculation would obliterate the loser.

"Grampa, nooo! Why would he do that? Why would Wind Burn enter a fast counter battle at this amount of power with Shock Wave when he is clearly no match?" asked Dante hysterically.

"I don't know, grandson. The question is, what are you going to do in this situation?" said Lou Shen.

Dante looked at the orb carrier in his hands and said, "Shock Wave must have a death wish for messing with my family."

Hellish flames came around Dante as he flew toward the battle like a fiery rocket. Lou Shen watched the devastating battle of power. Wind Burn showed great ability and power. One second, it was evenly matched. Then in the blink of an eye, Shock Wave sent a jolt of energy toward the energy battle. The ball of energy rushed toward Wind Burn. Wind Burn used every last bit of his life energy and will he had to stop the energy five feet away, but he could feel his hold slipping.

"So this is it, a date with Death," said Wind Burn through fearless laughs. Tears of regret blurred his vision, and then he closed his eyes...

Brother's past, ten years ago

Wind Burn would promise his father he would train harder if he would let Wind Burn take his poisonous spider wasp abomination to the park today to show all of the kids. Wind Burn was homeschooled by Lee Windol's trusted friend Alia, wedded in her spare time. Wind Burn could not be enrolled in any White Lotus classes, because it would raise too many questions and possibly lead to Wind Burn's death.

So Wind Burn was a lonely child. He could not wait for the weekends. Those days, Earth Nation Park was packed all day. So many games to play and so many things to do.

"Father, please…what's the point in having a pet if I can't show it to anyone?" pleaded Wind Burn.

"Well, I suppose, as long as you leave him in his container. If anyone gets bit, we're setting him free in the Lotus Forest. Are we clear?" said Lee.

"Clear as the Lotus Lake," said Wind Burn. He jumped for joy, ran to his room, grabbed the container, and ran out the door.

Once Wind Burn got to the park, he went straight to the merry-go-round where Dante was pushing the merry-go-round in circles. Dante stopped pushing when he saw Wind Burn approaching holding something.

"What's in the plastic box?" asked Dante curiously.

"A spider wasp his name is venom," said Wind Burn, showing Dante a closer look at the plastic cage.

"Can I hold him?" asked Dante as he tapped the cage three times.

"Sure," said Wind Burn as he sat the cage on the merry-go-round and opened the latch on the top.

The kids on the merry-go-round saw the mutated creature and ran yelling and screaming in different directions, except Elisha, who crawled over to the case and said, "Hey, guys, I don't think we should touch it." Then she jumped off the merry-go-round and stood by Dante.

"Why are you such a scaredy-cat? I hold him all the time," said Wind Burn in an aggravated voice.

"I'm not a scaredy-cat," said Dante as he hesitated and then slowly put his hand in the cage and grabbed the spider wasp. Before Dante could pull the creature out, he said, "Ouch," and removed his hand from the cage to see what the spider wasp did to him.

"Mommy!" yelled Elisha at the top of her young strong lungs as Wind Burn closed the cage, snatched it off the merry-go-round, and ran to laughing toward the Lotus Forest to torture his favorite pet for one last time.

Oh, the joys of pain, Wind Burn thought.

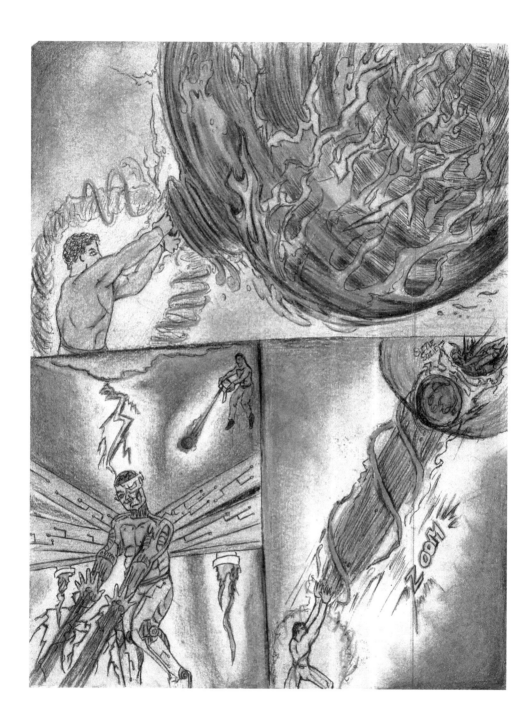

Present time

Dante flew so fast he bent reality around him, and then he teleported behind Shock Wave in the sky with the orb carrier in his hands. Dante knew when he opened the crystal cubed orb carrier, deadly power would seek the strongest energy source. Dante also knew from experience when he was forced to absorb his father's orb, no shield can block a power orb, and Shock Wave could not take his attention off the energy battle with Wind Burn. So they would be free to run, and Shock Wave would have to absorb the orb and hopefully get hit by all of the energy being battled. Dante opened the orb carrier. The orb spasmed in force energy and zoomed right to Shock Wave's back.

"Brother!" yelled Dante as Shock Wave's body absorbed the orb. In that exact moment, all of the energy that was about to obliterate Wind Burn hit Shock Wave and created an incredible explosion.

Booommm!

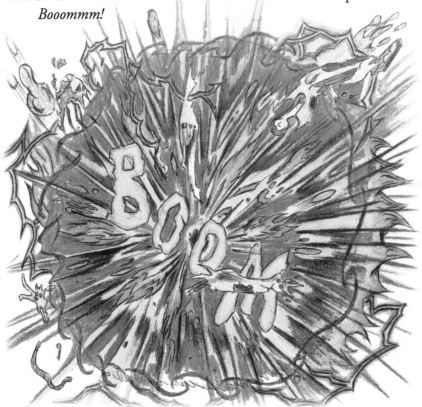

Chapter 10

Survival

Dragon Lord's fortress—Special Scouter Division

Dragon Lord sat on his throne chair in the Special Scouter Division looking at the 3D holo screens in front of him that played the events of last night's battle over and over again. The third screen to Dragon Lord's right showed a loop feed recording of Wind Burn's absorption.

The advanced computer system told Dragon Lord exactly how much power and essence Wind Burn now had. Dragon Lord guessed Dante's power was somewhere around the same, maybe more. Dragon Lord knew this would bring future problems. And what if the monk and brats find a meteor shard? Or maybe they would get killed by the many deadly creatures, them in the wilderness. All of these thoughts drove Dragon Lord even madder than he already was. The imperial king sat there in deep thought until he said, "Give me a VC with Dr. Volts. Put him on screen one.

"Visual conference on screen one," said a Dragon Lord guard. In twenty seconds, Dr. Volts appeared on the largest screen in front of Dragon Lord.

Dr. Volts was dressed in his usual violet doctor's coat; his computer-enhanced eyes were freaky.

"Yes, my lord," said Dr. Volts in a calm voice.

"Explain to me again why the Shock Wave was destroyed by an orb."

"Forgive me, my lord. This is a small problem I'm still working on."

"Seems like a big problem, Scientist," said Dragon Lord rudely.

"By binding so much power to a living specimen by alchemic scripture, more than five orbs will overload any clone Shock Wave's

94

power system. In which SW35 was the thirty-fifth clone of the original Shock Wave."

"The original Shock Wave that led my army in the hellfire war years ago. Where is he now?" said Dragon Lord.

"I have him here heavily sedated in my lab. I have been using his rare greater essence orb as the foundation for my Shock Wave cloning. It's hard to find live specimen who will willingly give their life to the advancement of alchemic technology."

"Prepare the original Shock Wave and five basic droids. I'm sending an execution team as soon as possible."

"Done, my lord."

"I'm also sending you an orb level 3 force human. Ki-claw, I think his name is. He will make a great live specimen for your experiments."

"My lord, I do have an idea to find a solution to the Shock Wave problem."

"What is it? My army cannot build itself."

"Perhaps if I could use a greater power source to bind orbs to live specimens, such as a meteor shard fragment or even Orian's god key. The shadow god surely could give you some sort of aid."

"I shall make time to take a trip to Shadow Empire City, to speak to Death face-to-face. Which would be more accurate to build my army, the shard or the lightning key?"

"Perhaps both if possible, my lord."

"We shall see, Scientist. I'll let you know," said Dragon Lord. Then the screens went back to playing the battle feed.

Dragon Lord's fortress: Prison cells

The head monk of the lotus clan lay on his bunk in his padded cell talking to Ki-claw for the past night. The cells had a random total of ten spots where the gray padding was missing, revealing clear crystal with alchemic writing on it that glowed and drained the prisoners of energy and power-blocked them. Ki-claw had his back to the wall of monk Gi Shen's cell wall that connected their cells. Ki-claw had his eyes closed with a look of hopelessness on his face. Gi Shen and Ki-claw talked about their lives and the past events that led them there, the family and loved ones they had lost and would continue to lose until Dragon Lord's reign over 7-Nations was over. But most importantly, the children of this world were born into a new wave of slavery called survival.

"Life is hard and unfair, but it is what you make of it," said Gi Shen.

"You wanna know what really angers me?" said Ki-claw, punching the floor.

"What is that?"

"How life is so cheap and meaningless nowadays no matter who you are or what your status is."

"We all have our parts to play in this game of life. I'm just grateful to have lived and enjoyed life this far."

"Not me. I'm not ready to die. I still have so much life to live," said Ki-claw on the brink of tears.

"If it's our time, so be it."

"My daughter just turned ten."

"What is important is that you raised her well. She will carry your legacy."

"I did my best to raise her, but being born to the force clan paves the way for one path, destruction," said Ki-claw.

"Not always. Would you like to hear a lesson I teach my students?"

"A monk's lesson. Gee, do tell," said Ki-claw sarcastically.

"Many years ago, when my brother's daughter was still young, we would walk through the Lotus Forest and talk. I would teach her the value of life, that everything in existence has a purpose. I would teach her the universal law, karma, right and wrong. Everything that you give and do comes back to you. So in all truth, you manifest your own reality by the choices you make, so the clan you are born to has nothing to do with what has come to pass. To take life and do bad things will darken your heart, and doing good will do the opposite. Either way, the universe will bring you back what you have given."

"Hold on a second, Monk. Some of us skipped your class growing up. What do you mean by 'heart'?" asked Ki-claw, confused.

"All elemental spirits are bound to an element of one kind, hence primary orb. This is the place of your soul and heart. Bad deeds weigh heavy on our being because of our connection to Gaia, which is connected to Fuzion. And Fuzion's presence on earth allows us to tap into the source on a greater level. The key is in our hearts. The gift of spirit in our hearts comes from the oldest god who is all."

"Where is this god now? I could sure use a blessing."

"All places, other dimensions, in the water, air, trees, and animals. If you look deep within, you might find the greatest gift that people die searching for. In most cases when an elemental dies, a tiny piece of the heart stays in the orb, and when someone absorbs it, they see visions of that being's life as it becomes a part of you. This shows and proves that life and spirit is universal. All is all."

"I never really understood or thought your monk classes to be of any importance when I was young. I wish I could have gained more knowledge wisdom and understanding about choice and purpose in life."

"Many never do. Their hearts and minds are tainted by wealth, ego, status, and power. Even a monk can get lost in the darkness."

"But you gotta admit, your monkish ways of life are weak and will get you nowhere, unless you're blessed with special scionic abilities like yourself."

"We all play our parts to survive as a whole, and like you said, we don't choose what element we are born with."

"Now I see my faults. You and your brother have taught me some valuable lessons about life, but still I don't see how my doing the right thing would have avoided me being here," said Ki-claw.

"It wouldn't have. In fact, you might have ended up on the run with my brother and grandsons, and look at me here with you. But at least you would die fighting for a positive cause! Don't beat yourself up over this. My brother has had decades to master self. It's not your fault his essence was greater than yours."

The entrance door to the prison quarters of Dragon Lord's fortress opened and closed with pressurized hisses. Gi Shen and Ki-claw both stood up and walked to their cell doors, attempting to look down the hallway. They could not see, but they heard two males' and a female's voices that anyone could not mistake as Dragon Lord's daughter.

"Open cells nine and ten. Ki-claw is in cell ten. Power-block restrain him, and prepare him for travel to Thunder Kingdom," said Halie to the two Dragon Lord guards with her. Halie entered cell 9 and stared at Gi Shen as he stood in the middle of his ten-by-ten feet cell with his hands behind his back. Gi Shen stared at Halie as if he had been touched by heaven.

Gi Shen saw a beautiful young lady who was twenty years old. What was strange was that she looked as if she had stolen his twin niece Raven Shen's face.

Her skin was tan like Raven's and Clara's. Her hair was long and silvery white just like Dragon Lord's. She had Dragon Lord's eyes with the stare of death that could kill. Halie had on a tight green leather body suit that had tiny platinum dragons all over.

This trance happened to Gi Shen every time he saw Halie.

"Monk leader...hello, snap out of it before I have your head," said Halie impatiently.

"I'm sorry, young lady. What is it you wish of me?" said Gi Shen.

"The fortress hall cameras three and four both spotted you giving the other monk a rare amulet of life energy. I want that amulet. Where have they gone?" said Halie.

"I don't know," said Gi Shen.

"*Fine*, rot in this cell forever, Monk," said Halie as Ki-claw and the two other Dragon Lord guards left the prison.

Chapter 11

Wilderness

Dante and Wind Burn walked slowly behind Lou Shen. Their travel gear and belongings seemed to weigh them down drastically. The sun was high in the sky, so Lou Shen guessed it was around noon. They had been walking nonstop since the battle last night to cover more ground, and still they were only in the middle of the deep desert. Lou Shen knew and could feel that both Dante and Wind Burn had used up most of their orb chi and they needed to rest. Lou Shen could simply use his life energy amulet and healing palm to heal them, but he wanted to teach them a lesson about pride.

"Come on, boys. We must hurry," said Lou Shen as he picked up his pace to a light jog. Dante and Wind Burn did not protest as they tried to keep up. After a half-mile jog, Wind Burn stumbled and fell forward.

Dante stopped next to Wind Burn and said, "Grampa, wait. We need to rest."

Lou Shen turned around and said, "Do you? I thought you would never ask," as he walked back to his grandsons.

Dante lay his bag down next to Wind Burn and flopped down in the sand. Wind Burn slowly sat up and removed his bags and said, "We need food and shelter."

Lou Shen looked at Wind Burn drenched in sweat and said, "We don't have time to set up camp. We need to keep moving."

"Grampa, can't you heal us?" asked Dante, out of breath.

"I could have healed you both before we left shadow tower," said Lou Shen.

"Well, why didn't you?" asked Wind Burn.

"Because neither of you asked. Lesson learned, especially for you, Wind Burn. Pride will get you killed out here in the wilderness. All we have is each other," said Lou Shen as he sat down next to Dante and grabbed some melons, dried meat, and a water canteen from his bag for each of them.

After they finished the food, Lou Shen stood behind Wind Burn, put his hands around his amulet in a praying gesture, and said, "Rejuvenating palm."

Lou Shen's amulet glowed with turquoise liquid energy that hummed. Lou Shen let go of the amulet and touched Wind Burn's shoulders. The glow around Lou Shen's hands disappeared, and Wind Burn's body glowed as it absorbed the healing water energy. Lou Shen did the same lotus healing palm to Dante, then gathered his things, stood up, and said, "Let's move." And move they did.

The boys followed with returned quickness and energy as they continued walking south in the middle of the desert. They speed walked side by side Lou Shen in the middle, Dante on Lou Shen's right, and Wind Burn on the left.

"Be conservative of your energy. We still have a long journey ahead of us," said Lou Shen. Wind Burn mumbled something under his breath. "What's that, grandson?"

"Nothing," said Wind Burn.

"Grampa, should we pick up the pace?" asked Dante.

"I believe we should," said Lou Shen as he started to jog lightly. Then Dante and Wind Burn did the same. The desert never seemed to end or change, thought Dante as they jogged at the same pace for about an hour until suddenly Lou Shen stopped. Dante and Wind Burn stopped next to Lou Shen.

"What's wrong, Grampa?" asked Dante, looking around but seeing nothing.

"We are surrounded, ready for battle, but follow my lead," said Lou Shen as he quickly sat his backpack on the ground, opened it, and pulled out a one-eyed glasses device that hooked on your ear. "On the piece that hooked on your ear had a small touch screen computer keypad." Lou Shen put the device on his ear and started pushing the screen while looking around them in a 360-degree turn.

Wind Burn grabbed his katana blade and got ready for battle. Dante took a closer look around, and about maybe eighty feet ahead all around them, he saw the sand moving in lumpy big circle that was closing in on them.

"I see them," said Wind Burn.

"Me too. What is it, Grampa?" said Dante.

"Dante, look in your bag's side pocket. There should be two more scouter devices," said Lou Shen. Dante sat his bag down and found the scouters and handed one to Wind Burn. At the same time, the brothers activated the devices and put them on their heads. In every direction they looked, the scouter eyeglass picked up different power levels.

"I'm reading orb level 5 and 6 energies. We don't stand a chance," said Dante.

"I will not become a slave," said Wind Burn as he grabbed two omega pill serums from his travel utility belt and ate them.

"Be humble, boys. Fighting is not always the solution. If we must, we fight, but first let me try and reason with them," said Lou Shen.

The sand circle moved closer around Lou Shen and his grandsons. Then eighteen muscular humanoid-looking sharks arose from the sand as if it was tan energized water. The sharklings kept their distance.

A large sharkling approached and stopped a few feet away from Lou Shen and said in a monstrous voice, "What reasons do you walk Sharkling Sand?"

"We are on a journey to Hell Mountain in the tainted lands. Forgive us for intruding on your land. We don't want any trouble. We simply wish to pass," said Lou Shen in a calm voice.

"Lie! You wear cloth of the dark dragon. You spy to find the secret Sharkling City," said the large sharkling, pointing a razor claw at Lou Shen.

"My grandsons and I are on the run from Dragon Lord. We seek Hell Mountain to join the rebellion," said Lou Shen. All of the sharklings roared in an unknown sharkling language as they jumped up and down hysterically.

One of the sharklings shouted, "Leader!" and all of the sharklings chanted leader in unison. The large sharkling known as Razel raised his right clawed fist, and all of the sharklings went silent.

"We take you to see Seastra in Undersand City," said Razel.

"And if we choose not to go with you?" said Lou Shen.

"Then you die now," said Razel.

Chapter 12

Under the Radar

Dragon Lord's fortress—air hangar

Halie, Mark, and the original Shock Wave waited for the full robotic droids and the new bioengineered Ki-claw to arrive from Thunder Kingdom. They were gathered around the master terminal, waiting patiently with tension in the air. The roof panel to Dragon Lord's fortress was open, revealing a sunset and darkening sky. They had been waiting for Halie's battleship to arrive from Thunder Kingdom. The enormous ship held forty medium passengers plus ten pilots, and the ship was packed with advanced technology and orb-fused weapons that could destroy cities.

Halie and Mark stood at the terminal holo screen with the same thought in their heads, what obstacles might they face on this mission in the unknown outside world? No one was above the many deadly abomination creatures created by Fuzion. The original Shock Wave was pure human elemental but only orb level 2, but he was a rare one in Dragon Lord's army. He had such great essence that he could defeat an orb level 7 elementals with no combined-elements attacks or stacked shields being used.

As kids, Mark, Halie, and Shock Wave had been friends; but from the years of alchemic experimentation on Shock Wave to make the Shock Wave clones, Shock Wave became evil, lifeless, and even creepy in his constant silence.

As young teenagers, Mark and Halie tried dating but later decided to remain friends due to Halie's explosive behavior and party-wild life. Mark was kinda angry at Halie for not saving his friend or at least attempting to save Ki-claw from the bio race change of power and technology that makes Ki-claw a monster in Mark's eyes forever. Mark hated the bioengineered race, and he hated Dr. Volts for creating it.

The bioengineered race got stronger and faster by alchemic modifications, but they paid the price because they are not able to reach an elemental's full potential. And now more than ever, Mark was begging to hate Dragon Lord for the evil things he constantly did. Ki-claw's family dedicated their lives to Dragon Lord and the force clan, and it was the payment for loyalty. *I won't let this happen to me*, thought mark. In the back of Mark's mind, he often thought of running away and joining the rebellion, if one even still existed, but the thought of leaving Halie made him discard that idea from his mind because he loved her too much. Mark looked over at Halie to see her staring at him. Halie started to say something, but Mark looked away.

"Aircraft Battleship Two landing through the panel," said one of the five receptionists at the terminals. The craft was metallic silver and was by far bigger than any ship Dragon Lord had in his ship inventory. The ship landed, and no one said a word as they boarded the great ship.

Desert

The sharklings seemed to pick a random spot in the sand. Three sharklings started digging together in the same spot with their clawed hands. They began to dig faster and faster until they moved in a blur. The sand turned to tan energy and uncovered a large tunnel that led twenty feet underground. The tunnel was slanted and fifteen feet wide and high. They walked down the tunnel in darkness. Dante first, Wind Burn behind Dante, and Lou Shen behind Wind Burn, then ten sharklings behind Lou Shen, and Razel last. The rest of the sharklings stayed above ground as constant guards always swam in the sands.

Wind Burn activated a compass and a high beam of light on his back holo net and said, "We're still traveling south."

"Good," said Lou Shen. They traveled on a downward slanted path for an hour until the tunnel broke into several different paths like an underground maze. They traveled through the maze until they stopped in a small circular chamber that had six different tunnels and a small pond that glowed light blue in the chamber's center.

"We rest," said Razel. The ten sharklings spread throughout the chamber in groups of two and three as they sat and spoke in their strange language to one another and pointed at Lou Shen and his grandsons as they stood at the entrance to the cave.

"Sit, rest," said Razel with his clawed hands crossed, standing by the tunnel they just came through. Lou Shen and his grandsons walked and located an empty spot by the glowing pond and sat down with their gear.

"Grampa, why are they laughing and pointing at us?" whispered Dante as they sat down.

"I don't know, grandson, but I'm sure we will soon find out," said Lou Shen.

"Yikes!" shouted a startled Wind Burn, who almost jumped out of his skin when he looked in the pond to see a female sharkling drinking the glowing water with her face in the pond.

The female sharkling pulled her head from the water and looked at Wind Burn and said, "Drink, long journey." Her body glowed for a second as she slowly backed away. Lou Shen and his grandsons looked at each other and then at the pond.

"Monk's healing waters with no alchemic scripture or monk's healing amulet, strange," said Monk Lou Shen. Dante leaned over and put his face in the pond and took a big gulp. When he pulled his face out, nothing happened.

"Breath waters of Seastra," said Razel, still guarding the entrance tunnel. Dante nodded and stuck his head in the glowing pond once more and took a deep breath. Surprisingly, Dante did not choke. The water energy flowed through him, and he could feel his life energy and orb chi returning to its max. By the time Dante raised his head from the pond, his body stopped glowing, and Wind Burn and Lou Shen had their faces in the water.

"We go now," said Razel as he pointed to the tunnel directly across from him. They walked and kept the same order as before.

"Grampa, can the sharklings see in the dark? Do they have special vision like Dr. Volts?" said Dante.

"I suppose so, grandson," said Lou Shen.

"Can you or I get special vision like Dr. Volts and become bio—" said Dante.

"Quiet, brother," said Wind Burn in an aggravated tone. They walked in total silence for the rest of the way guided by the light from Wind Burn's holo net…

Aircraft Battleship—pilot deck

It took eight full droids to fully operate the craft's flight systems. The pilot pit could hold ten medium humanoids and maybe two large creatures. The droids remained busy at their pilot holo screens. Halie slowly walked over to Mark's radar holo computer and said, "Hey, um, I just want to tell you I'm sorry," as she looked over in Ki-claw's direction. "My father was pretty angry about the whole situation, and even I know my limits to persuade him. Please don't be mad at me," said Halie.

"Don't worry about it. Let's just complete the mission and get home," said Mark while rubbing Halie's cheek and looking into her eyes.

"Mmm, 'kay," said Halie as she hugged Mark and returned to her head pilot seat, which was a throne surrounded by holo screens in the middle of the pilot pit. And the night seemed to only get darker.

Mark hadn't said a word to anyone since Halie spoke to him. Every now and then, Mark would glance over at Ki-claw to see him in a lost gaze, or Ki-claw would break out into a twitching seizure, or he would be opening and closing his mechanical hand looking at it with a sad look. Mark could not stand to see his childhood friend this way, and he planned to do something about it real soon. Mark loved his clan of the force element, and he loved 7-Nations. Dragon Lord guards could do whatever they wanted with the right skills and brainpower. Dragon Lord guards were the muscle, the law, and the richest nation thanks to Dragon Lord, but a blind elemental could see the obvious: Dragon Lord was a major problem in the equation, and someone had to solve it. In three hours, the massive ship had circled the desert. No human or human elemental could walk or fly faster than this ship that had three rocket thrusters that were powered by force energy. In all that time, the ship's radar still hadn't picked up any life heat signals.

"I still got nothing," said Mark.

"Well, let's give the desert another scan before we call my father with the bad news," said Halie.

* * * * *

Dante, Wind Burn, Lou Shen, and the sharklings walked for another hour deep down into the earth, traveling through the maze of mixed sand and earth tunnels until finally they entered an enormous chamber with two sharklings waiting at attention by the back wall directly ahead. Lou Shen and his grandsons stepped to the right inside the chamber, and all of the sharklings moved ahead to the middle of the chamber.

"Go to the middle," said Razel, who stepped into the chamber beside them. They all gathered around each other in the middle of the chamber. Razel said something in his sharkling tongue to the two giant sharklings by the wall. The two giant sharklings each put their right-hand claw over their chest and closed their eyes. In ten seconds, two medium-sized tan orbs of glowing energy appeared in their hands from their chest. At the same time, both giant sharklings inserted their orbs into the medium-sized hole in the wall where they stood. The wall and floor began to glow. Then the giant sharklings absorbed their orb back into their chest.

"Earth orbs, I've never seen them so big," said Dante. The sand and earth glowed brighter and disappeared around the earth where everyone stood, revealing a disk of earth that started to rotate and sink deeper into the ground. The earth disk dropped a hundred feet and landed in the middle of a small city made of earth and stone. Everyone stepped off of the earth disklike saucer, and it rose back to where it came from. Dante, Lou Shen, and Wind Burn could see the whole city of sharkling creatures staring at them.

"Fresh meat and orbs to eat," yelled a sharkling in the distance as hundreds of sharkling around the city came out of huts and stone homes to take a look. A great crowd of sharklings came around them with looks of hunger. Then out of nowhere, a medium-sized sharkling leaped at Dante, claws ready. Before Dante could react, Razel jumped in front of Dante in a blur of speed, grabbed the sharp-toothed sharkling by the neck, and roared in his sharkling tongue. Slowly the group of sharklings backed up and made path leading to the largest building made of fine marble straight ahead. As they walked on the dirt path, Wind Burn noticed that all the crowd of sharklings still followed them but kept their distance. When they reached the top of the hill, no one was there guarding the entrance to the marble building, nor was there a door to the cave-like entrance. Lou Shen, his grandsons, and Razel walked inside the marble building revealing another enormous chamber except this chamber was split in half. The half closest to the entrance was made of smooth brown granite. Crystals that formed stairs connected to the second half of the chamber which formed a pool filled with sharklings. The pool glowed and shimmered just like all special healing waters. Razel and his guests stepped to the first step, and Razel started looking for someone. Then a beautiful young sharkling woman appeared from the water and swam to the first step of the pool. The sharkling woman had no razor teeth or claws like the rest of the sharklings had. Instead she had humanlike features—long gray hair and smooth light-blue skin that matched the water. The scouter devices told Lou Shen the sharkling woman had a power level of 221,400.

"Razel, what reasons do you bring humans here to our secret city?" said Seastra. Razel bowed his head and spoke in his sharkling language and explained the events of the past few hours. Seastra listened to Razel, and every few words, she would take a quick glance at Dante and smile.

"Come swim, Razel," said Seastra. Razel climbed the steps and jumped into the water and blended in with the many sharklings in the pool. Seastra hopped out of the pool and sat on the first step facing Lou Shen and his grandsons. Seastra smiled, and her eyes glowed with white scionic energy as she gazed through her guests.

"My name is Lady Seastra. I am a sharkling scion, leader of this city and the sharkling race," said Seastra.

"My name is Lou Shen, and these are my grandsons, Wind Burn and Dante," said Lou Shen as he placed a hand on each of his grandsons' shoulders with a proud smile.

Seastra said, "Lou Shen two orbs water soul, Wind Burn four orbs storm soul, Dante four orbs very strong fire spirits to come."

"You can see elemental orb levels in beings. How do you have the gift of sight from the water god and you are not human?" said Lou Shen.

"I was reborn on Abomination Day just like everyone else. The will of Fuzion be done," said Seastra.

"Strange," said Lou Shen.

"What is strange is that dormant scionic energy sleeps inside yourself, Lou. Strange group you three are, indeed," said Seastra, looking at them as her eyes once again glowed with scionic energy.

"Why doesn't your race live in the sea? If you don't mind me asking," said Dante.

Seastra said, "Ask any question you feel you must know. I did not foresee this day's events in a vision, but Fuzion gave many gifts, along with the biggest curse to my people. We love water. Almost all of my people have earth souls, except me and a few others who have water or ice souls. But when we changed to this humanoid form, we lost our, um, how do you humans say…gills, and that is a big burden on us that life could ever deal, even worse than your Dragon Lord's army and war machines killing and destroying what's left of earth for his own personal gain," said Seastra.

"We are aware of this. That is why we seek the survivors of the rebellion at Hell Mountain to join the rebellion. We bring no harm to your city or people," said Lou Shen.

"I know this, or you would have been dead already. Dante's face, the son of Luke has saved your life today. *Rise of the hellfire storm*," said Seastra, smiling at Dante.

"You knew my father?" asked Dante.

"No, sadly, I do not on a personal level, but we are followers to some extent. Or should I say when the fire spirit and pure storm lead the rebellion, we will stand with them so the dark dragon will fall," said Seastra.

"My job is train such leaders," said Lou Shen, looking at his grandsons.

"Take a look," said Seastra as her right finger glowed with scionic energy. She stuck her finger in the water and stirred in a circle until an older, darker version of Dante dressed in red elemental hellfire plate armor appeared in the water like a movie and spoke.

SEASTRA.

Chapter 13

Memory Projection and the Scions

Seastra's memory

I am the hellfire clan leader of 7-Nations. I am calling out to my brothers and sisters of all races. We are one, and one is all that is in existence. I am making this holo recording in search of bravery, honor, and truth, maybe even leadership. I am calling brave souls to stand with me even though the odds may not be in our favor. How long shall we slave while Angel sits in his fortress with unlimited tech and wealth at the cost of your labor? How long shall we stand by and watch more of our people be killed for Dragon Lord's amusement? How long shall we bear these hunger pains of wanting to ascend orb levels to reach our true potential of elemental power? Because of him, this need to fill our spirit and be whole burns so deeply. Why do we die on death missions when he is the savior! The world cowers at the sound of Dragon Lord because the shadow god guides him. Well, the shard energy god of emerald light guides me.

The shard energy god is the true lord of the sixth element, and soon he will be freed. But first we must end Angel's reign of darkness and hurt, and we must do it together. The prophecy told by the fourth scion, Clara Saint, says that a great spirit warrior will surpass orb level 7 and have full control of all elements. He will become an ascended elemental god who will walk the earth and defy the gods of darkness. I stand before you today to tell you I am closer than ever. I have ascended powers of gods. The fire spirits have awakened within my being. So I ask the world to stand with me in the rebellion so that we may set ourselves free. I am searching for six human elementals like myself who also have ascended powers so that we may form an ascended council who will lead with me in the hellfire war. When Dragon Lord falls, we will reunite all life on earth and rebuild together. All races, all clans, all nations, and small cities will be equal. I have a secret headquarters in the tainted lands where a small army awaits my command. Dragon Lord's time is short. Which side will you stand on when the storm comes? *Rise of the hellfire storm…* I am Luke Saint Cipher. Stand with me now, or get lost in the storm…

*****

"How did you do that?" asked Dante, rubbing his teary face with his right arm.

"I can project memories I have in water," said Seastra.

"My father is dead," said Dante as he regained his composure.

"This I know. You have come to take his place, do you not?" said Seastra.

"My grandsons are in training to do so, but it is not as easy as it sounds," said Lou Shen.

"You must believe in yourselves and learn to tap into the higher states of Fuzion," said Seastra.

"You mean the hypermodes," said Dante.

"Yes, yes! Hahaha, and so prophecy takes route again. My, what a glorious day has come," said Seastra happily.

"We must be successful we stake our lives on it," said Wind Burn, angry at Seastra's sudden joyfulness.

"I know this, Wind Burn of the dark," said Seastra.

Dante said, "How many scions are there that you know of?"

"There are nine scions that are in tune to the source. Through the source, we are all connected. Sometimes, all scions have the same vision unless a certain god wishes to speak to a certain scion. The purpose of a scion is to bring the truth of all to the people. Some scions embrace their calling, and some don't. I will show you pictures of scions through memory projection and tell you what I know about them," said Seastra. Her finger started glowing again, and she stirred the water until a chart of pics and info formed into view.

Scion Chart		
Name	Race	Location
1. Nature, the first scion	human/pure water elemental (God)	unknown
2. Gi Shen (orb guardian)	Human scion	7-Nations
3. Raven Shen	race unknown	Shadow Hell energy signal reading
4. Clara Shen	human scion	unknown
5. Living wisdom	human scion	7-Nations
6. Alia Wedden	human scion	7-Nations
7. Trinity's Light	light scion human	Trinity City
8. Seastra	sharkling scion	Undersand City
9. Infinite Spirit	spirit human scion	Champion City

"Oh my, I just had a vision. Lou Shen will be the tenth scion," said Seastra.

"No, I won't," said Lou Shen.

"Even stranger, you deny your gift of sight," said Seastra.

"I am a conscious being of spirit. My true identity is all," said Lou Shen.

"So you don't need the gods. They're here to help us," said Seastra.

"Are they really?" said Lou Shen.

"Great day, indeed," said Seastra as she smiled and then said, "You all may stay here as my guest as long as you need. No harm will come to you."

"We are grateful for your hospitality, Lady Seastra," said Lou Shen with a bow.

"Razel!" shouted Seastra. Razel swam next to Seastra, and they spoke in their sharkling tongue. After they finished talking, Seastra said, "Wind Burn, may I have a word with you alone?" Wind Burn looked at Lou Shen as Lou Shen nodded in approval. Razel jumped out of the pool and led Lou Shen and Dante out of the marble building.

Chapter 14

Legendary Power Unlocked

The droids, Halie, and Mark flew the battleship over the never-ending desert while scanning the sandy floor. An hour later, Halie's computer screen went green, and she read a message.

> Message from: Dragon Lord
> Level Dry City
> Then come home

Halie walked over to Mark and said, "New plan: 'Level Dry City.'"

Undersand City

Seastra yelled a few words in her sharkling tongue as she stared at Wind Burn. Small, medium, and large sharklings jumped out of Seastra's glowing energy pool and left the tan marble building. Only Seastra and Wind Burn remained in the building.

"What's this about?" said Wind Burn.

"I sense a dark aura in your soul and heart. Why is this?" asked Seastra.

"I've had a troubled life."

"How so?"

"It's a long story that I do not wish to tell, nor do I have the time," said Wind Burn in a smug tone.

"Wind Burn of the storm, I am one you can trust. If you won't tell me your story, let me see for myself."

"I don't know if that's a good idea, Lady."

"I only wish to help. I sense another powerful sleeping storm soul on your person. Do I not... Please come sit. We must trust."

Wind Burn stood there in deep thought for a moment and then slowly sat his travel gear down except for the legendary weapon case. Then Wind Burn climbed the six steps and sat next to Seastra and placed the powerful sleeping weapon next to him.

"I'm going to take a small glimpse into your mind so that I will understand you better," said Seastra as she touched Wind Burn's forehead. Upon contact with Seastra, Wind Burn's body went into a spasm of violent shakes and seizures. Seastra's eyes rapidly played the events of Wind Burn's life as if a movie played through her head at the speed of light. Seastra removed her hand from Wind Burn's head and grabbed Wind Burn before he fell back into the pool, while he regained his consciousness.

"Wow," said Wind Burn while rubbing his temples, feeling a little drained.

"I see now," said Seastra, deep in thought.

"What did you see?"

"I see why your orb soul is so...dark."

"Why do you change the way you speak all of a sudden? You changed storm soul to orb soul and you're more proper."

"I have learned many things from your memories. Your way of life has elevated my intellect."

"You are a strange one, Seastra."

"You will meet even stranger beings than me on your journey to defeat Dragon Lord. And you must be wise enough to know who to trust."

"Dante asks a lot of questions, but he's wise."

"Not more than you. Wisdom is your attribute as wind. Now down to serious matters. Why do you keep your feelings and thoughts deep inside?"

"I guess I don't trust anyone."

"And why don't you have trust?"

"Because people only want to use you for their own personal gain."

"But being alone will only get you so far. Your younger brother has looked up to you since your childhood. Now you are not alone. Why don't you confide in him?"

"He's stronger than me, and I don't know his angle or what he seeks to gain from me."

"Maybe he has no angle and only wants the love of an older brother. Dante, as you call him, has one of the purest hearts I've seen in a long time. Your brother may be slightly stronger than you, but you are more wise and intelligent than he is. Strength is not everything in life. You must rise above the pride issues you have because you two need each other to defeat the dark lord."

"I don't know how to be a big brother. I've been an only child all my life. What am I supposed to do?"

"It is simple. Give him guidance and encouragement, share your opinions and thoughts, and don't be so mean and negative all the time."

"I'm just used to being an only child with no purpose. This is a lot on my shoulders. Just yesterday, I was stocking food in 7-Nations market. Now I'm training to lead a rebellion. It's all so sudden."

"I understand your troubles. A lot has changed. You have a new family, and you're soon to be an uncle. But let me ask you one last question, for this is unclear to me. Do you think you will ever be able to accept Dante as your brother and love him as so?"

"Strangely…yes! I've always felt a connection between us. When we were young competing in dragon tournaments, I've always felt compelled to show my strengths and expose his weaknesses. But Dante is born to the hellfire orb. They learn faster and adapt to their opponent quickly in combat. Tell me, Seastra, how am I supposed to compete with that?"

"How about don't compete just be there for Dante, as he has always been there for you. In this way you both excel, and not only in combat but in life as well."

"I'll try…but…"

"No buts, just do. Now you expressing your personal feelings and sharing your life with me has convinced me to help you awaken this powerful weapon you have," said Seastra.

"I can't activate it. It almost killed me nearly draining all of my LE and orb chi, and the weapon still didn't awaken," said Wind Burn sadly in defeat.

"I have heard stories of these—how do you say?—legendary weapons. Can I see?" Wind Burn grabbed the case at his side, opened it, and placed it on Seastra's lap.

"Wonderful art and crystals," said Seastra, amazed by the alchemy.

"Look, my real father left me some instructions. Maybe they can help us. When I channeled my wind energy through the sword when we were fighting Shock Wave, I knew I could never possess enough power to unlock the weapon," said Wind Burn as he began navigating through the holo net on his wrist.

"That is a holo net, correct?" said Seastra, amused at the holographic lights forming multiple computer screens.

"Yea, it's a holo computer device. It's an older version of the one I'm used to in 7-Nations. Dragon Lord can't track this kind."

"Before we go any further, you must promise me one thing."

"What is it?"

"You must protect your brother at all cost. And when he's afraid to move forward, you must push him through."

"I'll protect him with my life," said Wind Burn as he started the holo recorded message of his father...

Recorded holo message (3 of 3) 3 minutes, 37 seconds; date: 2060??

A 3D holographic image of Jonathan Swift stood in a cave lit by a small fire in the cave's center. Swift held the legendary weapon in front of him as it glowed and amplified a large razor sword made of storm. Swift spoke. "Hello, son, know that I love you more than you could imagine. Now a legendary weapon is like an overpowered battery. After so much usage, the weapon goes dead, and you have to recharge it. How much energy you put into the sword rewards how much power within the sword is unlocked. Before you yourself will be able to unlock the sword's lowest potential, you will need to be at least orb level 6. It takes a great amount of any energy source to awaken the sword to its full potential. *But* if your will is not strong, the weapon will drain you dry of all LE and chi until you die, so don't try until you know you're ready. I must warn you—don't let the sword control or turn you into a killing power-crazed junkie giving all of your energy to the sword. To deactivate the sword, you must drain all of the swords energy until it sleeps again. This weapon is not made by death. It's forged by the alchemist drake brothers if I'm not mistaken. They have a city in the wild lands called Port Shard Land. Now I know this is a lot, but this may be the only way for you to make it through the wilderness. I love you, son. Good luck! And *be swift*. Make it through the wilderness.

Wind Burn ended the recording and said, "My father was a fearless elemental but foolish as well."

"We all chose our own paths in life, so don't judge your father. Try and learn from his faults," said Seastra as she stood and walked down the steps to the marble floor. Then Wind Burn followed. Seastra held the swords case and asked, "Did you drink the healing waters today?"

"Yes, just once."

"Good, we are ready then."

Wind Burn stood in front of Seastra and grabbed the sword from the case and held it sideways with both hands. Seastra set the case down and then put her hands on Wind Burn's shoulders and said, "Once the sword has taken all of your orb chi, I'm going to give you half of mine or maybe more, so ready yourself."

"Okay, one with the storm," said Wind Burn as he channeled his orb chi into the weapon. The sword drained Wind Burn's energy faster and faster until a small aura of storm formed around the orb in the hilt of the sword. Wind Burn felt the sword drain all of his orb chi and then start draining his life energy. Seastra felt Wind Burn weaken, so she summoned her energy and gave it to Wind Burn with a jolt of shocking power. In a matter of ten seconds, the sword had drained all of Seastra's orb chi and almost depleted her life energy. The storm aura around the sword's orb got a little bit bigger and levitated Wind Burn and Seastra into the air.

"Get back!" shouted Wind Burn.

"I cannot break the storm's hold on me!" shouted Seastra.

"Ahhh! Wind tornado!" shouted Wind Burn, and a circular wind blew from the orb of the sword and pushed Seastra twenty feet across the room. Seastra fell to the ground and then quickly stood to her feet. She watched Wind Burn battle the sword while storm energy from Wind Burn's heart poured into the sword. Seastra could feel the deep depths of the sword's hunger, and she knew she or Wind Burn could ever have the power to awaken the legendary weapon.

"Ahhh!" shouted Wind Burn.

Seastra thought quickly and said, "Water control!" as she pointed hand at the water pool and grabbed from where she stood. Then she pulled toward her. A giant water hand-claw formed in the pool, and then the hand-claw swirled down and grabbed Seastra. In the same second, the sword's storm aura grew bigger and formed a sphere around Wind Burn that swallowed him whole. Seastra swam in the hand-claw and breathed the water as it healed her and then took her to where Wind Burn hovered in the air.

"Hang on, Windstin!" yelled Seastra as she grabbed another hand at the water pool, then threw the water at Wind Burn, and then controlled the water hand to grab Wind Burn's storm sphere. Once the giant hand-claw had Wind Burn, Seastra pulled him toward the pool. As soon as Wind Burn got pulled into the air over the pool, Seastra teleported into the water hand-claw that had Wind Burn clutched and then entered the storm and touched Wind Burn's shoulders. Seastra used more water-controlled claws and hands and willed the stored water energy in the pool and gave wave after wave of lotus energy to Wind Burn.

"*Not enough!* Take all I have!" yelled Seastra as hundreds light blue hands and claws formed from the pool, surrounded the storm sphere, and got pulled in. This went on for a minute or so. Then the deep pool of water got lower and lower until the giant storm around the sword stopped.

"*Muu-wah,*" said Seastra in a kissing gesture as she fell to the floor of the pool with the remaining water. Wind Burn teleported next to Seastra and caught her and pulled her close as she fell unconscious. Then Wind Burn's tornado aura came around them and slowly guided them to the ground of the ankle-deep pool. Wind Burn carefully laid Seastra down and bent down to drink.

Chapter 15

Newfound Ascended Power: Pure Wind

Dante and Lou Shen followed Razel down the hill to the village huts. Razel located an empty hut, opened the stone door, and said, "You rest. Yell if you need me." Then Razel turned around and walked toward the pond in the city's market. Lou Shen took his scouter device off and then grabbed a flashlight from his bag as he and Dante entered the hut. Dante closed the stone door behind them while Lou Shen sat the flashlight on the dirt floor facing up. Lou Shen unpacked his bedroll and rolled it out in the middle of the floor. Then he sat his travel gear in the corner of the small hut and lay down to rest. Dante watched his grandfather as he stood by the door with a look on his face.

"Grampa, are you sure Wind Burn is okay?" asked Dante.

"Yes, grandson. Now try and get some rest… We have a long journey ahead," said Lou Shen through a long yawn. Dante slowly unrolled his bedroll next to his grandfather and put his pack in the opposite corner. Dante's stomach growled, so he grabbed some dried melons from his grandfather's bag and lay down. After Dante finished the fruit, he reached over and turned the flashlight off. In seconds, his grandfather was in a deep sleep of calm breaths. Dante lay there in the darkness for what he thought to be at least ten minutes, and he could not sleep—too much on his mind. Dante felt for the flashlight in the dark and turned it on and then quietly walked over to his bag. He located his small black box and crept out of the hut to roam Undersand City.

Dante thought about Elisha and his soon-to-be son. He wished this was just a dream. He wanted to be there for his family, teach his son, and watch him grow up. But no, he had to lead the rebellion. Why him? On top of that, Wind Burn worried him so much. His brother's heart seems so dark and hateful. And what was crazy? As far as Dante could remember, Wind Burn had always been like this. But now that they knew that they were brothers, Dante hoped that Wind Burn's attitude would change. Dante felt a little bit down. In times like this, he would watch the info chips his parents had left him to raise his spirits. But he had no holo net. *Why so much rain on my life!* thought Dante.

Test the legend

Seastra's body absorbed the healing waters as soon as Wind Burn put her down. Seastra sat up and looked around as her body glowed and healed.

"Now I know the meaning of the word *wow*," said Seastra. Wind Burn and Seastra laughed as Wind Burn offered his hand, helping Seastra up. They stood in the bottom of the fifty-feet pool and looked in awe to see how much energy the sword could hold.

"Sorry about your pool," said Wind Burn.

"Don't be. In time, it can be regained. Now I must see what a legend of a weapon can do," said Seastra as she took a deep drink of the ankle-deep water.

"Lady Seastress, I don't think that's a good idea. I may hurt you. I don't know how to proficiently use this weapon yet," said Wind Burn.

"I am a level 6 elemental. I'm stronger than I look," said Seastra in a sassy voice.

"I know you're strong, but we don't understand the sword's power," pleaded Wind Burn.

"So let's get some understanding together. Now let's go," said Seastra. She backflipped twenty feet away from Wind Burn.

Wind Burn channeled a small amount of his orb chi through the sword. The legendary weapon hummed and vibrated in Wind

Burn's hands as the orb in the hilt of the sword glowed to life. Wind Burn waved the sword side to side in the air to get a feel of the sword. With each flick of Wind Burn's wrist, the sword amplified a large razor blade made of wind energy in its path. Wind Burn looked in Seastra's direction to see ten orbs of lotus energy headed straight for him. With swift thought, Wind Burn raised the sword, and a vicious storm poured out of the blade. With a downward slash, the energy blade and storm knocked all ten water orb blasts to the ground.

"*Ascended* wind state!" shouted Wind Burn as he raised the legendary weapon over his head. A powerful tornado of storm energy surrounded Wind Burn's body in a downpour from the weapon, turning Wind Burn's body into a large wind pure elemental.

"How do you like my new level 4 ascended power?" asked Wind Burn.

"I am aware of the human's godly powers, but I must admit I have seen better," said Seastra as she jumped in a somersault. While in midair, Seastra threw five combined level 3 force-water orb blasts at Wind Burn's new form.

Wind Burn gracefully sidestepped Seastra's attack and yelled, "Stop toying with me with weak attacks!"

"Just some fun, Windstin," said Seastra, laughing. When Seastra landed, she leaped right back into the air.

"Legendary wind scar!" shouted Wind Burn in anger, using his strongest attack. A giant long wind blade mixed with fire and water beamed at Seastra in the air with great speed and power. Seastra gathered every element she had and formed a water mirror shield. The mirror fazed into existence in front of Seastra and swallowed Wind Burn's wind scar.

Seastra's water mirror started to crack because of the intense power. Seastra pivoted to the left and pointed the stacked shield water mirror toward the ceiling. The powerful wind scar ripped through the water mirror and shot through the roof, slicing and destroying the smooth stone. In a blur of speed, Seastra ran toward Wind Burn and then teleported behind him.

"My strongest combined attack. *Paralyzing palm!*" said Seastra as she attempted to touch Wind Burn's neck. Her hand glowed with five different elements. Wind Burn's mind and the sword were one, and the blade glowed and zoomed in an arc of storm behind Wind Burn's back, blocking Seastra's attack.

"Impossible!" yelled Seastra with hurt in her voice.

"Wind slaughter!" yelled Wind Burn as he teleported behind Seastra, twirling the blade in a helicopter motion. Multiple large blades of storm shot in Seastra's direction. Seastra barely had time to evade as she fifty-five feet up to the highest step of the pool. The beautiful sharkling leader stood there for a second, amazed at the deadly power coming from the sword in the form of hundreds of large wind blades slicing up her home. A split second later, Wind Burn stormed into the air right above Seastra and swung the blade and yelled, "Wind slaughter!"

Once again, multiple large wind blades beamed from the sword, slicing holes where Seastra stood. Seastra evaded the attack by an inch, teleporting outside next to an approaching Razel and twenty of Seastra's most trusted warriors. Razel looked at Seastra's frustrated but unharmed face and said, "You will regret if Lady Seastress is hurt." Dante ran up the hill looking at the destruction of hundreds of large holes in the sharklings' main building.

"Brother, what have you done!" yelled Dante as Wind Burn's pure wind state flew out of the main building and then landed next to Seastra and powered his ascended power down and sheathed the weapon of death.

"It was my doing. Now, everyone, calm down," said Seastra, still a little shaken up.

"But, Seastress," said Razel.

"No buts. Assemble a group of lotus and earth sharklings to fix the main building and pool," said Seastra.

"As you wish, Lady Seastress," said Razel. He mumbled something, and then he and the sharkling warriors walked up the hill to the main building.

"Come, boys," said Seastra, gesturing with her hands for Dante and Wind Burn to come close to her. By now, most of the city had come out of their homes and formed a circle around them.

"Where were you headed, Dante?" said Seastra.

"To the market, until I looked up the hill to see giant wind blades slicing through the main building," said Dante.

"It was just a simple test of wonder," said Seastra as she led them to the market with her hands around their shoulders.

"What's in the black box?" asked Seastra.

"Crystals, platinum marks, and some recordings from my parents," said Dante. Wind Burn leaned in and made eye contact with Dante. "Bro, what type of new power was that?" asked Dante, changing the subject.

"My orb level 4 ascended power allows me to turn my body into a pure wind elemental state," said Wind Burn.

"And I see your legendary weapon works now," said Dante.

"Seastra helped me unlock the weapon and master its power," said Wind Burn with triumph.

Dante looked at Seastra and said, "I can't help but think that there's more to the reason you help us than my father's rebellion status."

Seastra said, "I believe in the prophecy. I can see both of your inner auras. Dante's is light and Wind Burn's is dark. Do you think this will be a problem in the times to come?"

"No!" Dante and Wind Burn said at the same time with confidence.

"What path do you live by?" asked Wind Burn.

"None or neutral as you call it. When I was first reborn by Fuzion on Abomination Day, I saw the results of the balance being unstable, when the shard energy god fell," said Seastra.

Then as they walked through the market, they stopped at a booth of glowing light fruit. "This is the fruit of the god of light," said Dante.

"Yes, it is, and you both can have one on me," said Seastra.

"Five platinum a piece, Lady Seastress," said a pure light elemental behind the booth's counter. "You can have mine, brother," said Wind Burn as he put fruit in his bag.

"How much for five more?" asked Dante.

"I'll give you a deal since you're with Lady Seastra, fifteen platinum," said the pure light elemental.

"Done," said Dante as he handed the tiny marks to the light elemental.

Wind Burn collected them and put them in his bag and said, "Dragon Lord bands light fruit in 7-Nations. You can only find shadow fruit in Earth Nation under the table. Over time, I have come to love the dark sweet fruit."

"That is one reason your heart is so tainted," said Seastra.

"Yes, I know. I have read the book of death many times in 7-Nations. I know what is expected of me. And I also know what not to do to avoid Dante getting in a bad situation," said Wind Burn. They walked to the market's pool and sat down at the edge.

Seastra dived in, came back up, swam next to them, and then said, "Windstin, what pact on your soul will you make with Death, or will you even sell your soul? You already have a legendary weapon, and it's not marked by Death."

"I won't sell my soul," said Wind Burn, in deep thought.

"Good," said Dante and Seastra in unison.

"The reason I'm helping you is this. The shadow god and many other obstacles in your lives will lead you off the path to stop Dragon Lord's rule. Do not allow your different faiths to be your downfall. Windstin, now that you have an unlocked weapon of death, the shadow god has no leverage over you. You can gain anything you want. Your soul is worth much more than anything Death could offer, especially when you can get material things yourself," said Seastra.

"And what if I choose the path of light?" asked Dante.

"How can you walk the path of light with intention to kill? Fate is the god of justice, love, and truth. Fate will help in troubled times. However, don't worship the gods, because, at the end of the day, you manifest your own destiny by the choices you make in life," said Seastra.

"You still haven't told us why you're helping us," said Wind Burn.

"Right, you are a wise one," said Seastra with a smile.

"My lady, the main building has been repaired, and the water gatherers wait for your guidance at the pool," said Razel.

"Enjoy your stay, and inform me when you are ready to leave," said Seastra. Then she jumped out of the pool and walked with Razel through the crowd…

"*Your* ascended powers are way cooler than mine," said Wind Burn to break the silence.

"Not really. I don't get my fire spirits till I'm orb level 5, and it takes forever to charge up an ascended fire beam," said Dante.

"I think all ascended powers take long to charge up, but this weapon is so powerful it activated my wind state in a split second. It was like everything I did was enhanced by the weapon's power brother. Our first mission is to get you one when we get to Hell Mountain," said Wind Burn.

"Sounds live," said Dante as he and Wind Burn dabbed fist.

"Bro, with this weapon, I almost defeated a level-6 elemental. I could sense her fear and anger," said Wind Burn.

"I wish I could have seen it. I can't wait to get one of my own," said Dante.

"But in all seriousness, I must tell you this. First, I apologize for the way I acted growing up. And second, I vow to protect you with my life. My heart is already dark, so when the time comes, I'll deliver the death blow to Dragon Lord so you won't have his blood on your hands. I battle a lot of demons in my mind, but I'll never let my shadow faith come between us," said Wind Burn.

"Okay, and I vow to protect you with my life," said Dante as they stood up and embraced. Then they returned to their hut to get some rest.

Chapter 16

God of Light

The sun just began to rise as Dante, Wind Burn, and Lou Shen emerged from the hole in the desert floor. The second they climbed out of the hole, sharklings jumped out of the sand and closed the hole using shape earth power. Wind Burn pressed the screen on his holo net and said, "Navigation." A compass holo image shined from the holo net.

"Distance and direction to Hell Mountain on foot," said Wind Burn.

"Travel west, six-to-seven-day journey on foot," said a female computerized voice.

"Sounds like we need a ship," said Dante as the started walking west.

"And where do you expect to find a hovercraft in the desert of 7-Nations south?" said Lou Shen.

"We will steal one from Dragon Lord. I have a feeling we haven't seen the last of that Shock Wave clone," said Wind Burn.

"How do you know it was a clone?" asked Dante.

"Because the original Shock Wave is a human elemental with no component mods. The original Shock Wave's power level is off the charts. We wouldn't last one second in a fight with him. He's mindless and even more deadly than Dragon Lord. And get this—the first Shock Wave only has two orbs. Dr. Volts keeps him drugged up in one of his alchemic warehouses hooked to alchemic computers to create the perfect killing machine," said Wind Burn.

"So you think you can defeat an orb level 5 Shock Wave by yourself now?" asked Lou Shen.

"I don't think—I know I can," said Wind Burn with cockiness as he grabbed the hilt of his legendary katana blade on his back.

"Or maybe we could buy a ship. I got like…1500 platinum marks, and Seastra gave me three pounds of corundum crystal," said Dante.

"Then we will travel to the closest city and address whatever situation that comes first. Our main objective is to get to Hell Mountain. Our second objective is to gain membership with the black market," said Lou Shen.

"Coo, GP, navigation closest city in walking distance," said Wind Burn.

"Travel south for one hour and twenty minutes to arrive at Dry City," said the female computerized voice from Wind Burn's holo net.

They walked in silence for the next forty-five minutes until Dante said, "GP, what's the balance that I heard Seastra say?"

"Something to do with keeping the earth's core and meteor shard's power stable. And since when do you address me as GP?" said Lou Shen.

"It sounds live, GP," said Dante, looking at Wind Burn for approval.

"You kids are going to drive me crazy," said Lou Shen, shaking his head.

"Don't be so grumpy, GP. Just chill. By the time me and li'l bro done showin' you what's good, you gon' be the coolist GP in Hell Mountain," said Wind Burn. Dante and Wind Burn jogged a few steps ahead of Lou Shen, dapping each other and laughing. Suddenly, Dante and Wind Burn stopped in their tracks, looking in the distance.

"What is it, grandsons?" said Lou Shen. He ran to catch up to see.

They saw a pure light elemental humanoid with hellfire hair and dressed in full-body plate armor that was made of compacted light. The pure light elemental sat on the desert floor stirring a wide red crystal pot.

"The god of light," said Dante as he dropped his bags and raced over to the being of light and fell to his knees by the pot. Wind Burn and Lou Shen grabbed Dante's bags and then slowly approached as

Wind Burn began to look in his bag for his eye scouter device. Wind Burn grabbed the device and put it on his ear; then he heard a voice in his head say,

"I wouldn't do that if I were you. Come sit and ask any question you like," Lou Shen and Wind Burn joined Dante around the pot and sat their bags down.

"I am Fate, the ascended elemental being of light. I bring truth and light to all souls. Light is information, and ignorance is darkness. I protect others and Fuzion from such darkness. I've come to you to ask the three of you personally if you would like to join the light faith and become orb guardians," said Fate. Wind Burn shook his head no.

"Are you positive, Windstin? It is not too late for you to see the light. You have made no pacts with Death. I can still shine light on your elemental soul to rid you of Death's flames of darkness," said Fate.

"*No*, the path of light will not allow me to succeed in my ultimate goal of killing Dragon Lord. Plus the light cannot exist without darkness," said Wind Burn, looking at Dante.

"What about you, neutral soul of water?" said Fate.

"I will stay on Nazareth's path to aid my grandsons," said Lou Shen.

"And you, Dante, you are one of my most-favored hellfire spirits," said Fate.

"I have some questions, but I don't want to anger you," said Dante.

"All is never angry. I will only try to help you see the truth," said Fate.

Dante took a deep breath and said, "If you're the god of light and you're the guardian of earth, why did you allow Dragon Lord to kill all those hellfire elementals seventeen years ago? Why does Dragon Lord constantly and meaninglessly kill and you do nothing about it? Dragon Lord has many orbs trapped in his orb vault, and so many are hellfire. Why haven't you freed them? The book of light and balance tells us you are the strongest god, the god of honesty, nobility, justice. You are the god of pure light and chi. I find it very hard to believe that you are powerless to stop Dragon Lord," said

Dante, running out of breath but still wanting to ask more questions but waiting for the answers to the many questions he already asked.

Fate said, "I do have the power to stop Angel. But I cannot violate the balance of existence, for all life will be at stake. Angel has certain ties with certain beings that the balance forbids me from intervening."

"So yet we suffer because of some balance that we barely understand," said Dante in frustration.

Fate said, "To truly understand the balance, you must come to the temple of truth in Trinity City. The orb guardian will allow me to show you through him. His name is Trinity's Light." Then the god of light fazed out of existence, the crystal pot was gone, and vials of light and dark elixir were left in the sand where the pot once was.

Chapter 17

Death Pact

Lou Shen and his grandsons jogged south to beat the coming darkness of the night. When they finally reached the remains of a destroyed city, Dante felt the weight of hopelessness heavily on his heart.

The city was a poor place and could barely be called a city. Dry City's floor was scorched sand. The buildings were made of weak gray stone. Rocks were piled here and there, and sharklings and panthrainians were helping the wounded and trying to rebuild the poor city.

"Dragon Lord has destroyed the city. We must keep moving west to the bridge of ice," said Lou Shen while changing directions. The two brothers said nothing as they followed behind their grandfather.

In less than twenty minutes, they reached a bridge of mixed ice, steel, and iron. As far as they could see, the icy bridge glowed with a yellow light.

"This bridge was created by Cazorof, the god of ice days after Fuzion's arrival. It's a five-day journey on foot, maybe less if we run. Also, we will be power-blocked from the god energies of the bridge," said Lou Shen. As soon as they each stepped foot on the bridge, a numbing cold came over their orb soul. Wind Burn pulled his legendary weapon from his back straps because it started humming and vibrating. Then they all stopped to look at the weapon.

"What's wrong, brother?" said Dante.

"I don't know. My legendary weapon's acting strange. And it's really hot," said Wind Burn. As they surrounded the weapon, Lou Shen took a closer look at the crystal-covered storm orb at the hilt of the weapon. The weapons orb glowed, and the alchemic writing around the orb rose to life. The orb was in a whitish-violet spell of energy.

"I see. The weapon still works on the bridge," said Lou Shen.

"How do you know, GP?" asked Wind Burn.

"It seems to me the weapon's spell somehow overpowers the cold-light power block aura of the bridge," said Lou Shen.

"For once we have an advantage," said Dante with confidence in his brother's ability.

"You don't want to get burned, so you will have to hold the weapon at your side as we travel," Lou Shen said to Wind Burn.

*****

They walked for an hour or so, and then they spotted eight medium-sized ice hounds approaching fast. Wind Burn charged at the hound in front of him and sliced the hound in half with his pulsing weapon. After Wind Burn brought his weapon to his side, the sword amplified a five-by-ten-feet-long storm blade that lay staked into the ice bridge. In seconds, the giant storm blade vanished, and the ice bridge magically repaired itself. The other two hounds ran and tried to bite Dante and Lou Shen. Lou Shen evaded and dashed away from the hound fifteen feet. Dante slipped on the slick ice as the ice hound bit his ankle. Dante fell on the ground, and the ice hound dragged Dante fifty feet southwest in the blink of an eye.

"*Ahhha, brother!*" screamed Dante.

Then the sky darkened, and a rift tore open by the blade of a shadow scythe. The rift was high in the sky over the battle. A dark shadow humanoid who wore a hooded cloak that roared with black-and-gray flames known as shadow energy. In a blur of darkness, the shadow humanoid flipped out of the rift and threw seven shadow energy scythes at the seven ice hounds with unseen speed. The shadow scythes split the ice hounds in half and vanished in the same second. The shadow humanoid landed with graceful ease. The shadow humanoid removed his hood and took an ice mask that had a changing face of scream and an icy smile. The dark humanoid wiped darkness where his face should be and then put the changing ice mask back on and looked at Wind Burn.

"The shadow god of death!" said Wind Burn as he approached the shadow humanoid slowly.

"I am Death Pact. The last of the four states of death, come close so that I see your past, present, and things that shall come forth in your life," said Death. Lou Shen tried to read Death's power level. Lou Shen saw a realm of shadow fire and death, millions of souls being burned in the shadow fire for all eternity. Then a huge death blocked Lou Shen's vision. The huge death sat on a colossal throne made of ice and shadow, and he held an hour glass of violet spirit.

"We will meet soon enough," said Death. Then Lou Shen fell unconscious to the floor.

Dante stood up and ran to Wind Burn yelling, "Don't talk to Death, brother. He will trick you into selling your so—"

Before Dante could finish his sentence, Death blew scorching shadow fire on Dante. Then Dante fell unconscious to the ground.

"Brother! Grandfather!" said Wind Burn with worry in his voice.

Death said, "They are well. I cannot harm them in the third dimension."

"Shadow god, our will be done," said Wind Burn as he stood five feet away from Death and bowed with his legendary weapon at his side.

"You will not sell your soul, correct?" hummed Death with a smile and then a scream face. Wind Burn shook his head no, and lightning struck the dark sky.

"I walk the path of darkness by choice," said Wind Burn.

Multiple of Death's voices hummed as Death said, "We have allowed you to benefit from the life energy of the shadow path for so long, and you have made no pacts on your elemental-bound soul. You have great life energy and essence. Your essence is almost equal to your brother's, and Dante has been chosen to harness a greater essence orb. We offer a rare opportunity to become Death's hand, to help lead the shadow army in the light and dark war."

"I'm going to Hell Mountain to lead the rebellion to kill Dragon Lord. It would honor me to be the hand of Death," said Wind Burn as he looked at Dante on the floor.

Death said, "You need not worry. What we have in store will bring no harm to your brother. When you are ready, go to Death's fortress in the tainted lands, complete the test and absorb the life orb. Then travel to my city Shadow Empire in the light and dark nations to get anointed by the shadow priest and have your Death's hand ceremony. Then you will lead the rebellion as Death's hand. I love to violate Fate's precious balance, so if you and you brother can kill the dark lord of the force dragon, my will be done, or as you have said, our will be done. Hahahahaha!"

"I have vowed to not fail, Death," said Wind Burn.

"I favor you so much. Black Storm we have named you. For you have great purpose. Do not fail us. All have much riding on your existence," said Death as he blew scorching black-and-gray shadow flames on Wind Burn's legendary weapon. The weapon hummed at full power.

Death said, "I have refilled your weapon of death for free. But just know that when you are ready to sell your soul in the face of Death, only Death shall come."

"The only way I will sell my soul is for my brother's safety," said Wind Burn. The ice bridge vibrated, and then Death's icy mask made an angry face and then changed to normal. A few moments of silence passed, and then Death said, "Love is an emotion that will get you killed. In time I'm sure you will see, and we know you miss your mother and father so, so much."

"Maybe I don't know them enough to miss them. That's why I must avenge them. Dragon Lord stole my life from me, and I hate him for that," said Wind Burn.

"Would you sell your soul to bring your mother back?" asked Death.

"No, I'm already a grown man. What can she do for me now? The time that I truly needed her love is long gone. I won't sell my soul, Death. I can do anything you need me to do but that. And after my revenge, I will ascend and join you in the universal realms of existence," said Wind Burn.

"So be it," said Death as the rift closed, and Death fazed out of existence. At the same time, Dante and Lou Shen woke up.

Dante jumped up first and said, "Did you sell your soul? What did Death say, Brother?"

"They want me to become Death's hand, and I did not sell my soul," said Wind Burn

"You will lead the rebellion as Death's hand?" said Lou Shen, standing up.

"Yes, now let's get moving," said Wind Burn.

Chapter 18

Cazorof's Bridge of Ice

After a full day of nonstop walking, jogging, and frequent stops to eat rations, the next day had come. In times of serious fatigue, Dante and Lou Shen ate light oranges, and Wind Burn drank light and dark elixirs. After a few more hours of travel, they spotted in the distance on the bridge a titan and ten medium ice hounds all sitting with and around the titan. The hounds and the titan sat and watched Lou Shen and his grandsons approach with eager happiness and wagging icy tails.

The titan waved excitedly and yelled, "I am the orb guardian of Cazorof's Bridge of Ice. Do you want to hear stories? Please come sit," said the titan.

"Orb guardians are okay. Let's hear what he has to say," said Dante as they approached.

"What are your names? I am Orb Guardian Cravis," said the titan excitedly.

"I am Lou Shen. These are my grandsons, Dante and Wind Burn," said Lou Shen. Dante and Lou Shen sat down with their travel gear in front of them. Wind Burn didn't sit. He just stood looking at the many ice hounds around them. Then Cravis formed two more icy hounds next to him out of the bridge's floor in a sculpting motion.

"Orb Guardian, do you know that Death, the shadow god, was on your bridge of ice and light," said Wind Burn in a rude manner.

"Nonsense. The god of light would never allow such a thing to happen. This bridge is for protection and safe passage over the chasm. The one of darkness cannot step foot on Cazorof's Bridge," said Cravis.

"Well, he was here, just seconds ago, Titan," said Wind Burn, resting the hilt of his legendary weapon on his shoulder.

"I do not like your negative energy, and you wield a weapon of death. I had stories and information for you all, but I will go now. Dante, perhaps we shall meet again to play, but I will not be in the company of evil," said Cravis. He and all of the ice hounds got up and walked in the opposite direction Lou Shen and his grandsons were traveling. Lou Shen and Dante picked up their bags.

"You don't have to be so rude, grandson," said Lou Shen.

"The orb guardians will be my enemies soon enough, so no sense in being friendly," said Wind Burn and walked ahead.

Day 3, Ice Bridge

The sun fell and rose again. More light fruit, rations, water, and healing elixirs were consumed from Lou Shen's bag. They drank, ate, and took quick rest and continued traveling. From behind them, they began to hear electric hums from a hovercraft coming in their direction.

"Looks like it's our new ride. About time," said Wind Burn, spinning his legendary katana blade in a helicopter motion from side to side.

The hovercraft came into view. It was a long transport craft. It flew over them and then turned around and landed, blocking the way. Six full droids fell out of the craft's side door, followed by a Shock Wave, who flew with rocket thruster boots and wings. The droids and Shock Wave landed in front of Lou Shen and his grandsons. The Shock Wave had all of his alchemic weapons active and infrared beams pointed on each of their heads.

"Lou Shen, Dante, Wind Burn—you have violated 7-Nations' laws and are considered rouge elementals! Please come with us! Do you comply?" said Shock Wave.

"Yes, we comply!" said Wind Burn with his hands and legendary weapon up in a freeze position as he slowly walked toward the Shock Wave and droids. As soon as Wind Burn got in reach of the Shock Wave, he charged the clone with an upward slash. Shock wave evaded and dashed behind Wind Burn. Then the battle broke loose. The six full droids shot laser beam rifles at Lou Shen and Dante from a distance. Lou Shen and Dante weaved red laser beams in blurry movements while Shock Wave and Wind Burn moved faster and faster, attacking each other and evading each other's attacks. Wind Burn was slightly faster. Shock Wave's laser chest cannon blasted close range at Wind Burn, who easily evaded and dashed behind Shock Wave and slashed his powerful weapon at the clone screaming, "Die!" but a wave of grayish-blue storm hit nothing. Shock Wave evaded behind Wind Burn a couple of feet and let off an arsenal of laser disk mines and rocket laser bombs at Wind Burn. Wind Burn jumped in a graceful somersault behind Shock Wave, and the red beams and rockets barely missed his face. Shock Wave swung a powerful dragon fist at Wind Burn as soon as the swift wind elemental landed. Wind Burn ducked under the fist and in the same moment sliced up Shock Wave's body. *Boom!*

Everyone stopped to look as the blue energy and smoke faded away to see Wind Burn with one foot on the neck of the Shock Wave, who lay lifeless on the floor.

"Don't kill him, brother!" screamed Dante.

Wind Burn quickly ran onto the ship, and then the full robotic droids followed behind him. A lot of commotion and explosion could be heard on the ship. *Booom! Thooom! Whack! Ahhh!*

"Do it!" someone screamed. Then as the droids reached the ship's steps, they each powered down and froze in their tracks. When Lou Shen and Dante finally entered the ship, they saw Wind Burn holding a holo pad in his left hand, in his right hand was his legendary weapon with the hot blade at the neck of a bioengineered Dragon Lord guard. A second Dragon Lord guard was unconscious on the floor of the ship. Hot raw energy was thick in the air of the narrow ship, and one side of the pilot pit was scorched and mostly destroyed.

"Don't kill him, brother…*please!*" begged Dante in a low hurt voice. Wind Burn slowly eased his weapon of death from the neck of his next victim.

"Ki-claw…what happened to you?" said Lou Shen sadly.

"Dragon Lord happened to me," said Ki-claw. Dante found some power-block restraints in the cargo hold and cuffed Ki-claw and the other Dragon Lord guard and then put them both in the prison cell in the back of the ship.

"You killed two of them, didn't you, brother?" said Dante, suddenly mad. Wind Burn nodded yes and then sheathed his legendary weapon as the glow calmed. Then Wind Burn used the holo pad to program the droids to get back in their transport seats.

"I told you I would get us a ship, and that's what I did. I had to make an example out of the first two," said Wind Burn as he gave the holo pad to Dante, then walked into the pilot pit, and took a seat. Lou Shen and Dante joined Wind Burn in the pilot pit and looked out of the front window to see twenty-five ice hounds and Cravis surrounding them.

"I'll go talk to him," said Dante as he went outside. Lou Shen and Wind Burn could see Dante gesturing and acting out events to explain the whole situation. Then Dante summoned his orb from his chest into his palms to show Cravis. Dante's orb glowed with hellfire and mixed hues of light. Then Dante put his orb back into his chest while still explaining and talking, and Cravis happily listened and laughed at Dante's acting and tale.

Dante and Cravis went on for a half hour trading stories until Wind Burn stood up with a look of anger and impatience.

Lou Shen stood up and said, "I'll get him, grandson." Then Lou Shen went outside and returned with Dante in less than a minute.

"Did you have to tell him your life story?" said Wind Burn.

"Just chill, big bro. Cravis really coo. Let's ride," said Dante happily.

Chapter 19

Hell Mountain Arrival

The damaged ship was blind from the sides and back. The ship also had no shields or artillery, because Wind Burn had destroyed most of the pilot pit's computer console. Lou Shen amazingly flew the ship by himself with ease.

In less than a day, they arrived at a dark-red colossal active mountain that had lava pouring from its top that ran down the mountain and split the dark-tainted lands as far as the eye could see.

Two masked humanoids dressed in black-and-red camos pointed energy cannons at the ship. Lou Shen landed the ship with a soft crash just as the ship lost all power. Lou Shen Wind Burn and Dante teleported through the window of the ship's pilot pit and approached the masked elementals.

Wind burn reached for his legendary weapon, but Lou Shen grabbed Wind Burn's hand and stopped him from unsheathing the weapon.

"We are from 7-Nations. We have come to join the rebellion," said Lou Shen.

Both masked elementals looked at Dante and then stood at attention and placed a closed fist on their chest and said, "Rise of the hellfire storm."

"Live." Dante laughed as he repeated the same chest gesture.

The masked elemental to the right shook Dante's hand and said, "Son of Luke, welcome home. Come into Hell Mountain. It's not safe out, especially when beings can see your human face. You need masks."

"Why do I have to wear a mask?" asked Dante as they walked into the mountain's cave-like entrance.

"Because humans are not favored by the wild beings of these lands. And we are the lowest race in earth's population. But most importantly, we are feared and hated because of our ascended powers, and Dragon Lord's image does not make it any better for us," said the hellfire soldier.

"So you're both human then," said Dante.

"Yes, we are some of the last of the hellfire clan who fought in the war as Luke's front line. There are ten of us here. There were eleven, but Karma's Dream left years ago. Oh, plus General Smoke is here. He leads us and keeps us alive," said the hellfire soldier as they walked out of the cave's tunnel to see a series of bars and alchemist spells. The bars where held shut by two red hot locks that made all of the bars hot and red, glowing with heat.

An alchemist walked over from a corner in the back of the mountain and used some type of spell from his Shock Wave gloves and opened the hot locks and barred gates. When they stepped in, they saw an unknown spell on the floor by a door's indention on the wall that no longer existed.

A tar and mixed hot mud pit was in the right corner of the small chamber. A light brown-skinned stocky human dressed in hellfire plate armor, black boots, and black gloves stood in the middle of the chamber.

Behind him stood seven humans dressed in hellfire clothes and black boots. The two masked elementals next to Dante took off their masks and joined the line of seven humans. The nine humans all stood at attention with energy cannons strapped to their backs. The human at the gate used alchemy to close the Hell Mountain entrance. Then he walked around everyone and stood in the left corner of the chamber by the red alchemist spell that was engraved on the floor. The alchemist had on Shock Wave gloves that Dante had not seen before in 7-Nations. They were slightly bigger. The alchemist wore a violet elemental war suit, and he had an elemental utility belt that had a holo pad on one side and a false meteor shard on the other.

Beep-beep-det. Wind Burn's black market holo net went off at the same time the alchemist holo pad started beeping. The alchemist human and Wind Burn made eye contact, but nothing was said.

Four large red drakes in dragon form stood along the wall at attention, eyes locked on Dante. The fire drakes had a fearless look in their eyes. They were strong and deadly, but somehow they had been civilized.

"I am an eight-star general in this rebellion. My name is Heat Smoke, but most call me General Smoke. Heat smoke was the name given to me by the great fallen fire warrior Luke Saint, the first to master the fire spirits within us fire elemental humans. To him, the fire spirits were like natural states he could enter at will, not mere ascended powers. These nine elementals behind me are the last of the front line who fought in the war with me seventeen years ago. Let us take a moment of silence in remembrance of our fallen clan of fire humans… Few seconds of silence. This is one of our alchemists, Cal, short for Calculate. Our second alchemist is in the Safe Haven City deeper into the mountain. Cal and Static run the Hell Mountain black market," said General Smoke.

Cal raised his Shock Wave glove and gave a thumbs-up to everyone.

"My name is Lou Shen. I believe we met many years ago, General. These are my grandsons, Dante and Wind Burn," said Lou Shen.

General Smoke stepped to Dante and looked him in the eye. Then the general grabbed Dante's shoulders.

"Hope lives!" said General Smoke, and he gave Dante a long hug.

"Umm, I don't know you, sir," said Dante as he hugged the general back uncomfortably.

"I'm sorry, son. You look so much like your father. Luke was my mentor and father figure for many years," said General Smoke, holding back tears. General Smoke looked at Wind Burn and said, "A legendary weapon of the wind element." General Smoke put his hand out to shake Wind Burn's, but Wind Burn shook his head no.

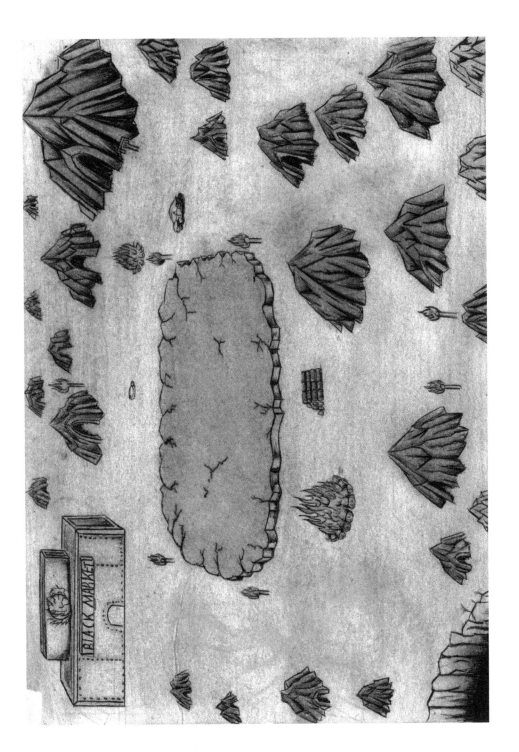

"Have you made any pacts with Death?" asked General Smoke while putting his hands behind his back.

"I have made no deals on my soul, but I am on the shadow path, and I am going to be Death's hand," said Wind Burn in a dark voice.

"Death's hand with no pacts…strange," said General Smoke.

"So let's not waste time. I have waited years for this one day for the rebellion to rise and build like a deadly storm and destroy all obstacles in our paths. Dante, you will lead the rebellion, unless…" General Smoke stopped his sentence and stepped back in battle formation on the right side of the front line.

"I *suggest*…we spar for the leadership position," said Wind Burn.

"This is the way Luke would have solved this situation. Let's go to Safe Haven City Arena to settle this change of events," said General Smoke. Cal used a small crystal copy of a meteor shard on his belt to conduct lightning around his Shock Wave gloves to activate the alchemist spell on the floor. The spell grew brighter and brighter until the strange symbols and writing rose from the floor glowing in red-and-violet light.

"It's a teleportation spell," said Cal; then he jumped in and vanished.

One by one, everyone followed. Then they walked through some maze-like tunnels for a short distance until they ended up at a giant hole in the floor of the mountain.

"The city is a one hundred feet up in one of the side chambers in the mountain," said General Smoke; then he turned on a hellfire aura and flew into the dark hole. Wind Burn and Dante activated auras and flew off in a race side by side.

Lou Shen looked at Cal. "Aren't you coming?" Cal said.

"No, I'm on door duty. Static and I switch shifts off and on, but here, catch." Cal threw Lou Shen a bark blue crystal storm amulet. Lou Shen caught the amulet and said thanks. Then he sent some chi into the amulet by thought, and a bright storm aura came around him, and he flew off into the hole to see his grandsons fight.

* * * * *

Safe Haven City was nothing but an enormous cave chamber with less than fifty gray stone huts, that surrounded a dark hard stone round arena. In the right corner of the city was a small black building with a sign over its door that read *Hell Mountain Black Market*. There were less than forty humanoid creatures in the city. Safe Haven population consisted of mostly pantharainians, a few pure elementals, and twelve hellfire drakes.

Over in the left corner of the city, in a large hut, a griffling was selling old rotten fruit and chasm worm meat. The city was poor and desperate.

General Smoke, the front line, Lou Shen, Wind Burn, and Dante landed at the widening hole of the city's only entrance and exit. Then they all walked and stood around the arena. Safe Haven City's population said nothing. They just stopped whatever they were doing and surrounded the ring like they knew something was about to happen. Dante and Wind Burn walked into the ring and stood twenty feet away from each other. They both began stretching and warming up as the crowd started to get amped up at the sight of a fight.

"Feels like the Dragon Lord tournaments, huh, brother?" said Wind Burn as he gave Dante a wink.

"Yeah, let's give them a show," said Dante.

Static came out of the black market building with a holo pad and an old scouter bot sphere that flew above him recording the fight.

General Smoke screamed and Static's scouter bot hovered over him and amplified his voice so that the city could hear him.

"You know the rules of Safe Haven City Arena fights. No legendary weapons, no consuming healing items. This is a test to see who is the strongest elemental. Above all forms of combat ascended powers are valued highly."

"I want to advance to orb level 6 before the fight," said Dante.

"So do I, but we don't have orbs," said Wind Burn, looking at General Smoke.

"I believe I have my last two special orbs in the Council's vault. What a coincidence," said General Smoke.

"Show us the fire spirits," someone in the crowd shouted.

"Yeah!" roared the crowd in great excitement.

"I'll be back," said General Smoke, and in a fiery tornado, the old general flew through the hole entrance in a race to get to the Council's chambers.

The creatures of Safe Haven City stood around the arena using their thought to read Dante and Wind Burn's power level, making bets, looking, and pointing at Dante and Wind Burn. And, of course, the topic of discussion was what element was better. What element would come out on top—wind, which was the fastest element, or fire, the element of balanced energy and strength? Then a panthrainian in the crowd shouted, "Son of Luke has come! Rise of the hellfire storm!"

Wind Burn walked to the edge of the arena where the panthrainian stood and said, "What is your name creature!"

"Shirock of the earth element. I am a member of the freedom pack that roam these tainted lands," said the dark-gray furred creature.

Wind Burn screamed, "Hell Mountain population, listen up! My younger brother cannot make the storm rise without me. I will become Death's hand known as the Black Storm. Let it be known from this day forward that I will be the one to kill Dragon Lord. The hellfire rebellion cannot, will not, rise without me. I am the storm that burns that you speak of. I have made no pacts with Death. I choose to be the will of Death. Soon you will fear me as you fear Dragon Lord."

Just as Wind Burn finished his rampage, General Smoke flew through the hole entrance to Safe Haven City and landed next to Wind Burn in the arena.

"This is an earth orb with the life special ability. I figure you might need it to keep those pacts down," said General Smoke as he winked at Wind Burn and gave him the orb carrier. "This will also save you the trouble of going to Death's fortress on the shadow god's life orb mission." Then the eight-star general walked over to Dante and said, "This is a force orb of memory. It will help you master many combined elements and other powers of other elements you absorbed and will absorb."

"Thanks, General," said Dante. Wind Burn nodded his head in approval and took a deep breath to calm his nerves.

"I have orb control, so if either of you don't absorb the orb quick, I will take the orb out before it's too late. I will have no deaths on my watch."

"I'll go first," said Dante in full confidence. Then General Smoke and Wind Burn both exited the arena. Dante turned the crystal latch and then quickly put his hand in the orb carrier before the orb could wonder away from him.

The force orb traveled up Dante's arm and entered his chest. In two seconds, silvery force energy surrounded Dante in a giant sphere and took him twenty feet into the air. It took less than twenty seconds for a hellish flame to swallow the force sphere in a fiery tornado from bottom to top. Then the energy around Dante got smaller and smaller until only Dante remained. In a flash of fiery speed, Dante teleported to the ground.

"Well done, grandson, a flawless absorption," said Lou Shen as Dante exited the arena.

"Yeah!" shouted the crowd. Then Wind Burn entered the arena and stood in the middle of the stone ring. He looked at the poor people of the city cheering his brother on as if he didn't exist. Wind Burn despised them for some reason he could not understand. Wind Burn scanned the city, looking in everyone's eyes with a look of anger until everyone quieted down. Then he slowly opened the orb carrier's crystal latch and quickly put the open orb carrier to his chest. The earth orb entered Wind Burn's chest. Then Wind Burn threw the crystal orb carrier to the side.

Wind Burn stood there for twenty seconds screaming, fighting the pain every time one of Wind Burn's knees would give and fall to the floor. Wind Burn would focus his vital life force and will and stand up again with newfound strength. General Smoke slowly walked up to Wind Burn and started to say something. But Wind Burn sent a blast of wind and will from his body that was wild and uncontrolled. The wind blew everyone back as the city had to shield deadly wind. Wind Burn kept trying to unlock the power of the earth orb. Then finally light-brown energy merged with the ground formed into a jagged ball of energy around Wind Burn.

"Fool! You're already drained of life energy!" shouted General Smoke. Dante walked next to General Smoke and pulled him back just as the ball of energy lashed at the general.

"Big bro can do it. He shows his best will when he's on the brink of death," said Dante.

"But special orbs have to be absorbed multiple times," said General Smoke.

"Let's not speak negative things into existence. He can do it," said Dante. Then Dante stood and watched with great faith in his brother.

✳ ✳ ✳ ✳ ✳

Wind Burn thought, *I have to get stronger…or at least as strong as Dante.* Damn! *Everything is given to him, while I work and slave for my power. I must show them I am worthy to lead this rebellion. I must become Death's hand. And I will…* I cannot, will not accept failure. I must, must…*tap into the wind element within my spirit. To overcome all obstacles in my path, I must tap into the all within my being…* So be it!

Then Wind Burn saw an emerald light that blinded him at first. Then it healed him. Then he looked up to see Fate and Death faze into existence in his earth energy sphere, and the gods of elements did not look happy.

Chapter 20

Tap into the Source

Wind Burn noticed the earth energy around him stop moving and burning him. He also felt the emerald light make him stronger and energized somehow. Time had stopped. *And why...is Fate and Death here?* thought Wind Burn. Death stood on Wind Burn's left. Death was large, and he had sharded gloves made of ice for hands. Death's shadow cloak hissed with black-and-gray flames. Fate stood on Wind Burn's right. Fate was the same size as Wind Burn, and he was dressed in full-body plate armor that was made of light. Fate's hair was made of red hellfire that remained calm and steady.

"I am the light and protector of Fuzion. We have met many times in other realms of existence. Why this unfortunate event came to pass, I know not. It seems my god sight fails me more and more as time moves on this planet. But...somehow you have tapped into the source of all... How did you do it?" said Fate.

"I don't...know... I just... I just thought... I believed in myself," said Wind Burn.

"I am Soul Taker, Death's third form. My job is to collect souls who violate the balance. Your soul is destined to journey through the depths of Shadow Hell," said Soul Taker.

"I don't take it kindly when being forced into things," said Wind Burn with an evil smile looking up to death.

"This we know, Black Storm, but you tap into power you do not understand. *Do not do it again,*" said Death as he cracked his icy knuckles.

"In a past life, you went into the center of Helios, earth's sun, to forge a boost orb of god energies because you had defied the laws of balance. You needed more power to fight higher beings in existence.

You lost so much. Do you remember?" asked Fate. Wind Burn shook his head no.

"*Do* not let this happen again. I will force you to ascend. And if I cannot force you to ascend, then Death will take you to Shadow Hell, and if the realm of darkness cannot hold your spirit, then you will seal your fate." Then the god of light disappeared.

"I despise the light *so…so…so* much. You did an excellent job. You must learn to harness the power of your will and desire and be more proficient in your power of thought to bring things into existence," said Death.

"But, Death, I don't know what I did in the first place," said Wind Burn.

"It is simple, Black Storm. You violated the balance by drawing energy that was unaccounted for from Fuzion, and Fuzion is pure source energy," said Death.

"And if I do this again, I could end up in Shadow Hell?" said Wind Burn.

"Yes, but Shadow Hell is not so bad. You will get really strong in all aspects of existence. We could teach you so much. We have so many gifts for you," said Death.

"How long will I have to stay?" asked Wind Burn.

"There is no such thing as time in the other plains of existence. Once the light and dark war is upon us, I will send seven chosen from the depths of Shadow Hell to earth to lead my army of darkness," said Death.

"I have things I must do here, in this reality, Death," said Wind Burn, getting a little angry.

"*So be it*, but I can only vouch for your soul for so long. Remember it is always your choice in whatever you do. If you draw power from the source again, Fate will put your soul in the Land of Lost Orb Souls' stream of spirit energy with the billions of sleeping souls. We will not allow this to come to pass. We need your soul… *One* way or another, we will have it," said Death.

"Ha-ha, Death, I control my own destiny. I am no pawn. It's funny how you want my soul but you have nothing I want," said Wind Burn.

"Listen and hear well, Black Storm. When Nazareth is freed and the light-and-dark war sweeps this planet, you will beg me to join my army. You cannot escape the darkness over your soul. Even the neutral energy you gained from the source cannot save you from the darkness. This is because you were born in it," said Death.

"I… I don't want to escape the darkness. I'll embrace the darkness and use it to get what I want," said Wind Burn.

Death said, "See? There it is again. When you think things like that, you turn the mental keys to gain access to the source. You are a rare elemental spirit. Your brother has similar gifts, but yours are better. To the gods, you have a gift known as the gift of thought to will things into existence. This special ability comes from your mother's scionic powers," said Death.

"So what did I get from the source?" asked Wind Burn.

"We are in your mind. Just think and you will know," said Death as he looked up and whispered something to himself. Then his icy face got angry.

"I have things for you, but I cannot give them until you are ready. Just know that we are on your side," said Death, and then Soul Taker vanished from Wind Burn's mind. Then a sweet hum of Death played in Wind Burn's mind.

* * * * *

(Hours to Death's Song of Truth)

Brothers' fight

All of Hell Mountain watched the earth energy sphere and Wind Burn's wind energy battle for control of the sphere. Then a powerful emerald wave of energy pushed the storm upward until it covered the earth energy. The sphere got smaller and smaller until Wind Burn stood in the arena. Three earth panthrainians quickly entered the arena and used shape earth powers to fix the damage Wind Burn's earth orb absorption had done to the arena floor. Then Dante walked into the arena looking at Wind Burn with concern.

Did Wind Burn become more evil while trying to absorb the orb? Dante thought.

Wind Burn's eyes met Dante's, and Wind Burn smiled and said, "Let's show them our new ascended powers, brother!"

"Bet!" said Dante.

Wind Burn first and then Dante a split second behind, both brothers activated auras and then summoned great energy around them. Power auras of their primary element covered their bodies. Then the auras got brighter and brighter until Safe Haven City could not see Dante or Wind Burn through their glowing energy auras. First Wind Burn turned into a large pure wind elemental humanoid and yelled, "Ascended storm devastation, I call forth acid rain, hail, and deadly winds. I am Black Storm!" Powerful storm circled around Wind Burn's pure elemental state in a thirty-foot radius around him. Dante's fiery aura turned him into a large phoenix of crimson fire energy. Then the pure wind elemental storm rushed at Dante's phoenix from and yelled, "Burning wind scar!"

The pure wind storm created and combined two storms of mixed fire, water, and wind, then shot the two storm waves at Dante. The large phoenix moved in a fiery blur of speed and teleported behind Wind Burn and countered with an inferno fist. Wind Burn evaded the fiery fist, and air dashed twenty feet back and up. The fiery phoenix brought his hands together, gathering red energy, and yelled, "Ascended fire beam!"

It took Dante ten seconds charge up the fire beam, so Wind Burn took the time advantage and sent three wind scar attacks at Dante in a blur of storm and speed. The storm devastation only made Wind Burn's wind scars bigger and stronger. Dante formed inferno shields with his mind and blocked the first two wind scars, but the third wind scar hit Dante's phoenix form directly in the chest. Dante ate the attack and then let off a compacted fire beam in the air straight to Wind Burn. The pure wind elemental tried to evade the fire beam, but he wasn't quick enough, and the crimson beam drilled into Wind Burn's head. The force of the compacted beam tried to push Wind Burn back, but the storm could not be moved in its ethereal form. Then the crimson phoenix flew up to Wind Burn with great speed while throwing five crimson giant hellfire orbs at the storm. Wind Burn easily weaved all five of Dante's attacks and teleported above and behind Dante. Then Wind Burn came down in a spinning diving tornado level 5 combined elements attack and yelled, "Black storm tornado!"

The combined elements and vicious storm tore at Dante's crimson hellish form and knocked him into the ground with great force, causing a cratered hole where Dante lay in the center of the arena.

Wind Burn looked at the faces of Safe Haven City and shouted, "This is your hope…! Ascended storm blitz!" Wind Burn formed two compacted orbs of hail, acid rain, and storm and then threw the first storm ball at Dante in the hole in the arena. A crimson fire beam met the storm ball in the air in an energy battle, but with a blur of speed, Wind Burn appeared next to Dante in the cratered hole and spun like a tornado while drilling the second storm ball into Dante's side. Wind Burn's storm devastation ripped the hole, expanding it wider.

"Inferno strike!" yelled Dante as a fiery crimson fist with the dragon fighting style swung at Wind Burn. Wind Burn evaded Dante's attack and teleported out of the hole and then landed in the arena that had not been destroyed.

"You must tap into the source, brother," said Wind Burn. Dante flew out of the hole in a red-orange dragon form and landed in the arena a few feet away from Wind Burn.

Dante yelled, "Ascended inferno tornado!" Wind Burn let Dante charge up and form his ascended power. Wind Burn took a quick look around the poor city to see most of the creatures of the rebellion mad and angry that Dante was losing the fight.

Right then, Wind Burn knew that leadership of this rebellion was not owned by strength and power. Dante's face was a symbol of hope and a fairness for the world.

Then a hellish orange flame tornado almost covered the whole arena. Wind Burn had no chance to evade or shield. The critical blow connected just as Wind Burn ran out of chi and energy. Wind Burn's ascended powers and storm auras powered down as Wind Burn got knocked into General Smoke's arms.

"I *lost*. My brother has to lead the rebellion," said Wind Burn.

"You will be his second-in-command, Black Storm," said General Smoke. Wind Burn smiled and then fell unconscious.

Chapter 21

Council Leaders

The next morning, General Smoke gave Dante, Wind Burn, and Lou Shen a detailed tour of Hell Mountain. They went to the dock first. The dock only had two beat-up ships that didn't look like they could fly. Two hellfire drakes in dragon form scraped off the spray-painted 7-Nations' symbol on the silver ship they had stolen from Dragon Lord. In the middle of the dock was a small lever and computer that controlled the dock's panel on the ceiling so ships could come and go.

Then they went to the Council's chambers. On the way there, General Smoke told them about the lava path that was located deeper into the mountain's maze. The lava path led to a blistering hot city known as Inferno City. This city was the home of an orb level 7 elemental being named Inferno. They finally arrived at a hole and sign that read *Council's Chambers*. Once again, everyone activated auras and flew up the hole. When they entered the Council's cave-like chamber, they saw the thunderbolt human known as Static working on a six-screen twentieth-century supercomputer in the middle of the chamber.

"Static, right? I need some things from the black market when you get a chance," said Wind Burn.

"Sure thing. We don't have much in stock. I need this super-computer up and running so I can get in touch with Merch. Just let me finish trying to get the system powered up, and I'll get you and Dante your own keys," said Static as he kept on working. General Smoke walked to the back of the chamber where the seven thrones were located. Each seat had a star and rank numbers of one through seven.

General Smoke stood by the middle chair with the one star and said, "The ascended Council is a group of seven human elementals who were born in 7-Nations. This group of seven will lead the rebellion. Our goal is to overthrow Dragon Lord's rule over 7-Nations and restore equal leadership to all elemental clans in 7-Nations. These elemental leaders are called the Council, but the creatures of the rebellion call them the Ascended Council because of their ascended powers of the gods. For unknown reasons, only human elementals have these powers. The Council governs the rebellion's decisions by vote and equality. There is only one Council member per the basic one to seven elements. That means light, shadow, lava, spirit, or shard energy cannot gain Council status. And there may only be one Council leader per one to seven basic element. The highest rank one can gain in the rebellion under the Council is the eight-star rank of a general. The eight-star rank are the Council's most trusted warriors and advisors. The front line and myself are all eight-star ranks. We fought with Luke long ago, and we will fight with the Council now. The Council knows the risk of death when leading this rebellion. We are well aware of Dragon Lord's special abilities from the shadow god. But to the Council, 7-Nations, the world's richest city and our home, is worth fighting for. Dante, your father gathered the freedom panthrainian pact of earth elementals to help the mountain's maze insides and chambers. As you can see, we don't have enough manpower or alchemist to run Hell Mountain properly. Static and Cal are great alchemists, but two of them are not enough."

Shirock came from the door of the soldiers' quarter holding three uniforms. Each uniform had a number and star surrounded by a fiery storm and seven hellfire orbs in a small symbol that was patched on the right shoulder. General Smoke grabbed the red uniform from Shirock first and handed it to Dante and said, "Creatures of this world believe in you so much, so blindly that once you put this on, I know things will change for the better." Dante put the uniform on and sat in the one-star seat in the middle of the thrones. Then General Smoke grabbed the two-star uniform and handed it to Wind Burn and said, "A leader is only as strong as his foundation, and what a great bonus to have a brothers' bond."

"Thanks, General," said Wind Burn as he put the uniform on and sat in the two-star seat next to Dante on his left.

Then General Smoke grabbed the last uniform and said, "Lou Shen, you have raised Dante well. I hope you will join the Council as three-star rank and help me train this rebellion."

"I will do so with all of my being," said Lou Shen as he grabbed the light-blue uniform and sat in the three-star seat beside Dante.

"The door to the right is the entrance to the Council's personal rooms. They're not fully furnished, but at least you'll have a comfy bed and your own personal space," said General Smoke.

"Who's going to fill the rest of the Council seats?" asked Dante.

"Bro, that's up to you," said Wind Burn.

"Oh yea, right," said Dante.

* * * * *

Dante, Wind Burn, Lou Shen, General Smoke, Static, Cal, and Shirock sat in the Council's chambers and got to know each other while Static and Cal worked on the supercomputer. Dante watched them and wanted to know their story… "So you and Cal are from 7-Nations? How did you two end up in Hell Mountain?" asked Dante.

Static stopped working and said, "Well, Dragon Lord kicked me and my brother out when we were teenagers for not wanting to help Dr. Volts's experiment on live creatures and humans.

REBEllioN
Symbol

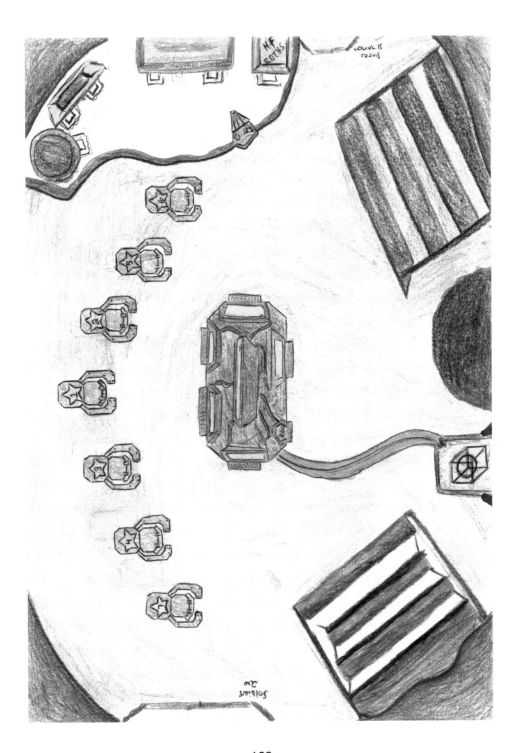

163

"So we ran away from 7-Nations and were living in Port Shard Land City helping the alchemist drake brothers when Luke approached me and told me of this mountain and how he needed alchemists to help build this mountain into a livable environment. I came here with my brother, Cal. We were orphans, so we don't know who are parents are. We don't even know if we are real brothers, but Elizabeth told us we are, so we believe her. But none of that really matters to us. We just like to build and create. I helped Luke forge the white flame cloak of power. It was meant to be a gift for you, Dante, when you got old enough, but sadly it got lost when Luke fell. I also helped design the mountain's architecture with alchemy and the help of the freedom pact. My main problem today is finding a significant energy source to power the mountain. General Smoke will tell you Cal and I drain ourselves daily just to maintain order in this place."

"Why don't you use a different energy source?" asked Dante.

"I use lightning because it's my primary element, and I use it proficiently while doing alchemy. We use our own chi for spell activation. Plus light, shadow, and shard energy are hard to come by," said Static.

"The orb guardian Cravis gave me this light orb and big orb carrier full of light energy. Can you use it as a better power source?" asked Dante.

"A big orb carrier is called an energy cell. I believe I could make it work. The light recharges itself in the day if you have the right spells in place, and I'll have to add solar panels on the top of Hell Mountain," said Static as he got back to work on the supercomputer. Dante went to his new room and then came back with the light orb and e-cell and handed them to Static and then sat back down in his one-star seat.

"Cravis gave me those light items to sell so I can have better bargaining chip for my hovercraft I plan to buy, but it seems like those light items are needed here more," said Dante.

"I'm going outside to install the solar panels," said Cal, and then he left the Council's chambers through the hole in a violet lightning aura. Static waited ten minutes and then wrapped and tied together some thick wire. Then Static drew some alchemic writing on the e-cell with his false meteor shard. Then Static set the e-cell full of light on a steel box by the hole entrance of the chamber.

"General Smoke, I need you to use orb control to put the light orb in the e-cell," said Static.

General Smoke walked over to the steel box and looked at the alchemic glowing spells on the e-cell and said, "Is it safe to touch this active energy?"

"It's fine unless you're shadow faith, but don't touch it for too long. It does get hot. Just calmly grab the light orb and place it in the e-cell nice and slow," said Static.

"No worries, I'm neutral faith," said General Smoke as he opened the orb carrier and willed the light orb into his hands and then slowly willed it into the e-cell full of light energy. Static closed the e-cells crystal top and added more alchemic spells to the e-cell and steel box.

"This en-equality spell I'm about to use might have a strong kick, so cover your eyes," said Static. First, Static connected the group of wires to the supercomputer. Then he connected the other end of the group of wires to the e-cell with his left hand and formed a strange spell in his right hand. Static pushed the en-equality spell of lightning into the e-cell and then stood back as the yellow light got brighter. *Woom!* The whole chamber lit up with a blinding light, and then the light died down as the six computer screens hummed to life.

"Well, they work, but they're so old, almost ancient. Where are the holo screens?" said Dante. Wind Burn just shook his head at his younger brother.

Each computer screen showed various camera feeds of Hell Mountain's insides, as well as the perimeter outside.

"This is the cheapest way for computer tech. Dragon Lord charges an arm and a leg for his famous holo computers. On top of that, he only does transactions with a select few nations and small cities," said Static.

"What cities?" asked Wind Burn.

"Shadow Empire, Champion City, Bounty City, and sometimes Port Shard Land. Other cities have to go through third and fourth parties to get goods. The tax ends up being too high. But now we can go through Merch, who is a pure shadow elemental who runs a secret black market that's under 7-Nations that Dragon Lord does not know about. We need to get in touch with Merch. That's why this supercomputer is so important for the rebellion," said Static.

"I know Merch. He's pretty cool. He will put you on, too, if you into making fast money," said Wind Burn.

"Well, now I can get our network online, so we can communicate with other nations and cities. What will our username be, General? It's been years since we have been able to get online," asked Static as he went to one of the computers and started typing.

"That's a decision for a one-star-rank Council leader," said General Smoke.

Dante looked around and thought and then said, "Hell Mountain," with a shrug of his shoulders.

"Hell Mountain sounds good to me," said Static, and he began to type faster.

Cal flew back in and said, "Since the system is up and running, I'm going to go update the black market computer." Then he flew off again.

"Good deal. Now I can run the black market in Safe Haven City more frequently and bring Hell Mountain some income," said Static. Wind Burn walked over to one of the computer screens and linked his holo net to the world network.

"I could use one of these computers in my room," said Dante.

"I plan on installing supercomputers in each Council member's room. Just give me some time. I got you," said Static.

"Static, why don't you take the four-star-rank Council seat?" asked Dante.

"Well, my brother and I are thinkers, not fighters. Plus, I'm over forty years old, and I'm not strong enough to reach orb level 6 or 7. I focus all my ability on intelligence. That's why I'm a decent alchemist and orb level 5, and I plan to stay orb level 5. But the rebellion has my mind to do whatever must be done. This is my life and second home," said Static.

The screen next to Static lit up and showed a dark air tank hovercraft land in the front of Hell Mountain.

"Warning, an unknown hovercraft has landed one hundred feet away from the Hell Mountain entrance," said a female computerized voice. Static and Wind Burn's computers showed four humanoids in dark hooded cloaks exit the hovercraft and wait by the big rock outside of the mountain. The two masked hellfire front line eight-star elementals approached slowly with their energy cannon rifles at aim. A few words were said, and then one of the fire humans ran into the mountain. It took him three minutes to reach the Council's chambers.

"General Smoke, I mean, Dante, sir, there's a beautiful young woman and three shadow humans here from Shadow Empire. The woman says her name is Skyla Breeze, and she wants to speak to Wind Burn," said the masked fire human.

Dante looked at Wind Burn and said, "The same Skyla you dated when we were young?"

"Yes, the same Sky, bro," said Wind Burn.

"Let her dock her ship. Then we will meet her in Safe Haven City," said Dante.

"Love is a beautiful thing," said Lou Shen as he got up and walked to his room.

"I'll go to the soldiers' kitchen and prepare a meal for your guest," said General Smoke as he walked over to the soldiers' quarters.

"Come on, bro, let's go see her. *Wifeyyy!*" teased Dante as he and Wind Burn activated auras and flew down the hole.

Chapter 22

A First Love, Skyla Breeze

Skyla Breeze ran and flew by herself to Safe Haven City through Hell Mountain's maze-like tunnels. She still remembered the way to the city from when she came here three years ago when she ran away from 7-Nations. Skyla had told her royal shadow guards and escorts that she wanted to talk to Wind Burn alone. She had butterflies in her stomach. She could still remember Wind Burn's last words to her.

"Our love is forever. We'll make storms that last forever because we are soul mates," Wind Burn would tell her. The last time she saw or heard from Wind Burn was so long ago, but her love for him burned so deeply, worse than Shadow Hell's eternal flames, or at least that what she thought. Skyla had met Wind Burn at Earth Nation Park when they were thirteen. Since then, they had been inseparable until Skyla's parents were killed by wild grifflings that had attacked Storm Nation's crop fields where her parents worked. On that day, Skyla prayed to Death to give her the power and chance to make the light gods pay for not saving her parents. She especially wanted Spirit, the god of wind, to pay the most. She felt like if the light was right, then her parents would still be alive. Skyla's parents prayed so much and did so much good they should have been the one the wind god saved. So many unheard prayers she thought, so she became a shadow collector. And when the light-and-dark war comes, she will ascend and have her chance to kill Spirit and absorb Spirit's orb, and she will be the goddess of wind and storm of the dark path, and the gods will pay.

Now Death's shadow priest had sent her to convince Wind Burn to come to Shadow Empire so Wind Burn could be anointed and become Death's hand. This whole situation excited Skyla so much she had no idea Wind Burn was on the shadow path, let alone how Wind Burn got enough favor in Death's graces to become Death's hand. Skyla wondered how many pacts Wind Burn had made with Death because the shadow god did not show his face unless Death is upon someone or unless they are a special elemental. She herself had only made one pact with Death. Now she used her wisdom and beauty to gain status and rank in the well-known and feared cult, the shadow collectors…

Skyla flew over a mud pit. Then she came to the hole and sign that read Safe Haven city. She willed her storm aura to get stronger, and she flew to her first love.

*****

Dante and Wind Burn stood in the door of the Hell Mountain black market in Safe Haven City and waited for Skyla. Dante was smiling, and Wind Burn was serious and nervous.

"So…you still love her?" asked Dante to calm his older brother.

"I don't know. I think," said Wind Burn, fidgeting with his holo net.

"So why did y'all break up?" asked Dante, looking through the crowd at the hole.

"One day, she just disappeared after her parents died. I never questioned it. People vanish from 7-Nations all the time," said Wind Burn.

"Did you ever get…to…you know?" said Dante, making love-making movements and thrusting with his waist.

"Come on, bro, chill. Don't embarrass me," said Wind Burn.

"Well, spill it," said Dante, still making love to the air.

"We only made it to second base. Plus we were only sixteen when she left 7-Nations," said Wind Burn. Dante burst out laughing, making more detailed lovemaking movements and thrusts.

Then Skyla Breeze flew through the hole entrance to Safe Haven with the looks and grace of a storm goddess. Then she landed and powered down her wind aura. Dante and Wind Burn's mouths both dropped when they saw her. She had the most beautiful face with light-tan skin. Skyla had on dark makeup and grayish-blue storm eyes and long black hair. She was dressed in a custom-made shadow clothes that glowed with shadow energy and crushed dark crystals. The dark pricey clothes hugged her curvy body tightly. She wore black sandals, and her toes and fingernails were painted with black-and-gray flames.

"Wind Burn!" yelled Skyla when she saw Wind Burn. They raced to each other, and Skyla jumped on Wind Burn with her legs wrapped around him and kissed him long and hard.

"Wow, you look so beautiful," said Wind Burn after he caught his breath.

Skyla got down and said, "You don't know how much I've missed you. I never thought I'd see you again. People in 7-Nations are so afraid to leave Dragon Lord's protected city and see the world," said Skyla.

"You look really good, Sky, healthy and wealthy," said Wind Burn.

"You too. You look strong. Let me guess… Orb level 5 and a fully unlocked storm legendary weapon. Am I right?" said Skyla.

"Right, are you orb level 5 also?" asked Wind Burn.

"Yes, unfortunately, orb level 6 is not easy to reach," said Skyla with her hands on her waist.

"Would you believe me if I told you a week ago I was orb level 2 in 7-Nations working like a slave with my father," said Wind Burn.

"No way you advanced to three orb levels in a week, no wonder," said Sky.

"*No* wonder what… Oh, I have someone I want you to meet," said Wind Burn as he led Skyla by the hand to the black market door. Dante stood there, still in half a daze.

Skyla giggled and said, "Dante, right? We've met a couple of times actually. I was friends with Elisha until I left 7-Nations.

"How is she by the way?"

"Fine… Well, I kinda got her pregnant actually," said Dante, regaining his focus and seriousness.

"No way. Are you serious?" said Skyla.

"Yea, it was my fault. I was curious, and one thing led to another… So now I'm going to be a father," said Dante.

"Well, I'm happy for you. So what are you two doing in Hell Mountain?" asked Skyla.

"To be honest, we live here now," said Dante.

"Really, this is such a dead city. You should both come live with me in Shadow Empire. I have an entire floor penthouse in one of Shadow Empire's skyscraper buildings. It has like six bedrooms. And I can help you guys make a lot of currency," said Skyla.

"Me and my brother are on a mission, Sky. And Dante can't go to Death's City," said Wind Burn.

Skyla said, "Dragon Lord is the last thing to be worried about. This is the world of Fuzion. There's a never-ending amount of opportunity. Wait, did you just say 'brother'?" Skyla ran her fingers through her hair and looked deep into Dante's eyes.

"Yes, we have the same mother," said Dante.

"How long have you known? No one even thought such a thing when we were growing up," said Skyla.

"We found out the day we left 7-Nations," said Wind Burn.

"I am so happy for you two. Family must stick together," said Sky on the brink of tears. Then she gave Wind Burn a quick kiss on her tippy toes.

"We've known each other since we were kids, so it's no big change," said Wind Burn.

"So are you staying till tomorrow? You look like you could use some rest," said Dante.

"Well, it's up to Wind Burn. I didn't plan on staying," said Skyla.

"I don't mind if you stay. The shadow elementals you came with can stay in the soldiers' quarters," said Wind Burn.

"Well, I just want to take a quick rest. I need to get back in the skies to catch the next shadow war vessel and get back to Shadow Empire," said Skyla.

"Okay, beautiful, it's your world. Come with me so you can rest. Brother, have Skyla's company shown to the soldiers' rooms and see if Static can refill her ships e-cells," said Wind Burn. Then Wind Burn and Skyla flew through Safe Haven City's hole in a beautiful storm hand in hand.

Must be nice, Dante thought as he watched them go.

Wind Burn's room, Council's chambers

Skyla Breeze took a shower while Wind Burn laid two bedrolls together. Then he stacked two more bedrolls on top of the first two. Wind Burn gathered some shadow cherries from Skyla's bag. General Smoke had sent them a basket of chicken, steamed potatoes, some baked bread, and two canteens of sweet berry juice from the soldiers' kitchen.

Wind Burn had taken a quick shower first, so once he finished arranging his room, he sat on his temporary bed and looked at Skyla through the shower's foggy glass. Every now and then, Wind Burn would catch glimpses of Skyla's body, or they would make eye contact, and she would smile while rubbing her body down with soap. She was tormenting him with this thirty-minute shower. She moved her curvy body to a beautiful song she sang, and she used some scented vanilla fragrance soap that drove Wind Burn crazy.

When Skyla finally got out of the shower, she wore a grayish-blue night gown, and her hair was wrapped in a towel. Skyla sat on the bed next to Wind Burn and said, "Someone cooked for us. It looks good. I brought those shadow cherries from Death's garden for you."

"Thank you. We can share them. What was that beautiful song you were singing?"

"It's called 'So Cool.' I wrote it for you a long time ago. It just popped into my head. It still needs work."

"I love it, Sky... So do you have a boyfriend back in Shadow Empire?"

"No, I don't, I've been waiting and hoping for my soul mate." Skyla whispered, "I'm still a virgin," in Wind Burn's ear as she took the towel off her head and grabbed a brush from her bag and brushed her wet curly hair. Wind Burn stared into her eyes and watched her every move. "Do you really plan to stay in Hell Mountain and lead this rebellion with your brother?"

"What did you really come here for, Sky...? Stop this act. I know you."

"Fine, I came here to ask you to take my virginity and come back to Shadow Empire with me for your Death's hand ceremony," said Skyla in a serious manner with her arms crossed.

"I'll answer your question after you answer mine."

"Mmm," said Skyla, and then she grabbed a shadow cherry and ate it and then sat closer to Wind Burn.

"What's your status in Shadow Empire?"

"I'm the fourth leading rank of the shadow collectors."

"Go on."

"Okay, um, I have a bounty on my head by Fate's orb guardians for stealing shard energy and shard energy shrooms and flooding the world. I have a great amount of currency saved up in Shadow Empire bank, and that's it."

"Okay," said Wind Burn, analyzing all of the information Skyla had told him.

"So answer my question now please."

"Okay."

Skyla screamed and jumped in Wind Burn's lap, giving him a storm of kisses.

Next day

Wind Burn grabbed his back straps and legendary weapon from his bed and put them on over his shadow suit Skyla had brought him from Shadow Empire. It was still early in the morning, and Wind Burn moved slowly while he thought about Dante and his choice to leave. Skyla had gone to Hell Mountain's dock to help ready the ship for the journey to Voyage City, where the shadow war vessel mothership would take them and their ship over the dangerous sea to Shadow Empire.

Wind Burn still hadn't told Dante he was leaving. But he had to leave. The rebellion needed him to lead with Death's hand status. Wind Burn thought, *I'll just go, do what I need to do, then come back.*

Knock, knock, knock.

"Bro, it's me," said Dante.

"Come in," said Wind Burn.

"I was watching the Hell Mountain supercomputer, and Skyla's ship hasn't left the dock yet. Is everything okay with you two?" said Dante.

"Brother... I have to go to Shadow Empire to meet Death's shadow priest."

"Okay...well, I figured something was up. She just shows up out of the blue, and no one knows we're here," said Dante sadly.

"I don't plan on staying long. Skyla says there's a three-day ceremony I have to go through," said Wind Burn as he grabbed his bag from the corner.

"Just be safe, and try not to kill anyone. Ever since you advanced to orb level 5, you've been mellow and more talkative. I like you better this way."

"For you, bro, I'll try."

"Did you get some last night?"

"Yea! I loved it, I mean her," said Wind Burn happily.

"I have a feeling you won't want to come back after you leave with her."

Wind Burn walked over to Dante and put his hand on Dante's shoulder and said, "Bro, I'm not going to Death's City because of Sky. I'm going because I need Death's hand status to help you lead the rebellion. No female could ever make me abandon my goal to kill Dragon Lord." Then he and Dante embraced.

"What do I tell everyone?" said Dante sadly.

"Tell them the truth. They will understand."

"Good luck then, big brother."

"Luck is not something I depend on, and I haven't forgotten about your legendary weapon," said Wind Burn as he left.

Chapter 23

Information Chips

As soon as Skyla's ship left Hell Mountain dock, Dante became sad and depressed. So he took a long nap. When he woke up, his sadness had not left, so he did what he always did when he felt down. Dante pulled the small safe from his bag, opened the safe, grabbed the three tiny black chips, and looked at them in his hand.

Dante had watched the chips videos many times, and he still didn't understand the meaning behind them. Dante walked out of his room to the Council's chambers to use the ancient supercomputer Static had fixed yesterday. He needed to watch the recordings on the chips. They were the only memories of his parents that he had, and they eased his pain of loneliness. Dante loaded the first chip, and the old screen came to life.

> *Recorded holo message (1 of 1) mini sec 38; date: unknown*
> Title: *Luke and Inferno Convo*

> It was a dark night at the entrance to Hell Mountain. Luke stood their dressed in a luminous white flame cloak of power that looked dark in the night. The white flames spewed from the cloak.
>
> "Inferno!" yelled Luke as he activated a fiery aura and flew up to the top of the mountain. Luke stopped at the peak of Hell Mountain's volcano hole, and lava burst out. Create your

safe haven. Luke used a level 5 stacked shield to block the deadly lava shower as a hellfire elemental being rose out of the mountaintop and looked at Luke.

Luke said, "Inferno elemental being, my name is Luke Saint Cipher. I am the son of a spiritual African king. I come from 7-Nations, and I come here to ask you to form an alliance with me to protect this mountain. I'm going to start a small Safe Haven City and rebellion in the mountain."

Inferno said, "No such alliance needs to be made, Son of a king. I already protect this mountain."

Luke said, "My close friend is becoming evil. My race needs refuge from our leader. His name is Angel, but he goes by Dragon Lord."

Inferno said, "I have met this Angel, so his mind has become corrupt. Do as you wish. Create your Safe Haven City. I have a test for you or anyone of your fiery element."

Luke said, "What is the test, Great Being?"

Inferno said, "First, come to my city in a dream, and find the realm guardian. Second, come to my city on Fuzion, and find the location of Blaze's god key. Then and only then, we will see the seven who find the universal bond."

Luke said, "Where is your city located?"

Inferno said, "At the core of this mountain."

Then the elemental being dove into the mountain's lava.

Transmission ends.

Dante thought, *The key of the fire god. The god keys aren't even real, are they?* Then Dante loaded the next chip.

Recorded holo message (1 of 1) mini sec 48; date: unknown
Title: *Vision and the Promise*

Dante's mother wore a fancy red dress that shined and glistened. She sat on a long lush black fur couch in the living room in Luke's mansion in 7-Nations. Baby Dante played on the floor on a lush red fluffy carpet. A young pretty woman in custom-fitted hellfire full-body plate armor came through the front door of the mansion with a look of deep concern.

Clara said, "Karma, I'm so glad you came. I had a bad vision."

Karma's Dream said, "It's okay, hun. Tell me the vision."

Karma picked Dante up and sat next to Clara on the couch.

Clara said, "Luke died. Dragon Lord found out about the rebellion. Dragon Lord killed me also. Then sixteen years later, Dante dies from trying to absorb Luke's greater essence orb. Then the shard energy god appears in Dante's energy sphere and helps him absorb the orb, and then everything went bright."

Karma's Dream said, "Scionic visions don't always come true. Just relax, hun." Karma hugged Clara and dried her tears while Dante pulled Karma's hair.

Clara said, "If Luke and I die, promise me you will look after Dante. I want you to be his hidden guardian angel—godmother."

Karma pulled her hair from Dante's strong young grasp and said, "No one's."

Clara said, "Just promise me please. You're my best friend and the only one I trust with his life if something happens to us."

Karma's Dream said, "I promise, but no one's dying. Our Fire Nation army grows! And mostly all of us are like level 4. Only the will of the gods cap stop the fall of Dragon Lord."

Clara said, "Well, let's pray that the gods don't get involved."

Karma's Dream said, "If the gods get involved, someone will have to ascend and even the odds for us."

Clara said, "I don't like this. I wish I could protect my boys from this."

Karma's Dream said, "They have to protect themselves, but I'll do what I can, I promise."

Transmission ends.

Dante thought, *The god of light helped me absorb my father's orb. I'm sure of it…strange.* Then Dante loaded the next chip.

Recorded holo message (1 of 1) min two sec 40; date: unknown
Title: *White Flame Cloak of Power and the Fire Spirits*

Luke stood in his room in Inferno mansion dressed in red hellfire clothes, holding a white-flamed crystal cloak of power that hummed and flickered luminous flames.

Luke said, "Son of a hellfire king, with the help of a skilled alchemist, I forged this cloak when I first found out about the three differ-ent flames of the fire spirits and how each flame excels in a different area of combat. The three flames are as follows.

"White flame, the liger spirit form, best used in hand-to-hand combat. This is also the best flame to use for alchemy spells. This is the flame of divine truth. It removes all illusion and darkness. Crimson flame, the phoenix spirit form, the best combat used in speed and range attacks. This flame makes you faster by energizing your restoring energy to your body. Orange and red flame, the dragon—the dragon's best combat damage and power. The strength of the dragon is explosive. Energy comes from your sexual energy and health. My son, you will learn to change into the fire spirits at orb level 5. This cloak was created to enhance the fire spirits, but I did not get a chance to fully master the cloak.

"The white-flame cloak was made by melting three pounds of hard level 9 crystals to an elemental cloak of power, and then Static placed an absorption spell on the cloak's melted crystals. I willed myself into the white flame fire spirit and sent all of my energy to the cloak in a white-flamed fire beam. I even used the forbidden fire perfection and used all of my life energy. The results were great. There are still many things to unlock within the fire spirits, but I feel that my time is short. I want you to have this cloak. I made it for a great king who will be honest and fair. He will have love for all life. I want you to be a hellfire king who has the love and compassion to make the ultimate sacrifices in life.

"*I love you, son, rise of the hellfire storm.*"
Transmission ends.

Dante watched the information chips a few more times. Then he ran down the hall into the kitchen of the soldiers' quarters and saw Static and General Smoke in a heated conversation about food and supply shortages. Dante turned away and went back to the Council's chambers to find Lou Shen in his three-star-rank seat.

"What's wrong, grandson?" asked Lou Shen as Dante took his seat.

"Nothing, GP," said Dante.

Then static and General Smoke came in the Council's chambers and joined them.

"Sorry, I've been away. I was a li'l down about big bro leaving. Can I ask why you were arguing?" said Dante.

"I don't want to lie to you, son," said General Smoke.

"But you don't want to tell him the truth either. Dante is not a baby," said Static while he started typing on the supercomputer.

"I can handle the truth. If I am to truly lead this rebellion, you must tell me everything—the good and the bad," said Dante.

General Smoke took a seat in the middle of the left bleachers and put his head down.

"Static, what's going on?" asked Dante.

Static said, "We have been low on power and supplies for so many years. We are barely surviving, living like savages. I'm so thankful you came with your 'light source energy' idea. We've been getting food and supplies from the hell thieves' black market. And we get power from the forest of balance, but both of those options have become too much of a hassle. The currency your father had saved is almost gone."

"How much is left in the vault?" said Dante.

"Six pounds of corundum crystal and one thousand and eight hundred platinum marks. And it's all yours, Dante," said General Smoke.

"I don't want the rebellion's currency," said Dante.

"Grandson, you need to help Static figure out a way to use the rebellion's currency to make more currency," said Lou Shen.

Dante sat in his one-star seat in deep thought for a few seconds and then said, "I have some ideas, but I have to go to the light temple in the wild lands."

"This is no time for worship and prayer, son," said General Smoke.

"Look, you're all just going to have to trust me. I'm the leader of this rebellion, right?" said Dante.

"Yes!" said General Smoke and Static at the same time.

Dante said, "Some changes have to be made around here, and I'm putting all my personal saved currency toward a new ship."

"Port Shard Land City has decent wealth and supplies. The alchemist brothers that lead the city could build you a custom craft, or you could buy one already made and trade in those junk ships in the dock," said Static.

"Sounds like fun," said Dante.

"You don't have to go on journeys and missions, son. You're a leader. We can simply send someone to do those things for you," said General Smoke.

"Nope... I have to talk to Fate myself. Plus missions build character," said Dante.

"I'll go with you, grandson," said Lou Shen.

"Coo, GP," said Dante.

"Take Cal with you. He's a good copilot," said Static.

Dante nodded while excitedly rubbing his hands together as more ideas ran through his head.

"Does anyone know anything about my father's white-flame cloak of power?" asked Dante, suddenly breaking his thought.

"No, it is lost. When Luke was killed, Dragon Lord sold it the liberators or the shadow collectors. Honestly, I'm not really sure where it is," said Static.

"I've heard rumors that it may be in one of the cities of light," said General Smoke. Then a silence filled the Council's chambers for a few minutes.

Dante broke the silence and said, "General Smoke, do you know the fire elemental being at the core of this mountain?"

"Yes, the strange being has a city in the depths of this mountain. I think the city is called Inferno City. The great being never comes out. But I know he's still here. I feel his fiery presence and great power. All you have to do is sense his energy with your mind. I don't know how, but he's been the only one to get the elemental being to come out," said General Smoke.

"I have to solve his test when I get back," said Dante. Dante gave the information chip with his father's convo with Inferno to Static and said, "See if you can gather more info for me. This chip has sentimental value, so please take care of it till I get back."

"I'll do what I can, Dante, sir," said Static.

"Now come on, GP. Let's go get packed and get in the skies," said Dante.

By sun fall, Cal, Lou Shen, and Dante were headed to the temple of light.

Chapter 24

The Temple of Light

Lou Shen was the head pilot, Cal was the copilot, and Dante was the assistant copilot. The old rebellion hovercraft was a small oval slow craft that Static and Cal had pieced together with parts from different low-tech ships. *Scrap metal, a piece of junk*, Dante thought.

In the back of the small craft was ten empty crystal e-cells, scrap parts, lots of wires, and the six full droids that Dragon Lord had sent with the shock to capture them…

Cal talked most of the way. He told Lou Shen and Dante that he was very good with numbers. That's why they called him Cal, short for Calculate.

He didn't have a real name, simply because his parents didn't name him.

Cal told them that the rebellion had a low number of fifty-two active members, give or take twenty travelers. Thirty of the active members are random hellfire elementals that came to Hell Mountain to follow Luke because of his fire spirits. Ten of the rebellion's active members were the hellfire humans or front line, including General Smoke who all fought with Luke seventeen years ago.

All of the front line were orb level 7 and pretty strong. General Smoke and the front line have kept the rebellion alive, fighting light, shadow, and random abominations at the forest of balance to fill these e-cells with power when the rebellion ran low. The other ten active members of the rebellion were earth pantharainians from the freedom pact.

"Then the only two alchemists of the rebellion are me and my older brother, Static. I predict a rise of two thousand members, give or take three hundred, once elementals find out the son of Luke has fire spirits and you absorbed your father's orb. Plus your brother's Death's hand status, and Wind Burn is almost as I strong as the son of Luke. You do know you're famous, Dante. It's crazy, right?

"So for us being humans and Dante being famous, I brought you two masks, hooded cloaks, and gloves. Some attention may be unwanted attention from certain creatures and beings. Our ascended powers are feared, hated, and envied. The wild creatures are threatened by what they don't understand. Heck, we barely understand our own powers of the gods. Some humans can't even tap into them. I don't know if it's because they're not strong enough, or maybe they lack the will to tap in to the source. Oh, Dante, I all most forgot to tell you. The ship you came in had a tracking device. I dismantled it and used some of the parts for…"

Dante wandered off in his mind as Cal talked on and on.

Dante's thoughts

So the rebellion needs currency. We need incoming wealth, so we need jobs—cooks, guards, alchemists. Oh, I could start a Hell Mountain mine for crystals and rare minerals like in 7-Nations. But I'd need to ask the fire elemental being first. I hope he's not mean.

I could talk to the light creatures at the forest of balance and ask them to form an alliance with me for constant drops of light energy to use for distribution, and Static and Cal could build more things with more power.

Maybe I could show of my fire spirits to the creatures at Port Shard Land City. I'll put on a show to raise some currency and members for the rebellion.

I could sell these droids for at least four thousand to fifty thousand platinum, I hope.

We need currency to buy goods in bulk from Merch's black market to start the Hell Mountain black market in Safe Haven City.

This is crazy. So many creatures depend on me to lead them to a better world and life—all because of my father. I wonder what he did that was so great.

I have to go see the hellfire elemental being and ask him about the key he spoke of. What key, Blaze's key, key to what? The keys don't even exist.

I wonder what Skyla Breeze and big bro are doing, probably sacrificing an orb in Death's name or going on a killing spree... I hope not.

Man, that Skyla was one beautiful lady, a walking goddess.

Beautiful women, I wonder were that beautiful hellfire woman is who was with my mother in the info chip. She looked to be about twenty something.

Karma's Dream—my guardian angel and godmother. She's about forty now. To still be alive. But I never seen her a day in my life that I can remember. That's 'cause she's your hidden guardian angel, crazy man.

Speaking of angels, I wonder how Elisha's doing. How long does it take for a woman's stomach to start showing?

Frost Bite's going to win the dragon tournament this week with ease now that big bro and I are gone.

Big bro said he's still going to get me a legendary weapon. He'll probably just get his rich girlfriend to buy me one... I don't even really want one, come to think of it. Death weapons make your heart dark.

But I'm leading a rebellion to kill. Two wrongs don't make a right. I'm so confused. Ahh, why so much rain on my life?

* * * * *

In a little under four hours, the rebellion hovercraft reached a hundred-feet-tall light temple that was surrounded by a small gathering of trees and bushes. The temple of light's walls looked light-yellow glowing glass, but you couldn't see inside. Cal landed the ship on the dirt path that led to the light temple's front doors. On the right side of the temple's dirt path stood a pure earth elemental in a yellow cloth armor suit. On the left side of the dirt path was a fifty-feet-high gray crystal pool filled with light energy. Dante looked at the beautiful scenery as Cal landed the ship and said, "Do y'all want to come in with me?"

"No, I don't worship gods," said Static.

"Neither do I," said Lou Shen.

"We'll wait for you here, Dante," said Cal. Then he and Lou Shen started a conversation about the neutral gods and Nazareth.

Dante opened the ship's side doors and ran outside to the pure earth elemental.

"My name is Dante. I need to speak to Fate," said Dante.

"Ahh, yes, Dante, we orb guardians have heard so much about you. My name is Nimble. If you seek the light, then you know what must be done to summon the light one," said Nimble.

"Right, what's in the temple of light?" said Dante.

"Inside the temple is a quest for those who are troubled in life and still want to become orb guardians," said Nimble.

"I have a simple question for Fate. I don't have time for quest," said Dante.

"You are a special one to Fate. I'm sure you won't have to take the quest. You will be automatically accepted as an orb guardian when you're ready, of course," said Nimble.

"Yea, yea," said Dante as he activated a hellfire aura and flew up to the top of the light pool. Then Dante raised his hands to the sky, and they caught fire. A giant hellfire orb of burning energy formed over him, and he threw the energy into the pool of light. The light energy absorbed the hellfire orb and turned into hundreds of light fairies. Then the light fairies merged and formed Fate, who sat in a meditation pose.

"God of light, I have come," said Dante.

"Your fire spirits have awakened," said Fate.

"Fate, I ask for the reason for this constant rain on my life."

"All has set a path for self to learn through your spirit."

"Who is this 'all,' and why me?"

"Why question the will of all? In the end, you're going to do as you wish."

"What do you mean?" said Dante, getting a little upset.

"You don't want to become an orb guardian, because you are blinded by revenge." Dante said nothing as he calmed his temper. "Do you deny that you are blinded by revenge?"

Dante said nothing as tears began form in his red fiery eyes. A legendary hellfire hammer formed in the air in front of Dante.

The weapon had a deadly fiery aura around it, and it dripped liquid scorching fire energy.

"This is for you. It is an endless burn legendary weapon," said Fate.

"Why would you give me a legendary weapon of death?"

"This is the path you choose. Why question the will of all?"

Dante understood as he stared at the weapon in deep thought. "No, I don't want my heart dark," said Dante. Then the death weapon disappeared. "Why did you help me absorb my father's orb two years ago?"

Fate said, "A greater essence orb obliteration could tip the balance given the right circumstances. If you would have failed, all in existence could have been destroyed. And you must know little help was given. Above all, my point in existence is to protect us all at all cost."

"So you really don't care about me, do you?"

"All truly does love all in existence. But sacrifices must be made in certain situations."

"Like my father and clan."

"Fire perfection draws dark energy from the source. This violates the balance. In the war with Angel, many hellfire used the fire perfection ascended power without understanding. This allows you to tap into power you don't understand. *Don't* use it."

"I won't. I feel so bad, like I'm hurting the planet."

"Yes, you can feel the all. You would make such a great orb guardian."

"Do you know where my father's white-flame cloak of power is?"

"Yes, it is in Pure City. I saved it for you once you are ready to become an orb guardian. This is your planet. Your human race must take responsibility for Gaia's pain. Dante, you and all life on this planet are temples of light. You must awaken from this dream and…"

Dante stopped listening to Fate and flew back to the ship.

Chapter 25

The Forest of Balance

Dante got back on the ship and said, "Let's go to the forest of balance," while wiping his face.

"Is everything okay, grandson?" asked Lou Shen.

"Everything is fine, Grampa, and I don't want to talk about it," said Dante as he took his seat in the pilot pit.

They flew south for a few more hours until the ship's old computer screen showed a lush energetic forest. Dante looked out of the pilot pit's window and said, "Wow, so much natural energy. It's beautiful!"

The forest was split down the middle by a fifteen-feet-wide lotus energy stream that glowed light blue and looked so pure and tasty. The left side of the forest had shadow energy pools and shadow apple trees. Ten dark-furred shadow pantharainians were in the shadow trees with powerful shadow auras active. On the tallest shadow apple tree was a large pantharainian in beast form looking eager and waiting for something to happen. The rest of the wild pantharainians stayed ready for battle while looking at the other side of the forest. The right side of the forest shined bright, with light energy pools and trees. A 110-feet-tall light-orange tree was surrounded by a circular 100-feet stonewall. Light ligers stood in the light orange tree and along the stonewall with light auras active, ready, waiting.

"It looks like a battle is about to start," said Dante.

"The forest of balance is one of the five places in the world where there are constant battles fought that never end. The prize is Fuzion's natural energy resources, which are light, shadow, and pure water energy. These battles are elite fights fought by orb level 6 and 7 elementals. Advanced beings who are on the brink of ascending only dare enter that forest," said Cal.

"We should land a good distance away, or our ship might get destroyed," said Lou Shen.

"No, fly up to three hundred feet, and activate the Hover Mode to save e-cell energy. I'll fly down and try to talk to the light creatures before the battle starts," said Dante. Cal did as Dante said and then opened the ship's side door.

"Be careful, grandson!" shouted Lou Shen through the strong winds as Dante willed his fiery aura around his self and then beamed down to the light side of the forest. All of the thirty creatures of the forest looked up at Dante's fiery being flying down with interest. The light and shadow creatures grabbed at the energy in their auras and formed shadow scythes and falchions of light and aimed their weapons at Dante.

"Creatures of this forest, I do not wish to fight!" screamed Dante with his hands up in protest as he slowed his flight to equal hover with the stonewall.

"Then you may have come to the wrong place," said a light liger on the stonewall closest to Dante. The light liger had a bow and arrow made of pure light energy aimed at a shadow panther who had a black-flamed shadow beam charged and aimed at Dante while moving in for a better view.

"I am on the light path! I mean you no harm! Let me speak to the leader of this forest!" shouted Dante while noticing everyone tensing up and moving slowly into better battle positions.

"No one leads us! Now speak quickly!" shouted an older-looking liger holding a light boomerang on his shoulders.

"My name is Dante. I come from Hell Mount—" Then it happened so fast. A lightning pure elemental teleported into the forest and ran to the stream in the middle of the forest and placed an empty e-cell in the water energy. Then all hell broke loose.

"War!" shouted the shadow creatures as they all started throwing shadow energy scythes, beams, and dark obliteration orbs at Dante and the lightning pure elemental.

Dante shielded and evaded over twenty-five shadow attacks. Then the shadow energy kept coming so hard and fast dark energy began to slice and burn him to the point where Dante started bleeding. Dante used an inferno shield and then flew back up to the ship and sat down in his seat.

"Well, that didn't work," said Dante as he drank a rejuvenation elixir from his travel utility belt.

"It seems to me that the only way to get the energy is to take it, grandson," said Lou Shen.

"No, I don't think that will work, GP. They're all so strong. I need to advance orb levels," said Dante.

"Then what?" asked Cal.

"I go dragon fire spirit and knock all of the shadow creatures out. Then there will be no war, and I can talk to the light ligers," said Dante.

"We don't have any orbs with us, grandson," said Lou Shen.

Dante looked at his computer screen and watched a shadow pantharainian form and launch a deadly shadow ball at the lightning elemental.

The black fiery energy exploded around the pure lightning elemental and threw him deeper into the light side of the forest. The pure lightning elemental hit a tree and then hit the ground still burning in black-and-gray flames. Seconds later, the lightning elementals body faded away, and five lifeless orbs came out of the lightning orb and hit the forest floor. The five orbs lay on the ground looking dim and drained of energy.

The lightning orb slowly flew southwest in the direction of the Land of Lost Orb Souls. And the forest battle continued on with explosive dark-and-light energy.

The battle seemed to be evenly matched, and it seemed it would never end. Both sides of creatures constantly attacked and shielded each other. No one crossed the river, so it was a bright-and-dark-ranged battle.

Every now and then, a creature would get hit a few times and start bleeding. That creature would run to an energy tree and consume an energy fruit and return to the battle fully healed.

"Looks like this is my chance. I haven't absorbed the lightning element yet," said Dante.

"Grandson, maybe we should wait and travel to Port Shard Land City first and buy me four or five orbs so that I may advance to level 6 or 7, then I can help and heal you," said Lou Shen.

"It's now or never, GP," said Dante. Then once again, he flew down to the forest and beamed straight to the lightning orb. Dante weaved a few shadow blast and then grabbed the lightning orb and put in into his chest.

"Ahhh!" screamed Dante as a sphere of lightning covered him.

The battle of shadow and light stopped, and the creatures watched Dante's colorful orb absorption in awe and amazement...

★★★★★

Dante thought, *Life is so unclear and full of misery and mystery all set by the gods. My father wants me to become a great leader and wear the white-flame cloak of power. But Fate has the cloak and wants me to become an orb guardian. But how can I live as an orb guardian with blood on my hands? Who is this, and what does he want with me, and where can I find him? It's funny how I find myself drifting off here a lot lately. But...something's different. I feel a soothing calm like a spiritual bliss, like my heart and mind have made a connection.* Live!

Dante looked around and saw his three fire spirits in the corner of his mind, standing there like large flaming ethereal statues, and they were all connected by emerald light. *I can shift between fire spirits at will now,* thought Dante. *I can see things more clearly now, but it's still blurry. Why won't the gods open my eyes completely?*

Dante focused his will to see Dragon Lord's exact essence and power, but Dante only saw death in the form of shadow darkness that blocked his vision. Fate fazed into existence in Dante's mind and said, "Some things are better left unknown. Sometimes, the soul is not ready to accept the truth."

"You're right, thank you," said Dante with a bright smile.

"What for?" said the god of elemental light.

"For giving me the gift of sight," said Dante.

"Your gifts are your own. I did nothing," said Fate.

"I know what I must do. Will you help me?" said Dante.

"You have always had the light. It is you who determines what is done with it," said Fate.

"Right," said Dante as he looked past his flaming fire spirits and saw three doors of energy—emerald, shadow, and light doors that led to the world. Dante turned around and saw other doors, and Fate was gone. The other doors gave Dante a feeling of the unknown, but at the same time, Dante felt like he had been there before, as if the unknown were forgotten memories of past lives. Then another door caught Dante's attention—a door that had a sign above it that said *Akashic.* Dante broke from his trance and flew to the phoenix and entered the fire spirits chest. Then the phoenix flew through the yellow door. *I'll be back to see what's in those other doors,* thought Dante.

* * * * *

The dark and light creatures of the energized forest watched the sphere of lightning savagely lash out lightning bolts in all directions as it hovered in the sky. The sphere of lightning moved with a glow of light toward the shadow side of the forest. When the sphere got close to the shadow creatures, bolts of lightning from the sphere shot at all of the pantharainians and knocked nine of them unconscious, except for the large one in beast form in the shadow apple tree. Who had blocked the lightning bolt with a shadowy orb level 7 stacked shield? Then a fiery tornado swallowed the lightning sphere from bottom to top. Then the sphere got smaller and smaller until only a large fiery crimson phoenix remained.

The crimson fire spirit flew with deadly speed to the shadow side of the forest while throwing inferno orbs at the shadow creature. The pantharainian weaved Dante's attacks in a dark blur and then teleported to the ground and formed a black shadow scythe from his aura and said, "Black fiery beam." As he whipped the dark scythe at Dante, a large scorching black-and-gray beam of energy shot at the ruby-red phoenix. The fire spirit formed a crimson shield around himself, blocking the black flames, and then Dante flew to the ground and took a blurred quick dash step and turned into a liger of white flame. The shadow panthrainian charged at Dante and swung his dark energy scythe, leaving a path of black flame behind it. Dante's fiery white form easily teleport-evaded behind the shadow creature and punched him with a level 6 dragon inferno strike of white luminous flame. Dante's punch connected and threw the shadow creature fifty feet deeper into the forest. The shadow creature hit a tree then hit the ground and then quickly stood up.

The shadow pantharainian looked at Dante's white-flamed fire spirit with hate and said, "Foolish human, roarrr!"

Dante stepped in a fiery dash and changed to an orange-red fiery dragon humanoid and said, "You seem to be the foolish one. You cannot win." The panthrainian changed to humanoid form and ran northwest toward Voyage City, roaring through the forest the whole time.

Dante powered down his fire spirit and flew over to the stonewall where the light ligers stood watching in amazement. The ligers powered down their weapons and auras that had been created by their light spirit.

"Will you kill the shadow creatures? They will wake in time," said one of the ligers.

"No, I don't kill," said Dante.

"Come sit in the orange tree of light," said one of the ligers on the wall. Dante flew over to the top of the orange tree of light fruit and sat with two old-looking ligers.

"Dante, my name is Knowledge Elder, and this is my good friend, Wisdom Elder. I would like to tell you a story of truth, a story on how the forest of balance came to be, so you may understand our culture and ways. On Abomination Day, three gods manifested from Fuzion—the god of light, the god of shadow, and the shard energy god. The first three gods fought over our faith and territory. But most importantly, they fought over control of Fuzion's power. This control of Fuzion's power was more like a partnership with Fuzion. The shard energy god was kindhearted and neutral. He rarely got involved in such battles. Nazareth would only fight when Death attacked him. But Death tried to kill Fate every chance he got.

"This forest was one of the main battlefields because Death wanted control over the tainted lands. The seventh scion Trinity's Light said there was a deadly energy battle between Fate and Death in the sky that covered 'these wild lands.' Death was so evil and heartless that he would rather destroy himself and all life before he would lose this battle with Fate. The energies of the gods became too much in the energy battle. God shadow and light fell to the floor of the forest and merged with various trees ponds and rivers, creating great sources of power.

"Sensing the deadly overflowing power, Nazareth willed himself to the battle of gods and saw that Fate nor Death could break from the energy battle or push the energy toward the other. So the energy grew and grew. Pretty soon, it could destroy the earth. Fate screamed to Nazareth, 'Push the energy into the sky, or we all die!'

"Nazareth watched the overflowing light and shadow god energy drip and rain down on the forest and wild lands. The shard energy god took a deep breath and pulled in emerald energy from everywhere and formed a shard energy aura and flew into the sky over the energy battle. Nazareth touched the ball of god energy and used the will of an ascended god and formed an emerald net around the energy and then pulled into the sky. Nazareth's power hummed and shook the entire earth as he took the great battle energy into the universal heavens. Then Fate and Death fazed out of existence. To the fourth dimension," said Knowledge Elder.

Then Wisdom Elder said, "I assume you want energy for whatever reasons, but let me tell you this. The forest and the god energies are connected to Fuzion to Gaia. Fuzion has so much to govern on this planet and in existence that energy on this planet is short. Every drop is accounted for. This is called balance of Fuzion on earth. The forest has a slow regeneration rate, but if too much energy is taken too fast, it will drain that certain energy of the forest forever.

"The balance of this forest must be sustained just like the meteor shard. The forest of balance has shrunk so much. It's ten times smaller than what it used to be. The shadow creatures don't care about the times to come. All they see are wealth, war, and energy from Death. We ligers live here and protect the rest of this forest. For your deeds of unknown power and noble righteousness, we will allow you to take light energy on this day only. The shadow creatures rest, which, in return, allows the forest to rest."

"Are you orb guardians?" asked Dante.

"No, we are not, but we walk the path of light. Light is information, and ignorance is darkness," said Knowledge Elder.

Wisdom Elder said, "This forest is not the solution to your energy problems. Some days, we and the shadow creatures lose lives protecting this forest from greater threats such as elemental beings, berserker lords, and the assassin lords from bounty city," said Wisdom Elder.

"I am grateful for what you will give me on this day. I am the new leader of Hell Mountain in the tainted lands. My soldiers will not steal from this forest again," said Dante. The ligers bowed and shouted praises to Dante for their day of peace, and then Dante flew to the ship.

*****

Dante flew back and forth to the ship, and the light pool filled e-cells with light and lotus energy. The elder ligers watched Dante and talked in deep conversation about Dante's realization.

Knowledge Elder is he the one who will fulfill the prophecy, much untapped power he has.

Wisdom Elder—I feel the light god's presence in him, but he is not conscious of his own spiritual and mental abilities to tune in to the all.

Knowledge Elder—maybe he must lose or gain something to perfect the gift of sight.

Wisdom Elder—or maybe he blocks himself from reaching true potential.

Knowledge Elder—his heart is pure with light. Do you think this rebellion will alter his fate and destiny?

Wisdom Elder—if he is the chosen one, he can manifest his own destiny. The dark dragon is simply an obstacle in his life. He must pass to get to his higher self.

Knowledge Elder—yes, yes, ha, ha. I see third eye. His higher self is selfless.

The ligers laughed as they waved Dante goodbye.

Chapter 26

The Alchemist Brothers

The sun rose and fell as the rebellion ship approached a small city that was surrounded by many different ships. Some ships were low tech and Frankenstein looking, and some ships looked like Dr. Volts himself had built them. Some creatures lounged around ships with tents and shops set up as if they lived out of the ships. The outskirts of the city looked like a busy market of creatures trafficking and trading whatever they could.

"Before we leave, I need to refill our ship's e-cells. We're down to one energy block of power," said Cal.

"How long will it take?" asked Dante.

"About half an hour," said Cal as he landed their ship outside of the city's wall of ships. Cal walked over to his bag in the back of the ship and started looking for something.

"Take this. It's dangerous territory for humans outside of Hell Mountain," said Cal, and then he found a red tribal mask, a cloak, and gloves and gave them to Dante. Then he found a green tribal mask and gave it to Lou Shen.

"Only color we have besides brown and gray. Sorry, Lou," said Cal. Dante and Lou Shen got dressed in their disguises. Then they grabbed the ten e-cells, five each. Dante grabbed his bag of crystals and platinum and the holo pad that controlled the six droids.

"Cal, I'll call you when I need the droids," said Dante. Cal nodded, and then he opened the ship's side door, and Lou Shen and Dante stepped outside and made their way through the crazy market to the center of the city.

As they walked, they saw mostly different-color drakes, pure elementals, and ligers, maybe a few hawk humanoids. Most of the creatures in this city had multiple bioengineered body modifications. The creatures showed off and compared the tech arms, wings, legs, and even entire chest plates with pride and happiness. "GP, creatures here equip bio-mods for fashion. Why?" asked Dante.

"It seems they need them. Some creatures lose body parts living in the wilderness or in open cities like this one. If a Kracktalark abomination would attack this city right now, many creatures would be eaten, and many would lose limbs if they somehow survived. You have been protected by Dragon Lord all your life, so you don't see this sad part of the world, but this is the real reality. To these creatures, Dr. Volts's bio-alchemy is their savior," said Lou Shen.

When Dante and Lou Shen arrived in the middle of the crowded city. An exotic custom luxury hovercraft was on a raised platform in the center of the city like a trophy.

"I want that one," said Dante.

"Looks pretty pricey, grandson," said Lou Shen.

"Psst, ay, you, Masked Elementals," said a hooded creature who stood in the corner of the city by the wall of the dock building.

"Yes, Hooded Creature?" said Dante as he stopped and turned around.

"Y'all tryin' to make some quick currency?" said the hooded creature.

"How so?" asked Dante, interested as he approached the creature.

"In a few minutes, a ship will leave this city dock to meet another ship at sea. All you gotta do is protect the ship and make sure it gets back here in one piece. The mission pays a thousand platinum per guard, per four-hour ride," said the hooded creature.

"This does not sound legal. What's on the ships?" asked Dante.

"You askin' too many questions. What y'all, OGs or somethin'?" said the hooded creature in a sassy tone.

"We are not orb guardians but I'm on the light path," said Dante.

"Then forget we even had this convo," said the creature as he disappeared into the crowd of the city.

Dante walked back to the custom-made ship in the center of free city. A violet scaled humanoid drake, dressed in morphing armor, black boots, and Shock Wave gloves came over to the ship. The drake alchemist walked around the ship with a holo pad checking the ship for scratches. The drake alchemist noticed that the masked elementals were checking the ship out, so he said, "Masked Warriors, my name is Blake. I am one of the drake alchemists who set the alchemic foundation of this city. May I ask what reasons your faces, and what are your reasons for coming to this city?"

"We hide our race, and we bring much to trade. I want to buy a ship," said Dante.

"Come into the energy-harnesser building to meet my brother Energy," said Blake. Dante and Lou Shen followed Blake to a dome-shaped building made of violet crystal. Dante could feel the compacted lightning energy in the crystal walls. When they walked inside, Dante saw three opal crystal beam projectors in the crystal wall that was separated in equal space, making a triangle. The beam projectors pointed to the middle of the room where an old two-screen supercomputer sat next to a metal table. At the computer's holo pad keyboard was another violet-scaled humanoid drake in violet morphing armor. Behind the drake was a circular staircase that led underground. Distant noise could be heard coming from downstairs.

"Welcome to the alchemist brothers' chi harnesser. I copied Dr. Volts's designs. It's not as big as his, due to lack of advanced tech they have in 7-Nations, but it gets the job done. My name is Energy. I'm the second oldest of the alchemist drake brothers. Now remove the masks and cloaks so we can do business," said Energy as he typed in a fast blur on his holo pad screen keyboard while still looking at Lou Shen and Dante.

"Brother, I think they're from 7-Nations. How else did they get full droids?" said Blake.

"I figured as much. I picked up strange energy readings twenty minutes ago. That's why I sent you to check on the ship. We cannot afford to get robbed right now. Big brother would be so angry at us," said Energy.

Dante and Lou Shen removed their masks, and Dante said, "My name is Dante, and this is my grandfather, Lou Shen."

"You look very familiar, Dante," said Energy, studying Dante's face.

"Do you have ascended powers?" asked Blake.

"Yes, would you like to see them?" asked Dante.

"No, that won't be necessary. I'll take your word for it. What do you wish to do with those e-cells of light and water source?" said Energy.

"I'll trade or sell them," said Dante.

"What are you looking for?" asked Energy.

"I need four special orbs of regular element, not water. And I want that ship outside. Plus, I have six full droids in my ship, and I want to sell my old ship," said Dante.

"Full droids…never heard of it," said Energy.

"Dr. Volts's new tech, top-of-the-line," said Dante as he turned the holo pad on that controlled the droids.

"Bring your ship into the city, and park it on the platform so we can take a look. Blake, move Corina Air Tank M50 to the shipyard, and put a brother on guard," said Energy. Blake nodded and left the crystal building.

"How did you get all of these e-cells of source? It's such a hassle for us," said Energy.

"The forest of balance was a new experience. It's a long story," said Dante.

"Do tell. We have nowhere to go," said Energy.

Lou Shen sat down with his bag and e-cells and started meditating as Dante told his long story with great excitement, and Energy listened eagerly.

*****

In a little under fifteen minutes, Cal and Energy entered the chi-harnesser building with the six full droids behind them. Gal had the rebellion ship's activation pad in his hands, and he spoke with the words of a man who knew what he was talking about.

"This is state-of-the-art high technology from the great mind of Dr. Volts, who has the first books of lost alchemic science. What we have is computer-programmed full robotic droids that can become self-aware. With this tech, one can explore the field of AI, or they can be used as mindless tools. Each droid's abilities and strengths can be modified max of eighty. This is stronger than most level 6 elementals today. These droids can equip biotech, and they are the perfect fearless soldiers," said Cal.

"So what are you pricing these full droids at?" asked Energy.

"Eight thousand to nine thousand platinum," said Cal with a serious look.

"What? No way," said Blake.

"This tech has not hit the market yet. How can you price that high of a value on the droids?" said Energy.

"Because you said it yourself—this tech has not hit the market. And I'm sure Dragon Lord will charge five times the amount we want," said Cal.

"Blake, contact chaos and tell him the situation," said Energy as he walked over and looked closely at the droids.

"Ten e-cells. They can go for five hundred and eighty-four platinum each for the light ones and one hundred platinum each for the water e-cells. That's three thousand and four hundred twenty plat total," said Cal off the top of his head.

Energy said, "Correct mathematics. The Corina Model50 is a luxury craft with a base price of three thousand platinum with no added modifications. The craft outside is maxed out at thirty-five modifications noted as follows: Four lightning e-cells which gives the craft thirty-two energy power blocks for two thousand and three hundred, thirty-six plat. A level 3 energy shield generator, radius of the whole ship for 150 plat. Five elemental turrent guns, a thousand plat for all five. A medical bay with five strap-in beds and two cabinets for a thousand plat. Decent cargo space on the lower floor, forty by forty feet about ten feet high. Two hover pad boosters for air combat evasion for a thousand plat and a pound of C crystal. A crystal bottom plate for optional ocean travel for a thousand plat. The craft's maximum passenger capacity is twenty-four medium humanoids. And three tenth-version holo computers in the pilot pit." Energy was still walking around the full droids in a deep study.

"Does this craft have a tracking device?" asked Cal.

"Yes, we will take the ten e-cells and your old ship, and you still owe us five thousand and eight hundred seventy platinum," said Energy.

"Take one of the droids, and call it even," said Dante.

"Done," said Energy, and Blake quickly hooked a holo pad to one of the droids.

"Do you have any special orbs in stock?" asked Dante as he and Lou Shen put the e-cells to the side.

"Yes, we only have three, an LE orb, an orb chi orb, and an orb of speed," said Blake.

"I would like all three of them, and any other two regular elements you have will be fine," said Lou Shen.

"We don't sell orbs here, especially special orbs. They are from our personal vault. But for you, one hundred platinum for the special orbs and forty for the regular. That's three hundred eighty platinum," said Energy.

"Is that all you want, GP?" said Dante.

"By any chance, do you have lethal poison?" said Lou Shen.

"Yes, ten platinum for a case of twenty vials," said Blake.

"Give us the five orbs and six cases of poison," said Dante as he handed Blake 440 platinum marks from his black safe in his bag. Then Cal and Blake switched holo pads for the ship trade since the deal was final.

Then the supercomputer in the middle of the room lit up in a 3D holo graphic display of a large violet drake in morphing armor that was stretched to its limits.

"My name is Chaos. I am one of the four assassin lords of Bounty City and the oldest drake alchemist brother. Energy, send me the stats on one of the droids," said Chaos.

"Already on it, big bro," said Blake.

Within the next thirty seconds, Chaos had analyzed the stats of the droids and said in a monstrous voice, "I am pleased with this tech."

"We have purchased one droid already, brother," said Blake.

"I'll give you thirty pounds of corundum crystal for the four droids," said Chaos. Dante looked at Cal and Lou Shen, who both shrugged their shoulders.

"Fine, you got it, Mr. Chaos," said Dante.

"The crystal payment is already downstairs, brothers," said Chaos, and then the holo screen powered down.

"I almost forgot. We need a shard energy cleansing wand," said Dante.

"You have made us so happy today. We don't deal with the shady Dragon Lord. He overprices everything. Sometimes, Chaos pays the tax but will not too often. You can have two wands for free," said Energy.

"Thanks," said Dante.

"Are you staying in Port Shard Land overnight?" asked Energy.

"No, I can't. I'm the new leader of Hell Mountain, and I need to get back," said Dante.

"Well, we must link nations to stay in contact... What is your username?" said Energy.

"It's just Hell Mountain," said Dante.

"You must tell us how you got these advanced powerful droids from Dragon Lord. Just one droids computer drive will advance our systems and the whole way we use alchemy. As of this day, we as nations can be called allies," said Energy as he walked over to Dante and happily shook his hand.

"Brother, we should give Dante back one of the full droids and show Cal how to merge the droid's AI with the Hell Mountain supercomputer," said Energy.

"Thank you, but that won't be necessary. I actually need a small favor," said Dante.

"What is it, my boy? Ask and you shall have," said Energy.

"The rebellion army has gotten so small. I need soldiers to follow me like they did my father," said Dante.

"Your father is Luke, the hellfire spirits. That's why you look so familiar. Do you have fire spirits? Let's run some test on the fire spirits right now. We could make white-flame cloaks of power crimson-flame cloaks of power. We could find a breakthrough in science and alchemic technology!" said Energy with great excitement.

"You sound like Dr. Volts. I don't think I want to be an experiment. But this is my favor. I want to ask your city's population and some of the random elementals here to join the rebellion of Dragon Lord. With your blessing," said Dante humbly.

"It's okay with us, but we need some white-flame energy as part of the deal and part of your speech. When you speak to the city, you can help me form a white-flame cloak of power or two. You can have one," said Energy.

"I'll help you forge one for you. I have one in Pure City. I'm just not ready for it yet," said Dante in a sad tone.

"We understand, young fellow," said Energy.

"I'll go prepare the false meteor shards and crystals for the spell to make the white-flame cloak. Cal, come with me to get your payment for the droids," said Blake, and he and Cal went downstairs.

"Dante, this is what I need you to do," said Energy as he explained the alchemy spell to Dante in great detail.

Dante's speech…twenty minutes later

Dante stood on the platform in the center of the city next to a black cloak with melted crystals packed on it. Violet alchemy spells glowed on the melted crystal. Most of the beings in Port Shard Land City stood around Dante with looks of confusion and irritation because Dante wore a red mask and hooded cloak. Dante spoke truth as he asked the city, "Elementals of this city, I've come to ask you to join me in a rebellion against a common enemy we have much hatred for… Dragon Lord."

"Why should we join you? You are weak," said a hellfire drake in the crowd.

"No one even knows who you are. You have no rep," said a pantharainian in the crowd. Then the crowd went into an uproar of name-calling and boos.

Dante removed his mask, and the crowd went silent. Then whispers came over the crowd. "Human, it's Luke. Remember the fire spirits?"

"Luke is dead, fool," said the hellfire drake. Then the creatures of Port Shard Land City got out holo devices and started recording Dante.

"My name is Dante Saint. I am the only son of Luke Saint. I absorbed my father's orb two years ago, and now I wield the fire spirits."

"Fire spirits!" shouted Dante as he powered up. Then a flame surrounded Dante and turned him into a large phoenix. "I call for fighters of every element to join this rising army," said Dante as he stepped to the left in a blur of fiery speed and changed to a large hellfire drake. "I call for brave warriors who will fight with me as we honor the code of battle," said Dante as he fire-spirit-shifted to a liger of white flame. "I, the son of Luke, will lead this rebellion. I will defeat Dragon Lord and bring equality to the world. No matter how you see reality or how you live life, we fight the same fight. Join me at Hell Mountain in the tainted lands so that we can train our minds bodies and spirits to do what must be done," said Dante.

Then three drake alchemists who stood around the platform in a circle brought lightning from the sky into their Shock Wave gloves and shot the lightning at the crystal-covered cloak. The alchemic spells on the cloak's crystals glowed and absorbed the energy. Then Dante summoned a ring of white fire in front of him with both of his hands and sent all of his energy into the attack while yelling, "Dante's inferno." A jet shower of white flame beamed from Dante's fiery white ring and hit the crystal cloak for five minutes straight. Dante's screams and power shook the city. Then the creatures of the wild lands stopped what they were doing and sensed the energy coming from Port Shard Land City. The white flame lit up the night sky.

Once all of Dante's orb chi was absorbed by the cloak, the violet alchemy turned white and shot rays of alchemic light off the cloak. Then a great white fiery aura caught flame around the cloak of power.

"Rise of the hellfire storm! Join me now, or get lost in the storm," shouted a weak and drained Dante.

"Rise of the hellfire storm!" shouted the packed city of creatures as they applauded Dante's show of power.

*****

Ships came and left Port Shard Land's busy sea dock. Even at night, the dock's traffic did not die down. This was odd because not many ships or sane elementals traveled at night. And the closest place to go from here by sea was Land Outlaw. *Who would want to go there, a place of prison and automatic power block?* thought Dante. Dante felt tired and drained of energy. Plus he wanted to sleep in a real bed, so he rented three rooms in the city's rest house after he helped Lou Shen and Cal load all of the thirty pounds of crystal onto their new ship. The whole time, his father's cloak fogged his mind.

Cal transferred all of their belongings to their new ship. And once he finished, Cal did a little shopping of his own. Cal bought computer hardware for the Council's rooms, some beds, new amplified Shock Wave gloves for him and Static, some light and dark elixirs, and a few spells he didn't know. Once Cal finished shopping, he decided to test out the new medical beds. It got really late, so Cal went to his room in the rest house to get some sleep.

Lou Shen took four of the orbs Dante bought him and went to the neutral shrine of Orian and Nazareth. The shrine was empty except for two bowls of violet alchemic energy mixed with shard energy. The silver bowls sat on fifth high pillars, on opposite sides of the wall. Lou Shen sat in the middle of the shrine and meditated for thirty minutes, and then he went out into the wilderness of the wild lands on foot with the orbs on his back in a bag. *I'll be back before Dante wakes up*, Lou Shen thought.

Chapter 27

Hell Thieves

As soon as Air Tank Clara (renamed by Dante after his mother) soared into the sky, the ship's radar system picked up three ships following them and forty to fifty humanoid creatures flying at a distance while trying to keep up with the line of ships.

"I assume they are your new followers," said Lou Shen while he operated his head pilot holo screen.

"That was quite a performance and speech, Dante," said Cal.

"Thanks," said Dante, watching all of the following creatures. "Maybe we should keep a slow speed so we don't lose them."

"Give me half-max speed and level 1 shield," said Cal at his copilot holo computer.

"Shield up, and we fly at half-max speed... Um, I'll be right back. I'm going to go check on our drake guest," said Dante, and he ran to medical bay. Ten red-scaled orb level 7 hellfire drakes in humanoid form stood at attention when Dante entered the bay.

"Dante, Lord of the fire spirits, we pledge allegiance to you and the rebellion. We can be your personal guards. We will die for the son of Luke and the hellfire spirits of all who wield the three flames," said Hell Drake 1.

"That won't be needed. I don't need—" said Dante, but another red drake cut Dante off.

"We insist. We search for the god of the fire spirits, and Blaze does not have fire spirits," said Red Hell Drake 2.

"I am no god, Red Hell Drakes. You are confused," said Dante.

"You are the fire spirits, ascended powers of the gods that the gods don't have. We are not mistaken," said Red Hell Drake 3.

"We were on our way to Land Outlaw to visit the shrine of the hellfire god. We ask for purpose. Now we have found it. We are the red hell drake brothers numbers one through ten. I am Red Hell Drake One. I am the oldest, and I speak for us."

"Okay, Red Hell Drakes One through Ten. Welcome to the hellfire rebellion. When we get to Hell Mountain, we will have basic training. Looks like it's going to be a big crowd," said Dante.

"We love competition and battles," said Red Hell Drake 4.

"Good. Does anyone have any questions for me?" asked Dante.

"No, Sir Fire Spirit Lord," said all of the red hell drakes at the same time.

"Call me Dante. If you guys need anything, Red Hell Drake 1, come to the pilot pit and ask," said Dante.

"Rise of the hellfire storm," said the drakes as Dante left the medical bay with a glow of happiness in his heart.

When Dante got back to his assistant copilot holo screen, Lou Shen said, "We have been half blind for the past ten minutes in your absence. Please give us a holographic three-sixty-degree projection around us, grandson."

"Okay, sorry. The drakes think I... I'll get right on it," said Dante. Dante operated a holo computer screen and said, "Looks like we got some trouble, GP. We have a transport ship gaining speed on us from behind. Holo image confirms that the ship has no weapon systems. I can see a symbol on the ship. It says *Hell Thieves* around a fiery red double mask. One mask is smiling, and one mask is crying." Dante was confused about the meaning of the ship's symbol.

"Bandits," said Cal.

"No, they wouldn't be so foolish to try and rob us with all of these elementals following us," said Lou Shen.

"I'm slowing to Hover Mode. Dante, send them a message, and ask them if they need help or would they like to have a holo convo," said Cal.

"I'm on it," said Dante. But before Dante could complete the message, the ship's radar computer holo screen showed a pure hellfire elemental teleport out of the transport ship, then fly in a fiery tornado toward Dante's ship.

"Warning, warning, an incoming fiery humanoid," said a female computerized voice.

Then in five seconds, the fire pure elemental teleported into the pilot pit of Dante's ship. The fiery elemental wore a dark-red beryl crystal armor, red custom elemental boots, an elemental utility belt, and a hellfire legendary hammer strapped to his back. As soon as the fire elemental landed, he said, "I come with no harm. My name is Faze. I am the leader of the Hell Thieves, and I wish to make an alliance with you, Dante," said Faze with his hands up.

"Whatever happened to a simple holo conversation?" said Dante, unsure.

"My apologies, my ship's communication transmitter got destroyed. We came from Land Outlaw on a fierce mission at sea. Orb guardians, sea abominations, and the sea climate have taken their toll on my ship. We barely heard your speech last night. But I downloaded it from a lightning drake for forty platinum," said Faze.

"So... I guess we should link nations. My username is Hell Mountain," said Dante.

"My username is the icon of the laugh-now-cry-later. The access code is 'hell karma.' Sorry for all the secrecy. I have so many enemies and stolen wealth that I must be careful of whom I trust. Plus other nations with trained tech thieves may try to hack your database, so be careful of who you give your user info to," said Faze.

"I'll keep that in mind... So the Hell Thieves want to join the rebellion?" said Dante.

"Not exactly. My band steals from Dragon Lord guards and Shock Wave clones when he makes big deals and trades with other nations. That's how we fuel our own self-sufficient black market. In this way, we can help each other. I have eyes in 7-Nations on the next deal. We mask up and fight the Dragon Lord guards and Shock Waves. Then we take the goods and split the shipment evenly. This is how we can become allies. As you said in your speech last night, we fight the same fight," said Faze.

"I'll have to think about it. I really don't condone stealing. Where is your nation located? I don't see Hell Thieves on the world map," said Dante.

"I have a secret base in 7-Nations south, in the highest mountain," said Faze.

"I see, a secret base of rich thieves," said Dante.

"How can you have morals when you build a nation on war? This is a new wave world of elemental power. All that matters is can you survive. In time, I'm sure you will see," said Faze.

"I don't want the rebellion crushed before it can stand," said Dante as visions of his clan and father being slaughtered by Dragon Lord and his force army flashed through Dante's mind.

Faze's black market holo pad started beeping on his waist. His dark holo pad was small and compacted so that it fit on his belt.

Faze took a quick glance at the black market holo pad and said, "I must go. When we link nations, we will talk more." Then Faze activated his fiery aura and teleported outside of Dante's ship.

"You should really consider the Hell Thieves goods robbery as an option. As the army grows, we will need more food, goods, and currency to sustain it. The crystals we got from the alchemist brothers will only last so long," said Lou Shen.

"I hear you, GP," said Dante in deep thought.

Chapter 28

Inferno, the Elemental Being

It took Dante and his followers a little under two days to get back to Hell Mountain. This was due to the slow speed they traveled for the sake of some of the followers who were not as strong but could make good warriors in time with good training from Lou Shen and General Smoke.

When they finally arrived at Hell Mountain, Cal docked Dante's new ship with the two other ships that followed. Hell Mountain's new recruits were twenty wolf-fox humanoids who were water elementals, five earth drakes, and ten random pure elementals had been on both ships. And over sixty followers flew by wings, hawk humanoid elementals of earth, ice, and wind—twenty each element. Plus the ten red hell drake brothers. Every creature who had come to join the rebellion was orb level 3 and up. Some creatures could be at higher orb levels if they had orbs.

The rebellion basic training was held at the battlefield. The battlefield was a drained part of the sea that had been built into a battle arena. The battlefield was located forty-five minutes north of Hell Mountain in a no-man's land. By the end of the day, 105 soldiers had successfully joined the rebellion as the lowest rank of a soldier. The rebellion's active member count went from 52 to 157.

Energy, the alchemist brother, had linked nations with Dante and told Dante that over 160 hellfire drakes came from Land Outlaw and were headed in Hell Mountain's direction. The five levels of the soldiers started to fill up fast. On top of that, Safe Haven's population count went up as well.

*****

Dante woke up early the next morning and told General Smoke and Masked Monk, Lou Shen's new name, to go on with the everyday soldier training without him because he had to travel to the core of Hell Mountain to talk to the hellfire elemental being. Lou Shen told Dante to do what he must do but be careful. No normal elemental could even get down there. Dante told his grandfather he would be fine, and then Dante went to his room.

Dante grabbed two light and dark elixirs and an LE elixir and put them on his travel utility belt. Dante wore his hellfire clothing set that was resistant to fire and no shoes. Dante watched the info chip with his father and inferno a few more times. Then he mustered up the courage to do what must be done. Dante made his way to the maze tunnels of Hell Mountain until he found the lava path. Dante saw that the lava path traveled upward, and it was slanted going deeper into the mountain.

"So traveling by crystal boat is not an option. Why does the lava defy the laws of gravity?" said Dante to himself.

Dante took a deep breath and calmed his mind. Dante could feel the lava sooth the fiery element that was bound to his spirit as he breathed.

Dante released fire around himself and turned into the dragon fire spirit. Dante began to jump in the lava, but a beautiful voice stopped him and said, "Use the liger spirit. You can walk on fire and lava, and you can run very fast. You need to save energy if you wish to make it to the fire city."

"Who are you? Where are you?" said Dante as he turned around looking. Dante saw a shimmer, and then a red crystal ball appeared held by someone invisible. "May the fire spirits guide you," said the heavenly voice. Then a violet ring of alchemy came around the crystal orb and vanished.

Dante felt the presence had gone, so he fire-spirit-shifted to white liger and stepped onto the lava path. "This is so live. How did she know?" said Dante as he walked down the lava path that flowed upward.

Dante thought, *Why doesn't the lava flow out of the path and scorch the mountain…? Strange. Does Inferno control the lava flow?*

Dante's white-flamed feet picked up the pace into a white fiery blur of speed. After ten minutes of fast running, Dante came to a colossal hole where the lava came out strong. The hole had a scorching heat coming from it. "This must be it, Inferno City," said Dante as he walked through the hole. Right then the heat got hotter and even started to burn Dante.

Dante saw a scorching city with buildings made of dark heated crystal. Hellfire berserker lords, fire soul bound armors, and hellfire pure elementals roamed the city on everyday tasks of fiery life.

Hellfire hounds were on heated crystal leashes being walked by medium and large pure fire elementals. Random fire creatures played and swam in the lava river. And all of the fire creatures seemed to be at peace with no worries.

When Dante entered the city as a luminous large white-flamed liger, the whole city stopped what they were doing and stared at Dante. Some creatures were confused, some were happy, and some showed obvious envy. "The white-flame fire spirit has returned from the dead," shouted a hellfire pure elemental. Two hellfire berserker lords crept up on Dante with level 7 combined searing orb attacks ready and fiery auras active. "You are not the bringer of the prophecy," said one of the berserker lords as both of the berserker lords attacked Dante at the same time.

Dante orb level 6 stacked shielded both searing orbs in a white-flamed wave of his hands. Then Dante formed two blast of white fiery energy and threw the energy wave at each berserker lord. The berserker lords easily evaded Dante's attacks and teleported five feet over Dante's head by the lava entrance. Dante reached up and placed a level 6 combined hell orb bomb on each berserker lord's foot. At the same time, the berserker lords tried to kick Dante's head with flaming stomps. *Boom!* Dante teleport evaded, and white flame exploded and sent a double wave of white energy over the city turning the whole city's red flames white for a few seconds. Dante felt energized by the city's hot air, and it wasn't the flaming city; Dante was sure of that. Both of Dante's hell orb bombs had hit the berserker lords head-on, and from the force of the explosion, the berserker lords fell into the lava.

"Hahaha!" Dante laughed. He activated a white-flame aura, fire-shifted to the phoenix fire spirit, and flew into the air and fiery sky of the city while yelling, "I am Dante Saint, son of Luke Saint. I've come to speak to the elemental being of this city!"

The core orb of hellfire at the center of the city started to lash out fire, and the scorching city got even hotter.

A fiery elemental abomination rose from the enormous fiery orb. What Dante saw was truly amazing. Dante wanted to get a closer look, so he flew to the big black fortress building next to the core of energy and landed. The elemental being was a huge mixed dragon-liger creature with seven fiery fox tails and beautiful fiery angelic wings with four large flame-thrower-like cannons linked to them. The cannons shot flames like active rockets.

The elemental being's whole body was made of compacted fire, and in the center of the being's forehead was a decent-sized emerald meteor shard. An emerald giant hand of energy came out of the being's head and pushed the lashing fire rays back into the core orb of the city. The elemental being had a deadly hellfire aura that had hues of shard energy within the deadly flames. The aura fueled the city's energies, and it was so strong it overpowered Dante's aura because Dante was so close. Dante fire-shifted to the dragon fire spirit to be immune to deadly fire. Then Dante looked closely to see thirty tiny hellfire fairies in the elemental being's aura. The fairies played, danced, and flew around in the great being's aura without a care in the world.

"Son of Luke, long have I waited for your arrival. My name is Inferno. I am the elemental being of this fiery city. Ask the question to gain the knowledge you seek," said Inferno.

Dante drank a light-and-dark elixir from his belt and then sat on the edge of the fortress. Dante thought for a second and then said, "What is an elemental being, and how does one come into existence?" The city's population slowly surrounded Dante and Inferno to hear their conversation.

Inferno said, "Elemental beings are manifestations of one concentrated element. I was a pure fire elemental at orb level 2. I was in the depths of Shadow Hell, the second heaven or realm. This was thirty-six earth years ago. I stumbled upon a meteor shard fragment, and I realized that the only way for me to escape Shadow Hell was for me to tap into its power. Then Death's second form, the element of darkness, came into being and told me to attempt to absorb another fire element orb while holding the shard fragment. I did as he told me, and it was a foolish act. I barely survived impossible odds. Now I can only absorb fire orbs, and I have attained the status of premature god. Only one elemental being of each element can be sustained by Fuzion."

"So where do the tiny fairies come from?" asked Dante.

The fairies answered in unison, "We are friends. We bound to Inferno's orb so that we can help each other."

"Wow, you fairies are your own intelligent beings," said Dante, surprised.

"Haha-hehe, we like you, Son of Luke. You're funny. Would you like to bind with some of us?" said the fairies.

"No, fairies, I'm sorry. Inferno, why is the energy level so high in this city?" asked Dante.

"This is an energized realm on Fuzion. It is the kiss of god. Natural energy is so great in the air that it enhances all life who breathe it. It is an unconscious form of meditation with great results," said Inferno.

"This city is one of the many energized realms on Fuzion," said the fairies.

"Why did Fuzion and the elemental gods come to earth?" asked Dante.

"The gods chose to come to earth to awak..." Inferno stopped in midsentence as his meteor shard blinked emerald once.

"My apologies, Dante, you must ask that question to Fuzion," said Inferno.

Dante got a little frustrated and said, "Inferno, will you allow me to start a mining project in the upper levels of the mountain? I need jobs and currency to fuel the rebellion of Dragon Lord," said Dante.

"Do as you wish, but do not get greedy and exhaust this mountain's natural resources," said Inferno. Dante gave inferno a fiery thumbs-up.

"We want to join the rebellion," said the fairies.

"We believe in the hellfire prophecy. We will fight for the son of Luke," said a giant hellfire pure elemental who stepped out of the lava river.

"Yeah!" shouted most of the city's population.

"So it seems to me you have at least three hundred fire creatures of this city at your command. Just yell my name from wherever you are on earth, and I will open a portal rift to meet you at a battle location," said Inferno.

"The riddle you told my father," said Dante.

"Yes, the riddle. You are one of the few humans who have the ability and will to come to this city and not be burned alive. But do you have the wisdom to find the location of Blaze's key of god fire," said Inferno.

"What are the keys exactly?" asked Dante.

"The twelve elemental keys are great energies of one element created by the first twelve gods to ascend. Some say they do not exist. Some believe they do. They can give great power to elementals, or they can be used to free the shard energy god," said Inferno.

"They do exist," said the fairies.

Dante looked around the scorching city at all of the hellfire elementals with open mouths and stares. Some creatures were confused, and some were excited about the rare conversation being held at this moment.

Dante sat there for a few moments in deep thought, and then his fire spirit dragon powered down. Dante had run out of chi. Whispers of the city could be heard: "Human, the son of Luke is human. How did he get so strong? Impossible. He should not be able to come here. He must be the chosen one of the prophecy, the lord of the fire spirits."

Dante drank his last light-and-dark elixir and quickly changed back into a fiery hellish dragon. Dante stared at the fairies and Inferno, and then he looked at the core of energy Inferno stood on. The core of compacted fire lashed out deadly beams and rays like a mini sun. Then once again, the emerald hand came out of the meteor shard on Inferno's forehead and brought stability back to the core by pushing the fiery beams and lashes and rays back into the core of Inferno City.

Dante focused his mind and sensed the energy in the core. Then great energy came the fortress he sat on. Dante closed his eyes, and he saw this same city in a darker place of death. The lashes and rays of the core were more deadly and not sustained. There were at least seventeen lashes, beams, and rays of fiery energy coming out of the core. Then Dante saw in the fortress on a fiery throne in a shield of god energy, Blaze's key. Then Dante came out of the trance.

"The key is in a fortress in a dark real of death," said Dante.

"Yes, the keys are not in this realm, but they do exist. Dante, you have done so well on this day," said Inferno as the emerald hand reached on top of Inferno's back and grabbed an emerald apple that hummed with shard energy and handed it to Dante.

"I'm low on energy. I have to go," said Dante sadly.

"I know, but if you need something or seek more knowledge, come to the top of the mountain and call, and I will come," said Inferno.

"What is this strange fruit? I've never seen one like it," said Dante.

"A shard energy apple. It will make you so strong," said the fairies.

"Thank you, Inferno, but strength is not something I long for," said Dante sadly.

Inferno's meteor shard flickered, and then Inferno said, "Your father's cloak is a symbol of growth in your life. Don't be so down all the time. Just enjoy life."

"Live, grow, happiness, love, light, peace, yay-e-e," said the fairies as they flipped and flew fast circles in Inferno's aura.

"I do live life, but there's so much strain on my shoulders," said Dante.

"If you want to bind with us, we can lift some of the strain for you, Son of Luke," said the fairies.

"No, I don't think energized fairies will solve my problems," said Dante.

"Rise of the hellfire storm!" shouted all of the fire creatures of Inferno City.

"Bye, Inferno City, I have learned so much today. I will come back soon," said Dante as he fire-spirit-shifted to a crimson phoenix and then swiftly flew to the lava path entrance of Inferno City.

Dante hovered five feet above the lava path and then changed to the liger fire spirit of white flame and ran the lava path to back to the tunnel mazes of Hell Mountain.

General Smoke, the masked monk, and Tage Serenity waited for Dante at the lava path with looks of worry. When they saw Dante's white liger humanoid form walking up the lava path holding an exotic-looking fruit, everyone calmed down and smiled. Dante powered down his fire spirit and said, "Tage, about time some light came in my direction. I'm so glad to see you, Superstar."

"You won't be glad to see me after we talk," said Tage.

"Okay, let's go to the Council's chambers," said Dante, drained of energy.

Chapter 29

Tage Serenity

Ascended Council's chamber

Tage had on a custom-made lightning clothes armor that had alchemic writing all over it. Tage had on a hooded opal crystal cloak and black-and-violet custom-made boots. Tage's Shock Wave gloves had mini holo screens on the top of each hand. Tage weighed about 190 pounds, and his skin was dark and smooth.

General Smoke, Cal, Static, Dante, Masked Monk, and the nine front line all stood around the Hell Mountain supercomputer while Tage downloaded various information chips. Most of the data being downloaded were alchemic scripture. Then blueprints of a large orb fused war machine suit lit the old computer screens in great detail. Recorded videos of tests and prototypes of the war machine appeared on two of the computer screens.

"Unbelievable. Look at the alchemic scripture. Impossible combinations," said Static while reading the complicated spell.

"The numbers and stats are crazy. I've never seen some of these hieroglyphics and languages. It's as if someone made them up," said Cal in deep study, walking around the supercomputer. The front line took seats in the bleachers. They didn't really understand all of this alchemic talk, and they didn't see why this meeting was so important.

"Dr. Volts built this?" asked Static.

"If he did, that's very bad for us," said Cal.

"What's bad for us?" asked Dante while coming out of the Council's vault, about to close the vault.

"Wait, the book of lost science," said Tage as he went in the corner to his bag, grabbed the bag, and gave it to Dante, meeting him at the vault.

Dante looked in the bag and saw a lot of corundum, beryl, and phenakite crystals, and a violet leather book titled *Alchemic Knowledge: Volume Four Applied Science.* Tage said, "You can have all of the crystal for the rebellion, but hold this book as the most valuable possession I have. I want you to hold it for me and keep it out of harm's reach."

"Follow me," said Dante as he led Tage into the orb vault. The Council's vault had four different-colored exotic-looking chest along the wall. Dante and Tage walked to the red chest. Dante opened the chest, and it had thirty pounds of corundum crystal and some platinum.

"How much currency is in this bag?" asked Dante.

"I'm not positive. I emptied out my secret savings in Earth Nation's secret bank in the underground caves," said Tage. Dante grabbed the book out of the bag and started counting the crystals as he put them into the chest.

"Seven pounds of beryl crystals for three thousand and one hundred thirty-six platinum. Nine pounds of corundum crystals for four thousand and five hundred platinum. Six pounds of phenakite crystals for one thousand and eight hundred platinum. And three teleportation crystal orb pairs for thirty pounds of corundum or fifteen thousand platinum," said Dante.

"All totaled to twenty-four and four hundred thirty-six platinum, and it's all yours, Dante," said Tage.

"Are you sure you want to do this? This crystal is all your hard-earned wealth from slaving for Dragon Lord in 7-Nations," said Dante.

"This is nothing. I left five times this amount in Dragon Lord's bank in 7-Nations. Plus Fate told me if I want to become an orb guardian that I must help you and the rebellion any way I can," said Tage as he grabbed the book from Dante and placed in the red chest with the crystals and closed the chest.

"I will only use it if we need it," said Dante. Tage nodded.

"Fate gave me the book of lost science, which helped me come up with the applied science alchemic arithmetic to create the serenity shield. As you know, this made me very wealthy and famous in 7-Nations. And Dr. Volts still can't figure out how I came up with the alchemic scripture," said Tage.

"You kinda lost me 'aritha' what?" said Dante as he locked the chest.

"Never mind. I have some important news to tell you and the rebellion," said Tage.

"Then let's get to it," said Dante.

"I'm kinda worried about my brother Knowledge," said Tage.

"I'm sure he will be okay. He raised you by himself, and you're all right. Hey, do you want to join the Council as four-star rank and leading alchemist?" said Dante as he and Tage walked out of the Council's vault into the Council's chambers.

"I would love to, but I'm only orb level 2. See, I was a serenity shield test pilot, and I have fallen in love with the Fuzion of element and technology. I have fair essence to advance to orb level 4 or 5, but I choose not to. I can aid the rebellion with my mind until I can find supplies to forge my own serenity shield," said Tage.

"I don't see a problem with you being orb level 2. We will vote on it," said Dante.

"The masked monk is Lou Shen, right?" Tage answered.

"Yes," said Dante as he took his one-star seat, and Tage went and stood by the supercomputer screen that showed the blueprints of the war machine.

"Everyone, please give Tage the floor. Council meeting in session," said Dante, and he gave Tage a thumbs-up.

*****

Tage spoke. "My name is Tage Serenity. I was Dr. Volts's apprentice for the last four years. By the graces of the god of light, a rare amazing book of lost science and knowledge from long ago fell into my hands. Knowing the book's power, I hid the book in the secret Earth Nation's caves with Esa and Elizabeth's help so Dr. Volts and

Dragon Lord wouldn't find it. To my understanding, there are six books of lost science. Dr. Volts has volumes one through three, and I have volume four. The fifth and sixth volumes locations are unknown to me. On safe nights, I would sneak away to the dark earth caves in my spare time and read and study the lost knowledge.

"One day, Elizabeth came to me in the caves and asked me the details of the book. She didn't understand how I would sneak down there just to read a simple book. I told her I had found breakthrough on how to forge an elemental suit of armor that could do our race great good. But I was not sure if I should tell Dr. Volts. Mainly, I knew Dragon Lord would surely take my invention and use it for war and destruction. Elizabeth asked me what my intention and vision were for the suit. I told her I wanted to use it to accomplish her dream, to reclaim earth back from the savage wild creatures who destroy our planet. And these days, human elementals destroy as much as the savage creatures. Elizabeth smiled and told me she would get me decent supplies, record my work, and do small tests without Dr. Volts and Dragon Lord knowing. Elizabeth did more than she needed to.

"She set up a good cover for me for the long hours I was spending in the caves. I was building an advanced healing machine for earth elementals who got drained of chi fast when using shape earth to constantly fix 7-Nations' buildings from the destruction of battles. In two days of time, my research and small project were complete. I told Elizabeth and I needed great amounts of activation energy for any further tests. I would have to tell Dr. Volts to continue. Elizabeth asked me if I knew anything about the rebellion. I told her I knew very little. Most people here don't believe a rebellion of Dragon Lord still exists after the fall of the fire clan. Then Elizabeth asked if I could leave some details out when making the suit and build an insufficient low-tech version for Dr. Volts and bring the mastered version to the rebellion. That was my plan when I approached my brilliant clan leader. But Dr. Volts is a true scientist. He would almost solve alchemic equations where I would leave out large pieces to the puzzle.

'On the third day of forging the suit with Dr. Volts, he confronted me and asked me how I came to mind with such unheard-of alchemic spells and equations. I told him I had a dream and the god of light spoke to me. Dr. Volts never questioned me again on the matter. When we completed the first serenity shield, I was allowed to be the test pilot. The suits armor could stand intense pressure and damage before the armor would crack. By the time an enemy would break the crystal-fused armor, I would have gunned down my opponent with the suit's alchemic gun I named SWING, meaning Shock Wave Incinerating Neutron Gun. I went on multiple recorded missions outside of the gates of 7-Nations. I even went to the seventh level of the Hellfire Nation crystal mines. I had great results and approvals from Dragon Lord and Dr. Volts. Then the inevitable happened. I was kicked out of the alchemic project called serenity shield. And I must admit I was completely heartbroken, with a broken spirit.

"Dr. Volts builds these war machines for the light-and-dark war, and Dragon Lord plans to use the first twenty-five serenity shields built to clear and take over the griffling lands known as Narrian. The day before I left 7-Nations, Dr. Volts had just finished a new alchemic assembly line that forges serenity shields at will… Rebellion of Dragon Lord, I am sorry. I apologize for making this fight with Dragon Lord and the world's richest city more complicated than it already is. On top of that, the Shock Wave and full droid army grows by alchemic assembly line also. Over five hundred Shock Wave clones are operational and at Dragon Lord's command, and the number grows by twenty every day. Also there must be something going on with Dragon Lord and Death. Dragon Lord went to Shadow Empire for some kind of Death's hand ceremony. I'm not sure what that means, but it doesn't sound good," said Tage.

"My brother went to Shadow Empire to become Death's hand," said Dante with worry.

"What brother? You don't have a brother," said Tage.

"Wind Burn and I have the same mother. We just found out recently," said Dante.

"From my conversation with the platinum assassins in 7-Nations, Dragon Lord is a high-ranked Death's hand. Death and Dragon Lord speak frequently," said Tage.

"I don't believe this. I'm really starting to get worried about Wind Burn," said Dante.

"It's almost been two days since I left 7-Nations. I left as soon as Dragon Lord's battleship left 7-Nations. Whenever Dragon Lord leaves to Death's City, he never stays gone for more than two days," said Tage.

"How did you get here so fast? It took us a week to get here, and we stole a ship from Dragon Lord," said Dante in shame.

"I used a teleportation crystal," said Tage.

Dante stood and addressed the high rank of the rebellion. "Eight-star generals and Council, Tage has donated a lot of wealth to the rebellion, and I would like to offer him the four-star-rank seat on the Council. If anyone objects to my decision or would like the position, please step up now." No one said a word, and then Dante sat back down.

Tage said, "I thank the rebellion for freedom of life. I want to forge serenity shields and legendary weapons for the rebellion. I must bring equality to this equation of war. I also feel confident that I can run the black market efficiently. Plus I have ties with the Hell Thieves and Shadow Merch for good deals and trades," said Tage.

"Getting goods from Shadow Merch is not an easy task. Dragon Lord's ships patrol day and night around 7-Nations. The Hell Thieves seem like a better option," said Static.

"I met the leader of the Hell Thieves. I'm not big on thievery," said Dante.

"Neither am I. You know I'm on the light path, but certain sacrifices must be made if we wish to survive out here. Does anyone have any questions for me?" said Tage as he took the four-star seat.

"What does serenity shield mean exactly?" asked the masked monk.

"My mother named me Tage Serenity because when I was born, I didn't cry. I was always calm and peaceful. The shields breakdown is as follows:"

> S—a *suit* of titanium alloys, armor fused with crystals and orbs
> H—equipped with advanced *high technology*
> I—and an *intelligent* computer self-aware system
> E—*empowered* by you and your ability essence

L—a *life-energy* protector

D—and *destroyed*, forged by the alchemist Tage
Serenity

"I got a question, son. How do you suppose we come up with the shards and thousands of activation energy for each shield you plan to build?" said Static.

"I don't have a clue. I was hoping Dante would help me with that problem," said Tage.

"Is the lotus clan leader still alive?" asked the masked monk.

"I believe so. he was forced to teach a chi-control class while in power-block restraints just before Dragon Lord left," said Tage.

"How is Elisha and Elizabeth?" asked Dante.

"Good. Elizabeth is still running the old underground earth cave with Frost Bite and Esa doing her illegal trafficking. She told me to tell you she is going to be sending elementals who are wanted dead by Dragon Lord to Hell Mountain. She said to send her an information chip and let her know everything is okay with you. Elisha is fine. She's showing, and it's a boy if you didn't know. Oh yea, she said, 'Rise of the hellfire storm,' with a smile."

Later that night

Dante and Tage stood side by side in the Council's chamber at the supercomputer. They watched some funny recordings of Tage's missions in the serenity shield suit. They talked about the good old times and their childhood together. Dante laughed so hard and long he cried and almost threw up his chicken dinner.

"Man, that was a crazy ride in the world's richest city," said Dante in a state of great joy.

"I know, bro. I'm going to miss it," said Tage.

"Is your big brother Knowledge still trying to drop knowledge?" asked Dante.

"Yea, in his spare time. Really he's always busy working for Dr. Volts. Do you know why Dr. Volts is such a great alchemist of this day?" said Tage.

"No," said Dante.

"It's because he has three books of lost science. The rebellion would be better off if we had another book or two," said Tage.

"So what's the deal with the books? Are they magical or something?" asked Dante.

"Something like it. They are alchemic compositions of lost knowledge from our ancestors who lived in the golden days of Atlantis. Advanced alchemic spells have been written into books to create things in the line of that book's focused science," said Tage.

Dante thought for a few seconds and then said, "How would we go about finding the last two books?"

"Well, I could send a hacked message on the world network to all of the major nations in search for the last two volumes. Five is formal science, and six is universal science. We could offer currency to buy the book, or we could make a deal to read each other's book. Just for a few notes and pointers, just a glimpse at one page will expand an alchemist's hieroglyphic alphabet and knowledge on that science greatly," said Tage.

"So send the message… Wait, what if a nation tries to hack us?" said Dante.

"Well, I'm pretty skilled at computer tech and hacks, but there's always a risk. It's your call. I don't want to bring bad karma on the rebellion," said Tage.

"We can't make advancements as a growing nation and rebellion if we don't take risks. Send the message," said Dante.

"This is a smart risk," said Tage as he began typing fast.

"I'm sending the message to the Hell Thieves, Port Shard Land, Shadow Empire, Trinity City, and Champion City under the hacked username 'red/alchemist,'" said Tage. *Beep… Beep… Beep…*

> *Message 4RM: Red/Alchemist*
> *Nation User: Hacked… Reply to Network*

I have the fourth book of lost science. I'm looking for volumes five and six. I am willing to pay handsomely, or we could read each other's book. Reply to the network, and I will find your message.

Red/Alchemist HACK sent to:—

"I'm surfing through the network looking for replies," said Tage as he typed with great speed.

"I got nothing yet… Oh, one just hit the net from Bounty City. They must have seen the message. Maybe they have one," said Tage.

Message 4RM: Chaos
Nation User: Bounty City

This is the drake alchemist brother Chaos, one of the assassin lords of Bounty City. I offer one hundred pounds of corundum crystal for a book of lost science.

—Chaos
Sent to: network

"Not interested, Chaos? This book is priceless. I just spotted a message from Shadow Empire, from a crystal flame," said Tage.

Message 4RM: Crystal Flame
Nation User: Shadow Empire

I have a lost book of alchemic science. My name is Crystal Flame. I'm one of the shadow children of Death, and I'm the leader of the shadow alchemist branch here in Shadow Empire City. I have volume 5. If you wish to read each other's book, reveal your true identity and location, Red/Alchemist.

Pic/Crystal Flame,
royal princess sent to network

Tage clicked on the posted pic to get a good look at Crystal Flame.

"Wow, she's beautiful," said Tage.

"An angel straight from Shadow Hell," said Dante.

"I just spotted a strange message, and everything is hacked with it," said Tage.

I have volume six: Universal Knowledge
Will Red/Alchemist make the selfless choice
to obtain it

—The Light One

"Fate has volume six. Great, the light one shines on us!" said Tage happily.

"Fate won't give it to us," said Dante.

"How do you know?" said Tage.

"Bro, trust me, I know," said Dante.

"Maybe we should ask before we make negative assumptions… typing. Oh, wait no username or network hacking trace. How is that even possible?" said Tage.

"Send the message to Trinity City with no block or hack," said Dante.

"On it," said Tage.

Message 4RM: Dante and Tage
Username: Hell Mt

We ask the god of light if we could we could
have the sixth volume of lost alchemic science.
Hell Mt. Sent to Trinity City

A message popped up on the screen before Tage sent the message.

Red/Alchemist—you can have the last book
when you both become orb guardians in the light
of all.

—The Light One

"See, I told you... Hey, one hundred pounds of corundum crystal sounds like a pretty good deal," said Dante. Tage pulled up Chaos's message on his own screen. "Not even close. The lost books can't be remade or copied. Dr. Volts has tried many times. These books are priceless artifacts," said Tage in a serious manner.

"All right, all right, just chill, bro. But I don't want to make any deals with Shadow Empire," said Dante.

"Neither do I, or maybe Wind Burn could help us when he gets back," said Tage.

"Maybe," said Dante through a yawn.

"Do you see yourself ever becoming an orb guardian?" asked Tage.

"To be honest, no...not really. I'm a free-spirited person. I was born into this role. The main thing I guess is I like to control my own life, you know," said Dante.

"Yeah, I know what you mean, bro," said Tage as he powered down the supercomputer.

"I'm going to bed. I got to get up in the morning and run soldier training and probably basic training tomorrow for a bunch of drakes who want to join the rebellion," said Dante.

"Okay, I'm going to contact Crystal Flame from my holo-fused scouter bot. It's a souped-up mini supercomputer. I'm going to reveal my identity to her. I'll block tracking transmissions, and I'll leave you and the rebellion out of the convo," said Tage.

"Coo, good night, bro. I'm so glad you came," said Dante as he embraced Tage with a strong hug of long-lost friends. Then they went to their rooms.

Chapter 30

Hellfire Prophecy

Dante woke as the sun rose around 6:30 a.m. for soldier training and then walked in the dock. Everyone was lined up, quietly waiting on him. Dante got in line in the front and led the exercises with the front line while General Smoke and the masked monk walked through the lines and gave pointers and pep talks to the ones who felt like giving up. The front line and Dante did a thousand push-ups and squats in less than an hour. The rest of the rebellion did five hundred push-ups, a few sprint races, and target practice. After that, General Smoke taught the soldiers combat march formation. Then the masked monk taught basic fighting styles, and General Smoke taught lost fighting styles to the front line and the few soldiers who were experienced.

After training, Dante went to his room and took a shower. General Smoke had brought eggs, sweet wheat bread, dried red berries, and lemon juice to his room. Dante scarfed down his breakfast and met General Smoke and the front line at the dock to fly to the battlefield for the soldier entry training. Today's entry rebellion training had the largest group so far: 163 drakes that were mostly hellfire and about 27 earth drakes. The red-and-brown-scaled drakes were orb level 5 and 6, so they passed the basic entry training with ease. And to Dante's surprise, nothing attacked them from the chasm. Dante was worried during the training because they were making a lot of noise.

By 11:00 a.m., basic entry training was finished, so Dante decided to call an open meeting at the battlefield. Over 390 creatures attended the meeting including Safe Haven's population count of 120, give or take 90 travelers back and forth. It was so packed one could hardly breathe or move under the hot sun. But the meeting had to be held here because everyone could not fit in Safe Haven City. A few fights broke out, and it took some time for the front line to settle the crowd.

Dante, the masked monk, General Smoke, Cal, Tage, and the front line stood on an eighty-feet-high dark-stone pillar in the middle of the battlefield while the crowd of the rebellion and Safe Haven City surrounded them.

Dante walked to the edge of the dark stone pillar and spoke as Tage's holo scouter bot hovered around Dante and amplified Dante's voice while projecting a large holo image of Dante so all here could see and hear him.

Dante yelled, "Brave noble creatures!" Dante's voice boomed across the battlefield.

"All hail the lord of the fire spirits!" shouted a group of hellfire drakes.

"Yeahhh, rise of the hellfire storm!" shouted the crowd in an uproar. Dante raised his hands to settle the energetic crowd. Then he spoke.

"Brave creatures, I thank you for joining this rebellion so that a worldwide enemy may fall and we may rebuild a righteous world. Together, we will train the hardest we ever have to build our minds, bodies, and spirits so that when the time of war comes, we will be prepared to deliver a justice that is needed to heal our broken wills to go on.

"Notice how I said 'we'? I cannot do it alone. This army grows and stands at six hundred fifty elementals plus Seastra's sharkling army of two hundred. We will offer our lives to bring equality to this world. I will wield the fire spirits with all of my being to lead this army to victory. The time to choose sides is now.

"Join us, or get lost in the storm. I am Dante Saint, son of a great fallen spiritual king. I carry my father's and my clan's death on my back as a great burden that must be lifted by Dragon Lord's death. Tell all you know to come join us and watch the *rise of the hellfire storm.*"

The crowd chanted with great energy, "Rise of the hellfire storm!" for thirty seconds. The masked monk walked next to Dante, and Tage's scouter bot projected him next to Dante as he spoke the words of a wise one.

"I am the masked monk. My face is not needed to be seen. Only my words must be heard today. The third scion once told me of the prophecy that a human of pure heart will pass level 7 and have control of all elements, even the sixth element known as shard energy. He will become an ascended god. He will be the chosen one, a self-chosen one who will defy the laws for the greater good of us. I have no faith in the gods, but I do understand that there is a higher power. And this higher power we do not fully comprehend. But know this: the fire spirits and all ascended powers may be the way for us to gain some kind of understanding. Dante absorbed his father's greater essence orb. Dante is more than some fill-in or some heir of this rebellion. He is the one who will bring this prophecy to the light. Thank you for listening… Rise of the hellfire storm!"

"Rise of the hellfire storm!" shouted the crowd.

Tage manipulated his holo screens on his Shock Wave gloves, and the scouter zoomed in on Dante as the masked monk stepped back next to page.

Dante spoke. "Besides training, this rebellion and nation need currency. I have traveled to Inferno City at the core of this mountain and spoke to elemental being deep within the mountain. I asked him to allow mining in the mountain for currency. He granted us permission, but he said we must not get greedy. Thievery will not be tolerated and will result in termination from the rebellion and Hell Mountain. If you need something, just ask. If the Council can help the situation, we will. You have my word. I have jobs available for those of you who wish to work. This goes for Safe Haven City and the rebellion. If you won't help yourself, then why should the Council help you? The jobs are as follows: kitchen help, one hundred positions needed. That's twenty jobs on each soldier floor. Hell Mountain guards, fifty positions. As the army's numbers grow, this position's number of needed guards will grow. Alchemists and tech assistants, thirty-five positions. Tage has asked if you apply for this job, please have some type of tech knowledge. Miners, minimum positions fifty. There is no limit to the number of miners. Once all positions are filled, all rebellion members will be paid five platinum daily and given a free full meal from the soldiers' kitchen daily. We also offer training every morning that will make you stronger. Any questions?"

A brown-scaled earth drake flew up to make eye contact with Dante and said, "I joined the rebellion this morning. Me and most of the drakes who came with me from Land Outlaw do not wish to sleep in the mountain. We wish to live on top of the mountain."

"I don't see a problem with that, but just so you know, we have five layers of soldiers' quarters, and we are prepared to expand. If you change your mind, just tell someone of eight-star rank or higher," said Dante.

"Very well, Lord of the fire spirits," said the brown drake, and then he flew down into the crowd.

"Let us see the fire spirits!" shouted a drake.

Woosh, Wa-woosh. Woosh. Woosh. Woosh. Woosh. From the north, fifty flying humanoid grifflings came flying toward the battlefield with great speed.

"Prepare for battle!" someone shouted in the crowd.

"No, calm yourselves," said Dante as he turned into a fiery red phoenix and took off like a crimson jet. With grace and speed, Dante met the grifflings halfway before they got to the battlefield.

"The hellfire prophecy of the fire spirits!" shouted someone in the crowd.

"Yeah!" shouted the crowd as they watched Dante's rare flame.

*****

Dante's crimson fire spirit and the fifty grifflings hovered over a dark-green jungle that bordered out sharply from the scorched tainted lands.

"Grifflings of Narrian, I am having an important meeting at the battlefield. It would not be wise to—"

235

Dante didn't get to finish his sentence, because an older-looking griffling cut Dante off and said, "We train at the battlefield at random times. This is no one's land. What race are you, ruby fiery one?" The older-looking griffling flew to the front of the grifflings with a strong flap of his beautiful wings.

"My race is human, and I am the new leader of Hell Mountain," said Dante.

"Human! Human! When did this come to pass?" said the elder griffin in a screeching bird voice. Then all at once, the forty-nine grifflings spoke to each other in an unknown screeching griffling tongue. Every few screeches the elder would point to Dante's strange form of fiery spirit. The elder griffling raised his claws and calmed his tribe. "Are you the son of Luke?"

"I am. You knew my father?" said Dante.

"My name is Gaheed. I am the leader of Narrian Cliff. I fought Luke so long ago—thirty-two years past I think, when Dragon Lord destroyed the many forest lands around 7-Nations city which used to be Great Narrian Forest. I was a boy when Luke and I had fought. I lost. Luke spared my life because he knew Dragon Lord was unjust and I was only trying to protect my home. Then a few years later, Luke came to Narrian Cliff and asked me to join his rebellion of Dragon Lord. For my spared life in his hands, I agreed. But then I hear Luke has fallen, and his army of hellfire humans are dead too. The rebellion is no more," said Gaheed with sorrow in his bird voice.

"Well, the army rises, I absorbed my father's orb, and one thing led to another, and here we are. Look, I'll end my meeting so that we can discuss your rebellion rank at Hell Mountain. And a good friend of mine has something he needs to tell you," said Dante as he powered down his fire spirit.

"It is the son of Luke," said the grifflings in amazed voices once they saw Dante's face.

"My life partner and queen of Narrian is named Niija. She is on the light path, and she is a believer of the hellfire prophecy. She will be happy to know the son of Luke leads the rebellion. I will send most of my tribe home to inform Niija. I shall cancel this day's training to go with you to the son of Luke's mountain," said Gaheed.

Gaheed said something to the grifflings in his screeching tongue. Then forty-four grifflings flew back to Narrian, and Gaheed and five grifflings flew with Dante back to his ship.

"What is your name, human son of Luke?" said Gaheed.

"Dante Saint. I am the—"

Gaheed cut Dante off and said, "I know, I know the son of a great spirit king. Yes, the fire storm rises." Then they entered Dante's ship and returned back to Hell Mountain.

The Council's chambers

Gaheed entered the Council's chambers first and walked to Dante's one-star seat, grabbed his spiked tail, and sat down. The five grifflings with him sat down in the bleachers on the left side of the chamber. The grifflings kept staring at the light orb and glowing alchemic spells hooked up to the supercomputer. The grifflings were drawn to the light like moths drawn to flame. Gaheed paid the light alchemy no mind as he moved around in Dante's seat and said, "Comfy seat, Dante. I like what you have done to the place." Dante sat in Wind Burn's two-star seat. Then Tage and masked monk flew through the hole of the chamber by storm-powered amulets of flight. Tage went to the supercomputer that faced Gaheed and started typing. The masked monk took his three-star seat next to Gaheed and nodded to the birdlike creature.

"How do you do, Masked Lotus Elemental?" said Gaheed.

Tage pulled up the serenity shield blueprints and said, "Griffling leader, Dr. Volts builds these war suits by alchemic assembly line—"

Gaheed cut Tage off and said, "What is assembly line…? Wait, I destroyed one of these big robots yesterday on my flight across 7-Nations north and south. I must admit it was a tough battle."

"Alchemic assembly line is a computerized droid—one-manned line that builds one thing fast and proficiently," said Tage.

"Ah, so many words I don't know. Robots built fast. Got it," said Gaheed in a deep raspy voice of frustration.

"Dragon Lord builds these machines as we speak, and the first mission for the first group of completed machines will be to destroy

Narrian. I am sorry, griffling leader," said Tage. Gaheed had a worried fearful look on his face, and he looked down.

"Don't worry, Gaheed. I won't allow Dragon Lord to destroy Narrian. I will fight Dragon Lord beside you," said Dante with hurt in his voice.

Gaheed said, "I do not worry. We attack Dragon Lord's city less and less as time goes by. It seems to me that I must lead more savage attacks on the city to keep Dragon Lord busy. My father was killed in the war between grifflings and Dragon Lord's army of human elementals when Dragon Lord destroyed the many Narrian forests around 7-Nations city so long ago. I will not let time replay itself!"

"It says here in the supercomputers old records that Gaheed has major rank with ten stripes," said Tage.

"I have five hundred trained griffling warriors at my command," said Gaheed. The masked monk went into the Council's vault and came out with a morphing armor that had ten stripes over the rebellion symbol, a charging device, and holo pad. Then the masked monk gave the items to Gaheed.

"The holo pad is so we can keep in touch. I don't want to bump heads with using the battlefield again," said Dante.

"I will give this gadget to my oldest son. We must not bump heads, as you say. My warriors need to train at the battlefield more to sharpen our elemental abilities," said Gaheed.

"Why not train at your homeland? I'm sure it's big enough," said Tage.

Gaheed said, "The griffling race is one of the first and largest groups of creatures changed by the emerald light. My race did not have the knowledge of this world and our elemental powers. Plus with Death's corruption, the god of shadow almost started a world racial war that would have killed us all if the balance was to break from too much power and destruction. Without the knowledge of the humans to civilize us, we are nothing more than savage beasts. So when I was a child, I watched the god of the light draw a spell. It is what you humans call alchemy around Narrian Cliff. This spell power-blocks my homeland. So I teach a chosen few to control their mind and powers at the battlefield. I believe in the hellfire prophecy.

Dante, you have my army to do as you please. Now I must go and tell my race this terrible news."

The masked monk escorted Gaheed and the five grifflings out of Hell Mountain. For the rest of the day, Tage, Dante, Static, and Cal assigned jobs and housed creatures in the Hell Mountain supercomputer.

Chapter 31

A Brothers' Conversation

Council's chambers

Five days had passed since Gaheed received the horrible news of Dragon Lord's plans. But the thought that was heavy on Dante's mind was, *If Dragon Lord destroyed Narrian, then Hell Mountain would be next, right?*

Dante knew deep down in his heart he could not defeat Dragon Lord in a war or in battle at this time, even though things looked good for the rebellion.

The rebellions active members grew to a little over 1,300 from the word of the ascended fire spirits. And the army continued to grow in strength, as well as in numbers. Dante hoped Dragon Lord didn't hear of all of the commotion Dante was making around the world. An early war is what got Dante's parents and clan killed. That hurt Dante just even thinking about it.

Daily training went smooth this morning. The 160 earth and fire drakes did not attend the training session, which was kind of a good thing; everyone couldn't fit in Hell Mountain's small dock. But Dante still wished they would come. But no, the crazed drakes just flew and stood on top of Hell Mountain day and night. They didn't even ask Dante for anything to eat.

So it was late afternoon. Dante sat in his one-star seat with a hundred thoughts drifting through his mind. The masked monk sat quietly next to him, not moving in a deep meditation state behind the green mask. Tage, Static, and Cal stood around the supercomputer on some task or study that Dante didn't understand. General Smoke and the front line were in the soldiers' quarters showing the savage creatures how to be civilized and live accordingly. *General Smoke and the front line really have their hands full,* Dante thought.

Dante thought about his older brother, who had been gone almost two weeks with no call or message.

"GP, do you think big bro is okay?"

"Yours or mine?" said Lou Shen.

"Mine…well, I guess both," said Dante.

"I'm sure Wind Burn is fine. It's Gi Shen I'm worried about."

"It's just so boring. It's so live to have a brother."

"I know what you mean. The last time I spoke to Gi Shen, he gave me our father's amulet. As the amulet hangs around my neck, it's a constant reminder of our mission… We have to get stronger, grandson."

"We will train harder, mind over matter, pushing our mind and spirit to the limit until we reach the highest potential."

"I don't think you understand what that truly means… We need to talk to Fuzion. Certain questions must be answered."

"Why not just ascend?"

"We don't know what awaits us if we do that, grandson."

"I wish I could save Wind Burn from the dark path."

"I wish I could show you the universal neutral path, or maybe it is not that anyone needs saving. It's more of the realization what a person must go through in life. This molds us into the person we become. It is like food for the soul in a learning aspect."

"Hey, I just found a message from Wind Burn on the network from an independent user holo pad," said Tage.

Message 4RM: Wind Burn
User#: Holo Pad 1083

Hey, bro, it's me. I'm using a teleportation crystal and alchemist spell to get back. Meet me outside Hell Mt. at the big rock. Leaving now!
Black Storm sent to network

Dante quickly read the message. Then he ran to the Council's vault, punched in the code, and ran to his chest. Dante opened the red chest and grabbed the shard energy apple. Then he raced to the hole and beamed down the hole in a fiery blitz of speed. Lou Shen calmly closed the Council's vault and then walked to the hole and activated his storm flight amulet and flew down the hole after Dante. Static stopped navigating through the computer screens and said, "Should we go welcome Wind Burn home?"

Tage said, "Na, let them have some family time."

"Yeah, you're right," said Static.

Then he continued moving through the computer screens of alchemic scripture in a blur.

"How did Wind Burn come up with ten pounds of corundum crystal for a teleportation crystal set and spell?" said Tage.

"Wind Burn's rich girlfriend probably bought it for him," said Cal.

"How did she get so rich?" asked Tage.

"She's a shadow collector," said Cal.

"I wonder if she knows Crystal Flame. She has the fifth book of lost science, and she will let alchemists read it for a small fee. But I think I'm falling in love with her dark beauty," said Tage.

"Having children with her could get you in trouble," said Static.

"Who said anything about children?" said Tage.

"I know how things go," said Static.

"Yeah, just be careful," said Cal.

"I got things under control," said Tage.

"All right, if you get her pregnant, a child born with a lightning and shadow element will violate the balance. I'm just trying to save you the trouble," said Static.

"Why can't regular elements mix with advanced elements?" asked Cal.

"I don't know, but the orb guardian bounty hunters don't play around with things like that," said Static. Tage went into deep thought.

As soon as Dante exited the cave entrance to Hell Mountain, a shadow alchemist spell came into existence above the big rock. A dark crystal orb shimmered into view. Then dark energy came around the orb, and Wind Burn appeared holding the orb in his right hand.

Wind Burn had on a fancy clothes armor and black-and-gray force shoes that Dante had never seen before. Wind Burn had a stuffed back pack over his right shoulder. Under his left arm, Wind Burn held two long items wrapped in dark cloth. Wind Burn smiled when he saw Dante.

Dante flew to the rock and landed next to Wind Burn. The masked monk came out of the cave, flew over, stood next to the rock, and said, "Welcome home, grandson."

"It's good to be back, GP," said Wind Burn.

"How was your trip? Did you make it? Are you Death's hand?" asked Dante.

"Of course I made it, and the trip was crazy. I love Death's City. I met the shadow family. The shadow children basically runs Shadow Empire, and they're all our age. Oh, and Dragon Lord's Death's hand also. We had a talk. It was very awkward. But I'm still going to kill him," said Wind Burn.

"Bro, why didn't Skyla come back with you?" asked Dante.

"Her life and situation is complicated. She has a bounty on her head from Fate's orb guardians. Death's City protects her. But she sends her regards, and I convinced her to buy you two of these," said Wind Burn as he put the crystal orb on his belt and handed the wrapped items to Lou Shen and Dante.

Dante and the masked monk unrolled the dark cloth to find fully unlocked legendary weapons that were not marked by Death. Dante's weapon was a war hammer made of red crystal, and it was light as a feather. Masked monk's weapon was a glove which was a staff-like weapon with a sharp blade at the long weapon's tip. In the center of the blade was a tiny lotus orb.

The masked monk rolled his legendary weapon up and whistled...

"These cost a pretty crystal. Tell Skyla I said 'thank you,'" said the masked monk. Dante stared at the weapon with uncertainty and slowly rolled the weapon of death up in the cloth, then gave it back to Wind Burn.

"Bro, I want you to have it. You don't have to attack with it. Use it to unlock your ascended powers faster," said Wind Burn. He sat his bag down, opened it, found some red back straps, and helped Dante put them on.

"You have an orb level 7 power level, and what's that great dark energy I sense on you," said Dante.

Wind Burn sheathed Dante's legendary weapon between Dante's back straps and said, "It's my Death's hand amulet. Death touched it and made it powerful. I don't use chi anymore. Now I use LE for powers. If I do use chi, I use it all at once in one deadly attack. This amulet of death allows me to use LE for powers and not be pow-er-blocked or drained from energy loss," said Wind Burn as he took the dark crystal, hand-shaped amulet out of his shirt to show Dante.

"Brother, question. Why haven't you eaten that shard energy apple yet? I've seen shadow elementals in Death's City kill for that rare fruit," said Wind Burn.

"I went to the core of the mountain, and a fire elemental being gave it to me. And now I'm giving it to you," said Dante as he gave the emerald apple to Wind Burn.

"Thanks, bro," said Wind Burn as he scarfed down the energized fruit in two bites.

"Wow, what an energy rush. Okay, bring it in for a quick hug. I actually missed you guys," said Wind Burn with open arms. The masked monk grunted as he climbed up on the big rock, and they stood in a group hug for a few seconds.

"I'm glad you're not evil," said Dante.

"It was a hard test of will not to kill in a city of killers. The elementals in Shadow Empire test your kindness and G card at every corner. I grew tired of having to watch my back. So many shadow elementals are jealous of my Death's hand status because I'm human and not shadow, and I'm not Dragon Lord," said Wind Burn.

"Sounds like an evil city of hatred. Why would Sky want to stay in a place like that?" said Dante.

"Like I said, Death's City protects her from the light guardians. Sky is an emotional wreck. I couldn't live with her if I wanted to. So, anyway, fill me in on what's been going on since I left. I can feel that you two have both gotten stronger. And, GP, what's up with the crazy green mask and lethal poison on your belt?" said Wind Burn.

"Perhaps a discussion for another time, grandson. I'm feeling a little low on energy. I need to go meditate in my personal quarters," said the masked monk.

"GP, here," said Wind Burn as he threw Lou Shen a light-and-dark elixir from his belt.

The monk took the small vial of light-and-dark energy and said, "Thank you, grandson, but the natural way to regain energy is the best way. In time, you will learn this," said Lou Shen as he teleported toward Hell Mountain's entrance and walked in.

"What's up with GP?" asked Wind Burn.

"I don't know. Ever since we came back from Port Shard Land City, he won't take off the mask. He went orb level 6 so fast. And he leaves on late missions. I think he's doing assassination jobs for Bounty City," said Dante.

"Na, GP wouldn't do that," said Wind Burn in a surprised tone.

"I don't know what to think, but something's going on. So, bro, look, I need to talk to you about a few things that have been bothering me," said Dante as he sat down on the edge of the rock facing north with his legs dangling over the edge.

"What is it, brother?" said Wind Burn, joining Dante.

"Well, first, I don't want to be in competition with you. A lot of creatures look up to me because of the fire spirits. But I'm still a kid, and I still have a lot to learn. I look up to you and GP. So I want you and the Council to lead this rebellion with me equally. I know I don't always make the right choices, so before I make the final decisions, I'll ask you, or the Council can put it to a vote," said Dante. Wind Burn looked behind him and saw the many drakes that flew over their heads. Then Wind Burn noticed hundreds of drakes on the mountain. Wind Burn drew his legendary weapon, but Dante stopped him and said, "Bro, it's cool. They're in the rebellion."

Wind Burn sheathed his katana blade of death and said, "Bro, this is your army. Do whatever you want. I'm not in competition with you anymore. At first, I thought I had to prove myself to you and Hell Mountain. I was wrong. Now all I care about is killing Dragon Lord," said Wind Burn.

"But I value yours and all of the Council's opinions. I'm not a corrupt leader like Dragon Lord," said Dante.

"Look, bro, above all bs, the final word falls on you. That's why you have the highest-ranking star on your arm. Your father's and clan's blood sweat and tears built this. Remember that, little brother," said Wind Burn.

* * * * *

For two hours, Dante and Wind Burn filled each other in on the details of their separate journeys. They laughed and joked as they told their stories. They acted out events and scenarios with great emotion as if they lived the scene once again. Wind Burn showed Dante all of the cool things Sky had bought him—a mini holo pad, a false meteor shard for Static and Cal, and an invisibility cloak of power. She had bought him a variety of dark aura shadow fruit, death melons, shadow apples, and shadow cherries. All of these items were packed into Wind Burn's bag.

Wind Burn closed the bag and said, "Let's go spar, get some fresh air. I'll teach you how to use your legendary weapon."

"I know the perfect place—the battlefield. Just send Hell Mountain a message. I don't want to worry them," said Dante.

Wind Burn grabbed the holo pad from his bag and sent a message

Message 4RM: Wind Burn
User#:1083

We will be back in a few hours, going to the battlefield to spar
Black Storm sent to: Hell Mt.

"Hey, soldier!" screamed Dante to the rebellion guards who stood at the entrance to Hell Mountain.

"Yes, sir, Dante, sir," said the soldiers as they flew over to the rock in fiery auras.

"Take my brother's bag and give it to the masked monk," said Dante.

"I'll race you there," said Wind Burn.

As the brothers flew off, the soldiers yelled, "Rise of the hellfire storm!"

Chapter 32

Orian, the God of Lightning

The two brothers flew and soared through the air circling around each other, creating a beautiful tornado of grayish storm and flames from their auras. Dante and Wind Burn flew with great speed as they laughed and tested the limits on how fast they could fly. It was obvious Wind Burn was faster, so the older brother slowed and kept his pace with Dante.

"Brother, I sense some lava energy to the northeast. Let's check it out!" shouted Wind Burn through the wind of their speed. Before Wind Burn could switch directions, Dante had already somersaulted and twisted in midair and zoomed in a fiery tornado toward the lava pool. Wind Burn laughed and yelled, "Good one, bro!" Then he quickly caught up to Dante.

In the distance ahead, the rebellion brothers spotted a spasming lightning vortex appear before them... The vortex of energy formed a humanoid drake made of pure god lightning. The brothers slowed their flight to a hover a few feet away from the unknown drake.

"I'm sensing strange energies," said Dante.

"Me, too, so much power," said Wind Burn. The lightning drake seemed to faze in and out of existence in violet-and-yellow lightning hues. It looked as if his ethereal form did not exist in this realm. The drake's aura was mixed with lightning and emerald energy that electrified and hummed a soothing melody.

"So much great power with no depths. I've never felt anything like it," Dante said.

"Who are you, and what do you want with us?" said Wind Burn.

"Greetings, human elementals. I am Orian, the first of the lightning element to reach ascension. It is a great honor to finally meet your consciousness. Nazareth has told me so much about you two while I've been away," said Orian.

"You're the lightning god. Why do you look that way?" asked Dante.

Orian said, "This is a tiny fragment of my true form and power. True god sight would obliterate any nonascended elemental."

"Did we do something wrong?" asked Dante.

"No, fire spirits. I am a neutral god, and me being here violates the balance. I would have come to see you sooner, but you were both not ready for the truth that I have for you. I do not have much time before Fate—"

Boom! Boom! Boom! Thooom! Before Orian could finish his sentence, loud bangs on energized crystal could be heard coming from the Land of Lost Orb Souls. The vibrations of booms sent tremors all over earth. Screams of torment and pain could be heard from all aspects of life who were connected to Fuzion during each bang.

Dante and Wind Burn both grabbed their chest as they fell to the ground from three hundred feet in the air. With each boom and bang, the brothers felt intense pain in their spirits and orbs. They lost control of their powers, and they could hardly breathe. Dante and Wind Burn hit the ground with great force that cratered them into the earth.

Orian looked toward the Land of Lost Orb Souls and closed his eyes. In the next second, Orian came into existence on the ground next to Dante and Wind Burn. Both brothers were already climbing out of the deep holes in the earth. Then Orian said, "Death must be trying to steal shards from Fuzion again by attacking the source of earth. Fate will be busy fighting Death, so we have time to play a game. I want to help you two ascend. To do so, you must both realize a few truths. What I want for all life on this planet some gods do not. You know this, don't you? Hmmm... I can see that your mental judgment is clouded by self-doubt. Well, know this—if you choose to ascend, no matter what path you're on, you will need my help. In this realm or the next. Sometimes in elemental life, the only way to survive may be to land critical blows. Anger, frustration, giving up, and not believing in your own will and self are all qualities that will not allow you to reach your highest potential. You must believe anything is possible in the face of death against impossible odds."

Dante dusted himself off as he stood and said, "It's not that simple."

"But it is that simple. In time, your third eye will be opened. So I call this game hit-the-god! The first of you to land a critical blow of any kind on me wins," said Orian. Wind Burn summoned all of his orb chi into a great wind scar level 7 attack. Orian simply sidestepped the attack and moved behind Dante in a sonic dash of speed.

"The shadow within you has been unleashed, Windstin," said Orian.

Wind Burn's aura came alive in the form of light black-and-gray flames mixed in the storm that surrounded him. In a movement of fiery speed, Dante launched five giant hellfire orbs at Orian. Orian moved in sonic speed, weaving all five of Dante's giant attacks without moving from where he stood.

Wind Burn quickly drew his legendary weapon and yelled, "Wind slaughter!"

Wind Burn spun his weapon of death from side to side in a helicopter motion. Ten large amplified blades of dark-bluish storm shot from the blade in a time frame of two seconds. Orian slowed time as he evaded dark storm blades like a swift ninja, jumping and walking on the blades in a stride.

Orian landed on the last blade and kicked it around, then kicked it back at Wind Burn, and yelled, "You waste so much power over something so small."

Wind Burn fast countered the attack with an amped wind scar. The two blades of storm met and collided in a great explosion that sent Wind Burn back one hundred feet... Dante charged Orian with hellfire hammers and swung the fiery will calmly. Eight fiery hammer heads only hit air. Orian moved in sonic speed behind Dante. Dante combined the fiery hammers together, leaned back, and launched them at Orian with great will.

The hammer missed Orian's cheek by an inch as the lightning god weaved to the side.

"Good, my young fire spirits, learn to tap in. Try harder. Know you can hit me," said Orian.

Then Wind Burn teleported above Orian with his legendary weapon amplifying a deadly storm while yelling, "Diving wind tornado!" Wind Burn dived down headfirst while spinning in the air with the tip of his death weapon swirling storms of large wind blades... As Wind Burn came down, he descended and destroyed the area where Orian stood. Orian's body burst into tiny mixed emerald lighting fairies. The fairies surrounded Wind Burn and formed two shard energy apples in his hands. Then some of the fairies formed one shard energy apple in Dante's hand.

"If you choose to ascend, this will not be a game but a battle of life and death." Then Orian's presence faded out.

Chapter 33

Pound Fist Storm Technique

The sun started to set. Wind Burn landed with such grace and sheathed his legendary katana blade behind his back. Then Wind Burn tossed a shard energy apple to Dante and sat down on the cold scorched floor of the tainted lands.

"Now we're even, two and two," said Wind Burn as he scarfed his emerald fruit down. Dante caught the apple and then ate them both, smacking and talking between bites. "Um…good, tastes…like liquid energy."

When Dante finished the apples, he sat next to Wind Burn and said, "That was strange."

"Strange doesn't surprise me anymore," said Wind Burn.

"Do you think we should ascend first, then defeat Dragon Lord?" said Dante.

"It doesn't sound like a bad idea. I'm with it if you are," said Wind Burn.

"I'm so confused. Why don't the gods want us to ascend?" said Dante.

"I don't know, brother. I guess we'll have to ascend to find out," said Wind Burn.

"It just seems like a big leap into the unknown," said Dante.

Dante and Wind Burn heard someone approaching, so they looked behind them to see a womanly humanoid with long light-brown hair, red gloves, custom red heeled shoes, and a tight-fitting hellfire leather suit that covered her whole body. She had on red tech mask, and she had two legendary hellfire war hammers strapped to her back. The tight leather suit showed her curvy body off and topped it all off with a stylish belt that was stocked with all kinds of cool things Dante had never seen before, and the woman carried a sweet smell of strawberries that moved in the wind.

"Hey, boys," said the beautiful voice of an angel as she approached. Dante and Wind Burn stood and faced the woman.

"Do we know you?" said Wind Burn.

Dante thought the voice sounded familiar, from the mountain tunnels when he went to see Inferno. *This can't be just a coincidence.*

"Hey, by any chance, did you boys see the lightning god around here? My supercomputer picked up some heavy energy readings from this location. Then my system went crazy and shut down on me," said the woman as she stopped ten feet away from the brothers with her hands on her waist and hair blowing in the wind. Dante read the woman's power level, and he knew she was more experienced than Wind Burn and Dante put together.

"Um…yes, we…he, my brother, hit Orian, and green lightning fairies turned into shard energy apples in our hands. Then Orian was gone," said Dante.

"Darnit, I owe Orian something. Oh well, I'll catch him eventually. So…what are you guys doing out here by yourselves? It's not safe. No matter what orb level you are, there's always something stronger, bigger, and even worse than you are," said the woman.

"But what if we ascend?" said Dante.

"Don't be silly. Have you seen any elementals come back to earth after they ascend? No! Orian violates the balance when he comes here. If you ascend, the gods will force a path orb on you," said the woman.

"What? I don't understand," said Dante, looking at Wind Burn, then at the woman.

"*Look,* the shard energy elemental being in Land Outlaw said if a being on earth ascends, they must choose a path by absorbing a path orb such as a light orb for the light path, a shadow orb for the dark path, or shard energy for the neutral path. Oh, and for some reason, even as an ascended god, shard energy neutral path still violates the balance. Crazy, right? Either way, the journey of higher realization will not allow you to influence life on this planet, and anyway, no human elemental has ever ascended," said the woman.

"The water god nature ascended," said Wind Burn.

"He doesn't count. Something happened to him in space on Abomination Day," said the woman.

"How do you know so much, and I never heard of you?" said Wind Burn.

"What is your name, Lady?" said Dante.

"Just call me Red," said the woman as she circled around Dante and Wind Burn, looking them up and down. Then she turned on a fiery aura and formed a chair from her aura's energy and sat down. "Come sit with me. I guess I have some things to teach you," said Red.

"Why? You owe us nothing," said Dante, getting a little angry.

"I want what the consciousness of earth wants, which is Dragon Lord removed from the highest position of power," said Red.

Dante and Wind Burn slowly sat down a few feet away from Red's fiery throne.

"Can this day get any stranger?" said Dante.

"Red…what about shadow, light, and shard energy elementals? They only have one element. How do they advance orb levels? And how does path orbs work with them?" asked Dante.

"The advanced elements are born to a path without choice. In most cases, they stay on the path they are born to, or they may choose to become neutral. In rare cases, you hear of a light elemental on the shadow path because he loves to kill. Or a shadow elemental may be on the light path because he likes to heal and help. Only the god's path of your primary element can truly help you, but in the end, that may not help you at all, especially if you plan on ascending to get to the next heaven. So how I see it, neutral is the best way because you learn to help your own self. When one of the three path elements ascend, they can choose one of the regular one through seven elements to absorb. That's why you see Death with an icy mask and Fate with hellfire on his head," said Red.

"Are you a human from 7-Nations?" asked Dante.

"No, sweetie, I'm from Land Outlaw, Spirit Forest City," said Red.

RED TECH MASK AND SUIT.

"You lie! Why do you hide your face and body?" said Wind Burn.

"I hide my body so some fights may be avoided when I travel," said Red.

"You're human. I know you are. I'm just looking for my guardian angel," said Dante sadly.

Red giggled and then said, "You must be your own guardian. What orb levels are you, guys?"

"I'm level 6, and big bro's level 7," said Dante.

"Well, I have a special energy combiner orb of earth," said Red as she grabbed a tiny cube from her belt. The cube expanded in a violet-glowing alchemist spell until it grew into a palm-sized orb carrier with an earth orb inside.

"Where do you find that type of tech?" asked Dante.

"I've got to get Sky to get me one of those," said Wind Burn.

"I keep an earth orb on me just in case I need to ascend to avoid Death," said Red in laughter. Then she got serious and said, "Wait, you mean Skyla Breeze, the shadow collector? You're *dating* her!"

"Sort of. Why?" asked Wind Burn defensively.

"Humph, no reason. We've run into each other from time to time," said Red.

"My brother's Death's hand," said Dante.

"Bro, we don't know her. Why would you tell her that?" said Wind Burn.

"Relax, Windstin, your secret is safe with me," said Red, laughing at Dante and Wind Burn.

Dante said, "Obviously, we don't have any secrets. She knows a lot about us, and she's not telling us a lot of what she knows and how she knows it."

"Look, boys, I want to show you something really cool and important. But I need you both to be orb level 7," said Red.

Red and Wind Burn both looked at Dante.

"Fine, fine, fine. It's just I don't like rushing into advancing orb levels. I like to build my mind body and spirit to be sure I can do it. I want my heart to stay pure," said Dante as he grabbed the orb carrier from Red and then walked a great distance away to not cause any harm to Red or Wind Burn while he absorbed the orb.

"Okay, here I go," said Dante, and then he opened the orb carrier.

Dante's mind

Dante walked up steps made of earth for what seemed like eternity. In time, Dante's step got hot, so hot that they engulfed into flames, and then Dante's steps turned the earth steps into lava as he moved.

I need to go faster, thought Dante, and then he turned into the liger fire spirit and dashed up the steps in a blur of white fiery energy. When Dante finally reached the top, he saw the doors again. Dante entered the door that read *Akashic*. He couldn't believe what he saw, endless rows of books on shelves. Dante walked over to the alchemic section and saw nine books of lost science. He saw the six Tage spoke of, plus a volume 7—transmutation science. Volume 8—the source science, and volume 9—the science of all. Dante looked at the books and then moved on. He stopped when he saw the books of the gods.

Dante saw the book of death, the book of balance, and a glowing emerald book that was covered in meteor shards that was titled *Shard Energy Book of Conversations*. Dante reached to grab the emerald book, but he stopped when he heard a voice that said, "I wouldn't do that if I were you," said the voice.

"Who are you?" said Dante as he turned around to see no one.

"I'm you but in a higher place," said the voice.

"So…you're my higher self," said Dante.

"The mind at its highest potential. Wait, how do you know that?" said Dante.

"Ah, yes. Vast knowledge at the speed of thought all stored here, since time first set in motion. Um…you shouldn't be here. But since you're here, think of any question, and you will know the answer," said the voice.

"Why ask a question if I already know the answer?" said Dante.

"You're such a strange one to be on the path of light. Why?—is the greatest question of all. That is why, all is all, so all can find the answer to why. You really need to tap into the source like Windstin does," said the voice.

"I know I'm working on that tapping-into thing. Death stole meteor shards from Fuzion today. It hurt so bad when Death hit Fuzion. I could see it, feel it, as if I was Fuzion or a small part of him," said Dante.

"All that exists is connected to the source. The next time we meet, I hope you're ready for your greatest test," said the voice.

"I will be because you live and you learn," said Dante as he walked over to the book that said the source science and picked it up. Then it got really hot, and red flames filled the library of all's knowledge.

*****

Wind Burn and Red watched the earth orb enter Dante's chest. Within seconds, the scorched dark ground around Dante glowed into earth tannish energy and formed a giant sphere around him. The giant sphere sank a little bit into the ground. It hummed and pulled the earth in around it.

It only took Dante twenty seconds to summon all of his fiery orb chi and bring it over the earth energy sphere and bring all of the power into his being.

"Flawless absorption, as usual," said Wind Burn.

"Well done, you're very strong, Dante," said Red while clapping her gloved hands.

Dante walked over to Red with Red hellfire in his eyes and said, "I know who you are. Just take off the mask, and let me see you!"

Red laughed, crossed her legs in her fiery seat, and said, "And what if I don't!" At the same time, Dante and Wind Burn leaped at Red and tried to grab her mask. In a red fiery flash, Red teleported and appeared above Dante and Wind Burn in her fiery aura with her hands crossed.

"You're both way too slow. You guys will never beat Dragon Lord at your current essence. Why don't you boys have hypermodes?" said Red. Wind Burn tried to grab Red again, and Red teleported behind Wind Burn and countered Wind Burn's grab with a lost fighting style. "Muchido kick!" screamed Red, and she landed a powerful kick in the middle of Wind Burn's back and threw him one hundred feet, sliding him across the tainted earth.

Dante calmed the flames in his eyes and then sat down Indian style on the floor and thought about this mystery woman's motives.

"And he's supposed to be the wise one," said Red.

"I know a little bit about the hypermodes. GP hasn't finished teaching me, though," said Dante.

Red said, "Well, you need to tell your GP to teach you and Wind Burn as soon as possible. The hypermodes may be the only way to touch Dragon Lord." Red still hovered in the air in her fiery aura as she watched Wind Burn fly like a bat out of Shadow Hell in his pure wind state ascended power form with his legendary weapon drawn.

Red pulled both of her legendary hellfire hammers from her back straps in a quick blurry motion. Red spun around in the air, and great flames roared from her weapons in a fiery tornado that turned her into a large hellfire dragon.

"I wouldn't do this if I were you," said Red with her arms spread wide at her sides in her fiery dragon state.

"Bro, you trippin'. Calm down," said Dante.

"No! You need to turn up! I need both of you in ethereal ascended form to teach you the pound fist storm technique. It's a powerful combined form of will I learned in Champion City, from the ninth scion. If the hypermodes fail, this can be a second option that will give you the upper hand against Dragon Lord," said Red.

"Then get on with the teaching. I grow impatient with your games, Red!" shouted Wind Burn.

"Okay, okay… Geeze, so angry. Relax and breathe, Windstin," said Red.

Dante drew his legendary hellfire hammer and raised it above his head. A white tornado of flames poured onto him and turned him into a white liger fire spirit.

"All right, meditation and mudras are not just for crazy scions and monks. It is an art and means to gain and channel universal energy. Fuzion allows us to use these energies at a small scale unconsciously. But with great focus of will, we can attain higher levels of power that are hidden deep within us. Mudras are physical postures and gestures with the hands and body movements that guide energy through the body," said Red as she slowly put her weapons of death behind her back and then landed on the ground. Red's fiery aura vanished as she said in a serious tone, "Put your legendary weapons away, and come close. Windstin, do not attack me... You cannot win!" Wind Burn huffed in anger and did as Red said while eyeing her down.

"Stand side by side, both facing south. Your hands must stay connected in a mudra called Jnana. This is the most common mudra used in meditation. You both will lock this mudra together after the two pounded fists, which are daps. You know, as you kids say 'to dap' someone. The pound fist connection and the power of your ascended form energy will cause a chain reaction and sonic explosion of energy. Then once the pound fist energy is activated, you will both spin while holding the mudra lock in connection to each other. This will turn your ethereal forms into a deadly mixed storm of your primary energies and ascended states. So let's try it."

"We're both right-handed," said Wind Burn.

"I can use my left hand if I need to," said Dante as the two brothers got into position. Red thought just like their mother, left- or right-handed.

"Lock the mudra first while standing side by side, then turn and face each other to pound fist with your free hands. Remember you must keep the mudra tight and connected to stay in this technique. Wind Burn, put your fist on top. I'll have to get back once you spin. The wrath of the pound fist storm technique could do some serious damage. Remember two-pound fists is okay... Three is even better. You must both be sturdy and be sure in your stance and put your full force into the pounds," said Red with her gloved hands on top of Wind Burn's and Dante's, walking them through the movements.

Dante said, "Red, wait. Won't we get dizzy from spinning so long and fast?"

"After the seventh spin, stop spinning and focus on the mudra lock, but keep spinning the storm with your wills. If you do it correctly, your ascended forms will keep spinning and merge into a powerful being. Ready… Activate your auras," said Red as she activated her fiery aura. "Try to pound fist as a test run so you know what to expect."

Dante and Wind Burn nodded, and then Wind Burn's fist came down, and Dante's fist came up. *Pound* and then *boom*. The collided fists made a powerful chain reaction like a visible white-and-blue sonic boom in the form of ball of energy around their fists. Dante and Wind Burn tried to pound-fist again, but they could not break through the ball of sonic energy. The boom expanded and threw Dante and Wind Burn back thirty feet.

"Come on, boys. The fate of 7-Nations rests in your hands. Try harder. Get back over here!" screamed Red.

Dante and Wind Burn flew back into position and locked the Jnana mudra.

"Use a simple hand-to-hand power to break the sonic sphere on the second pound fist. A fluid motion of pure will must be used by both of you to break the sonic sphere," said Red.

"Are you ready, brother? We must tap in," said Dante. Wind Burn nodded, and then his fist came down, and Dante's fist came up in a collision.

Pound and then *boom*. Again the colliding fist made a chain reaction in the form of a white-and-blue sonic ball of energy.

At the same time, Dante yelled, "Inferno strike!" and Wind Burn yelled, "Storm fist!" Then the brothers' energized fists came down on the sonic sphere of energy. Dante and Wind Burn's fists compacted the sonic energy around their mudra-locked hands.

"Now hold in the energy and breathe deeply. Then spin as fast as you can," yelled Red as she teleported one hundred feet away.

As the brothers spun, a vortex of white flame and blue storm combined with the pound fist sonic energy and made Dante's and Wind Burn's ascended forms bigger and stronger as they merged into one. It was as if the brothers' separate forms took turns every three seconds, showing itself through the white-and-blue storm.

"You can hold this form as long as you don't let go of the mudra lock. Aha, oh my god, I…the ninth scion's prophecy comes to light. Let's test it out with a fight," said Red.

Pound fist storm technique

Chapter 34

Karma's Dream

Red fire shifted to a crimson phoenix, and then she used a series of unknown mudras with her hands. Her hands moved in a ruby-red blur, and her crimson fire spirit grew from large to a giant phoenix.

"Don't use your legendary weapons. You must test your wills in the pound fist storm technique!" yelled Red as she pulled both of her legendary weapons out. Red's crimson form was one size smaller than Dante and Wind Burn's huge storm. But Red showed no fear as she spun around once with her weapons of death stretched out at her side. The weapons grew large engulfed in ruby-red flames.

"God hellfire orb!" yelled Red as her two legendary weapons let off a crimson tornado around her, and she spun once more in such grace and speed that the crimson flames rose and formed a huge death star that hummed with the power of a dying planet's core. Red's crimson fiery light looked like a dark-red flare as it lit the darkness of the tainted lands. In a blur of fiery speed, Red teleported behind her god hellfire orb and hit the energy with her two legendary hellfire hammers. Red's death weapons made the god hellfire orb bigger and more vicious as it beamed toward the storm. *Zoom.*

The white-flamed liger appeared from the storm and bit and crushed the death star. The death star's explosion made Dante and Wind Burn's storm energy spasm and electrify and grow more deadly as it absorbed the fiery power. Then in the next second, the pure wind appeared in the storm and shot a colossal storm of multiple wind scars at Red. Red orb level 6 stack shielded the storm attacks, and then the wind in the storm got very dark with shadow.

"Very cool, Hand of Death. All your chi, huh? Well, try this— inferno strike!" yelled Red as she flew above Dante and Wind Burn's storm, then flew down like a crimson phoenix bullet. Red had both of her legendary weapons in front of her side by side as she shot the level 7 combined flaming strike at the storm. *Eee-r. Pr-i-pp. Thoom.* A mixed fiery storm hand swatted the elemental energy into the sky. Red's flame energy lit up the sky like a red sun.

Then the white fiery liger appeared from the storm and shot a white hellish rain of eight large inferno orbs at Red. Then in the next split second, the liger vanished, and the pure wind elemental showed his face throwing four large bladed scars of dark wind at Red. Dante's and Wind Burn's powerful attacks flew from the storm two seconds apart from each other. Red's legendary fiery hammers lit with even greater flames and met with each attack from the storm with dead-on speed and accuracy as she yelled, "No, no, no, no, no, no!" while hitting each deadly attack. Dante's and Wind Burn's energies bounced off Red's legendary fiery hammers, hitting random places on the earth and beaming into the sky. Dante's and Wind Burn's energies exploded with the power of the pound fist sonic boom. On the last attack from the storm, Red spiked a wind scar blade down and teleported next to it and hit the storm scar with both of her weapons of death. Wind Burn's storm scar engulfed in flames and beamed back at Dante and Wind Burn with the power of a sonic boom.

A white fiery hand shot from the storm and swatted Red's smooth counter away. Then the dark storm hand appeared and tried to grab Red.

"Oh no, you don't," said Red as she teleport-evaded to the stomach of Dante's and Wind Burn's storm, then once again put both of her legendary weapons together in a powerful flamed blow while yelling, "Inferno strike!" *Thoom.* Red's crimson strike landed a critical blow on the storm and knocked the storm down on one knee. Then the dark storm's hand spun in a circle and formed a giant wind tornado and hit Red's crimson fire spirit, knocking her one hundred feet away.

"Really, Windstin?" said Red as she teleported over the head of the storm and yelled, "Red's inferno!" A ring of crimson flame formed from Red's legendary hammers and poured intense heat at the storm that poured and poured some more.

"Ahhh!" screamed the storm, and a dark hand made of wind grabbed through the pour of flames and grabbed Red. Then a hand of white flame crushed Red with the power of a white inferno strike and drilled her into the ground. Then the hands of the storm punched the ground so hard and fast that ripples tore through the dark tainted earth. Then the storm raised its hands and tried to combine a...

"Nooo!" yelled Dante because he felt the mudra lock break.

Then Dante went flying in one direction, and Wind Burn went flying in the other at incredible speeds, ripping and tearing through the earth with their bodies for a thousand feet. Dante and Wind Burn lie in cratered holes of the earth unconscious. A dark seven ring shadow alchemy spell shot from Wind Burn's Death's hand amulet and covered his body in a cocoon of healing.

Red climbed from the rubble she had been punched into and looked at her legendary weapons to see that they were fully drained and dead. "Darnit," said Red as she powered down her ascended phoenix and put her lifeless weapons behind her back. Red couldn't see clearly through her tech mask. It was cracked, and the computer screens in the mask's eye lens kept blacking out. Red removed her mask, and she was bleeding from her neck and forehead.

"Nothing too serious," Red said to herself as she activated her aura and flew in Dante's direction guided by the pure flame she sensed in his spirit and also the rips in the earth that were left in his path. When Red found Dante in the cratered hole, she stared at him in amazement. *No one can hold a pound fist storm technique for more than thirty seconds. Fine set of boys you got here, Clara. They just might do it—defeat Dragon Lord and free the shard energy god. But they still need more time and training... I don't have much time before I ascend,* thought Red. Red flew down into the hole and put an information chip in Dante's hand, and then she flew out of the hole and looked in the direction of Hell Mountain and saw ships and hundreds of drakes flying in her direction. Red quickly grabbed a red crystal orb from her belt and willed some energy into it. The alchemic letters around the orb glowed to life and rose off the orb in a violet aura of strange symbols, and then Red and the crystal orb vanished into the dark night.

Dante woke up in his room, in his bed. It was dark, and Dante felt as if someone was pounding on his head. Dante slowly sat up, and the world was spinning. His stomach felt so empty it seemed as if he hadn't eaten in weeks.

"Lights on," said Dante.

"Lights on," said a female computerized voice. A light shined bright from the top of Dante's supercomputer, and the brightness made Dante's head hurt even more.

"Day and time," said Dante as he grunted from an aching body and walked to his shower and turned the water on.

"March 8, 2081, 1:00 a.m., forty-two seconds," said the female voice from Dante's supercomputer.

I've been sleep for three days, thought Dante as he let the water soothe his body. Dante brushed his teeth and then got out of the shower and walked over to his supercomputer. Dante noticed a Red tiny information chip on his computer touch screen pad. "What's this?" said Dante as he inserted the red chip into his computer. The old computer hummed and loaded the info on the chip.

"A hack done by the Hell Thieves," said Dante.

6 Files—Liberators Database Hack

File 1: Pound fist storm technique
File 2: Outlawed lost fighting styles
File 3: The shard energy book of conversations
File 4: The twelve elemental god keys
File 5: The lore of the twelve gods
File 6: The liberators, real or fake?

"Load file one," said Dante.

"Loading file one," said the female computerized voice.

"The pound fist storm technique was so live. Who comes up with this stuff? How do they come up with this stuff?" said Dante.

File 6: Pound Fist Storm Technique

Many elementals don't know about meditation or the positive effects that simple calm, controlled breathing can do for the mind, body, and spirit. Below are some daily meditations and mudras that can help you in everyday life, as well as in combat. The pound fist storm tech is the ascended art of mastered will, founded by the spirit triangle, who found teachings of the art in a recovered Egyptian scroll.

The pound storm fist technique was later perfected by infinite spirit and faith, who were only able to hold the mudra lock for thirty seconds. Many masters of the art have only been able to last ten seconds before they are ripped apart. This art is much more than physical. It's a mental connection to the partner and the will of all. Some Spiritual masters can't even get past the first pound fist. As time went on, some spiritual master arose and showed simple mudras that advance combat ability in ethereal form, but those same masters could not perform combined elements while in the pound fist storm technique state. This is because you need both hands to physically combine the elements. Practice and breakthroughs can be found at the famous Champion City. Strong-willed elementals are encouraged to travel to Champion City and Spirit Forest to help the spiritual masters find new attacks and perfect this one further. Fuzion will help brave elementals who come see him at the Land of Lost Orb Souls.

It is said by the scions that Fuzion waits for the chosen who can stand in the storm.

Free Nazareth…by Faith

Meditations and mudras

"Well, I can't go talk to Fuzion. That violates the balance," said Dante as he went to his personal vault and grabbed a light orange and scarfed it down. Dante went back to his supercomputer and ejected the red chip and put it in his vault, and then he grabbed a new chip and inserted it into his supercomputer. "I need to send Elizabeth this message," said Dante.

Message 4RM: Dante

Elizabeth, everything is okay here. The army's number soared over a thousand. Wind Burn is my brother, just found out. He's cool. Tage got here a few days ago. He hasn't stopped working since. Send all the humans that want freedom from Dragon Lord to me. We will need their ascended powers. I learned a new technique that will have all of us free of Dragon Lord's reign of terror in no time. I just need to practice and get stronger. Tell Elisha I love her.

Do you know any female from my clan named Red?

—Dante, rise of the hellfire storm.

Dante thought, *What happened to big bro!* Dante recorded the message to the chip, ejected the chip, grabbed it, and ran to Wind Burn's room across the hall. *Knock, knock, knock.* No one answered, so Dante quietly cracked the door open and took a peek in his older brother's room.

Dante saw that Wind Burn's room was empty. The masked monk came out his room and said, "Grandson, you have awoken. Are you okay? We were so worried about you. If you didn't wake by tomorrow, we were going to take you to the world hospital."

"I'm fine, GP! It's late. Do you really need that mask? It's only us," said Dante.

"Yes, grandson," said Lou Shen as he took off his mask and hugged Dante.

"GP, where's Wind Burn?" asked Dante.

"He woke up as soon as we got here. When we found him, his amulet had this crazy shadow alchemy around him like a creepy tattoo. I guess it healed him fast. He's in Tage's room. They are having a double holo convo with Skyla and Crystal Flame," said Lou Shen.

"Oh, okay. I won't bother them then. I need something to eat and some fresh air. I'm gonna go sit on the big rock," said Dante.

"I'll have someone bring you something from the soldiers' kitchen, grandson," said Lou Shen as Dante walked off, suddenly depressed.

*****

Dante sat on the big rock with the information chip to Elizabeth in his hand and his thoughts to himself. *I know that was Karma's Dream. It has to be. How many other hellfire humans wonder around with fire spirits? Not many. This is crazy.*

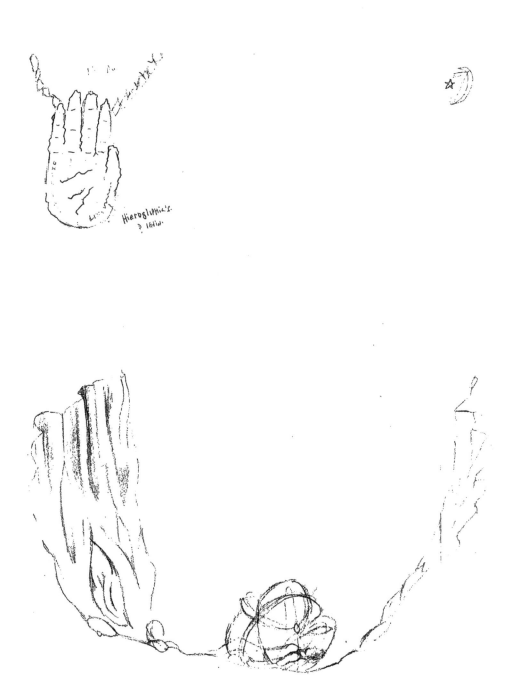

Hieroglithic's.
? Indin.

I'm really glad big bro is back. We were so in tune with each other back there. Just like always. Big bro just goes overboard sometimes. I don't understand why he lets his anger control him.

Dante looked up at the stars and thought, *I wonder what awaits me if I ascend. I'll do it right now… No, I won't. I can't. So many will be hurt and let down if I just… They depend on me so much, so much hope placed on my essence, choices, shoulders, and life. Darnit!*

What if Dragon Lord kills Wind Burn because of his short temper and obvious weakness? Big bro can't think straight when he gets angry. My heart will be ripped apart if I lose big bro to that monster. I'll never let it happen. I'm done losing loved ones to that evil person.

Red was very strong and highly knowledgeable about a lot of things. She used two or three mudras so fast they made her fire spirit bigger and tougher. I figure we were doing legendary damage to each other. I admire her strength and feminine energy. I wonder why she doesn't kill Dragon Lord. She must know something we don't.

So many thoughts on my mind, so much rain on my life. Mother, Father, I wish you were here to lead this rebellion as you intended to. I want to be with Elisha and watch my son grow.

Maybe I should go to Land Outlaw. It seems there's a lot of important people to meet, as well as things to learn. I wonder what the price is to learn an outlaw fighting style. Maybe I'll run into Red. Hey, that doesn't sound like such a bad idea.

General Smoke came out of the Hell Mountain main entrance with a plate of food and a glass of orange juice. When General Smoke got closer, Dante saw seasoned beef and potatoes with smoked onions and carrots, and two bread rolls on the side.

"Are you ready to eat, son?" said General Smoke as he walked over to Dante.

"I'm starved more than one of Dragon Lord's hostages," said Dante. General Smoke laughed and handed Dante the plate.

General Smoke said, "Wind Burn won't tell us what happened. He said a red-masked elemental knocked you and him out. We don't believe that story."

"Big bro left a lot of details out, but it's true. She was very strong, and she had the cutest laugh," said Dante between bites as he scarfed the food down.

"Slow down, son. Nobody's going to take your food," said General Smoke in a joking manner.

"Do you think there's a possibility that Karma's Dream could still be alive?" asked Dante.

"Yes…very small possibility. I mean where would she have been all of this time? Me, the front line, Static, and Cal came here after your father…you know. We haven't heard one word from her in all these years," said General Smoke.

"I'm going to find her," said Dante.

"Don't waste your time chasing ghost, son," said General Smoke.

"I have this information chip I need delivered to Elizabeth in 7-Nations. Can you send a pure earth elemental to 7-Nations, have him sneak in by elemental phase, and tell Elizabeth to meet whoever you send in the Earth Nation caves?" said Dante.

"I'll go myself. I'll take Wind Burn and a few hellfire drakes. We will use one of Tage's teleportation crystal spells. It will be a quick trip," said General Smoke. Dante nodded and then handed the info chip to General Smoke.

"Son, I know this is not the best time, but I thought the decision belonged to you on this matter," said General Smoke.

"What is it, General?" said Dante while looking in the sky.

"The force elemental Ki-claw, he…um… We have had him prisoner since you came here with him in Dragon Lord's stolen ship. Static and Cal took the video link to Dragon Lord's computer system out of Ki-claw's processor. It was life treating alchemy, but they managed. He's still bio-e, whatever you call it," said General Smoke.

"If he means no harm, let him go, or stay in Safe Haven City," said Dante.

"Very well, son, I'll leave you to your thoughts," said General Smoke as he put the info chip in his pocket, then grabbed the plate and went back into the mountain. Dante let the silence settle in. Then he drank the orange juice in three gulps and looked to the sky again.

After an hour of quiet and peace, Dante realized Red had used a hellfire power that Dante had never seen before. She called it *god hellfire orb*. *It must be an orb level 7 ascended power*, Dante thought. *If Red can do it, then so can he.* Dante stood up and then raised his hands to the sky and summoned great lashing fire from his core. Reality began to warp and bend around Dante as he powered up and released every bit of orb chi he had.

"Ahhh! Ascended god hellfire orb!" yelled Dante.

The hellfire energy around him rose in fiery beams and formed a fiery orb that grew and grew until it was colossal sized. When the god hellfire orb was done forming, it looked like a fiery death star and supergiant with mixed hues of yellow light.

"Ahhh!" yelled Dante as he threw the deadly energy into the sky, releasing his frustrations into the dark universe where it faded away.

★★★★★

Red fazed into existence on a red crystal plate in a lavish enormous base that was located deep in some mountains in 7-Nations south. Faze came out from behind a series of long supercomputers that were lined along the walls of this breathtaking base.

Faze reached to Red's side and said, "Karma, are you okay? Why are you bleeding?"

"I missed Orian, but I taught Dante and Wind Burn the pound fist storm technique, and get this—they held the mudra lock for like five minutes. They almost beat me. But they're too weak to face Dragon Lord, or even think about freeing Nazareth, so they need a boost from the keys. So this is what we are going to do. Call in a favor from the assassin lord Glacier. Ask them to let you buy a large supply of goods from them so they will have to buy from Dragon Lord to restock and feed their city. Hell Mountain's supplies will run out fast, thanks to Dante's little speeches and fire spirit shows. His growing army will drain his little accumulated currency. Then the Council will have to join the Hell Thieves on a petty thievery mission to survive," said Red as she took of her body suit, gloves, weapons, and custom heeled boots, leaving a trail behind her.

"But, Karma, the Council may steal the assassin lord's goods," said Faze as he walked behind Karma, picking up her bloody, beaten clothes and items.

"That's what I want. Then the rebellion will either go to war with trained assassins or Glacier will want the Council to find the keys," said Red.

"Lady Karma, you are such of a brilliant manipulator and a supreme master of puppets," said Faze.

"Yes, I know. Now prepare me a teleportation gate to land in Outlaw, Champion City. I need to tell infinite spirit about Dante and Wind Burn's pound fist breakthrough," said Red as she went to her room for a quick shower and change of a new red costume.

Glossary

abomination. Strong creatures of mixed mutated beings or energies that wander all over earth. Some abominations wander aimlessly through the wilderness, and some have their own personal gains in mind. Some abominations feed on elemental orbs and gain no orb level. And some abominations lead cities as civilized powerful lords.

Abomination Day. The day that Fuzion, the meteor shard, came to earth to elevate life (2030).

akashic: A collection of all past, present, and future events; records of all that have always been and all that ever will be; the collective consciousness of all.

alchemy. A lost science used to create or forge.

alchemy experiment. This is the result of an alchemic made to bind an elemental orb to any form of stability. These creatures are deadly in combat, but they fall short compared to an original elemental. This alchemic power and spell makes these beings crazy and evil, and they forget all memories of their past.

aura. An aura is the energy field around a person. Most elementals can send powerful energy into their aura to help them in combat. The power of your aura has a light color of the path a creature walks. Light path is yellow. Shadow path is black-and-gray flames. Neutral is shard energy.

creator's oil. An alchemic mix of enhanced vitamins and minerals that have been sprayed with nonlethal shard energy.

Death's hand. This elemental has unquestionable faith in the shadow path and will fight in the name of death no matter the cost.

elemental. Any creature with a power orb and elemental abilities.

elemental fairies. These beautiful creatures are created by large amounts of energy of one element. At some point in time, the gathered energy made contact with a meteor shard. This created many small pixie-like fairies. Elemental fairies are intelligent beings with childlike behavior. They need a host of a constant energy source of the element they are made of. This is why they stay in a natural element or in their host aura. Elemental fairies don't have orbs. They are simply concentrated conjurations of spirit and energy.

elemental code. A prideful elemental who lives by the code of battle and honor. This warrior loves to test his body and spirit to go past the limits of reality. This elemental knows that all battles cannot be won by power alone. The mind is also a valuable key. This elemental trains for one day he may have his chance to ascend.

essence. The pure will and ability that allow a creature to do and act. Elementals go above and beyond normal essence. This is simply a sign that, that elemental is on the path to ascension.

fifth element. Violet spirit energy, the vital life force of all living things.

Gaia. The collective consciousness of all life on earth. The earth mother.

god greed. When an elemental absorbs too many orbs that they are not supposed to, this violates the balance and is called god greed.

greater essence orbs. The first twenty-four orbs given to a select few. These orbs have great power because they awaken the twelve DNA strands of the creatures.

legendary damage. Regular life of an orb level 1 or 2 elemental would be seventy to one hundred LE. Life of a level 7 elemental could be a thousand to two thousand, maybe more.

legendary weapon. Power orb fused weapons created by alchemy.

liberators. A cult of neutral elementals whose sole purpose is to help land our law creatures escape Land Outlaw to Death's City. In most cases, these creatures want to find the twelve keys to free Nazareth.

life energy. Life energy is any creature's amount of life points. When an elemental has less than one-fourth its life energy from damage, that creature starts bleeding.

light-and-dark elixir. An alchemy spell that bound shadow and light together to be the perfect healing elixir.

light-and-dark war. The shadow path will fight the light when Death calls. In the chaos of this war, Death will try to kill Fate to gain control of the meteor shard.

light path. Creatures who follow the god of light.

meteor shard. Emerald and mixed hues of blueish light and dark energies that are compacted inside an astral diamond.

neutral path. Elementals who follow no god and practice the universal teachings or Nazareth. These teachings are mastery of self and ascension.

orb carrier. A cube made of quartz crystal that has alchemic writing drawn all over it. This cube is made to contain and hold power.

orb chi. The energy elemental has in its spirit to use powers of the elements it has absorbed. Orb chi color is always mostly the color of the elemental's primary orb. But orb chi also has small amounts of light dark or shard energy depending on that creature's chosen path.

orb foundation. An elemental must absorb their primary element before they can absorb other elements. This is a needed foundation of power so one's energy may be strong enough to bring other energies within.

orb guardian. These elementals walk the path of light. They are the warriors of Fate who use their powers to keep balance on earth and in the universe.

power orb. A power orb has all of an elemental's life energy and orb chi bound to spirit. Then these three energies are compacted into an orb of element. Through training, strong elementals can absorb other power orbs to reach the next level of power. Power orbs can be taken by Death or used as a last stand weapon. Elementals are born with a primary power orb. Regular creatures cannot absorb power orbs. Orbs are passed down through bloodline, and the male orb is always dominant.

prophecy of the chosen one. A vision foretold by the fourth scion: A human elemental of pure heart will surpass orb level 7 and have full control of all elements with the power of pure will. He will become an ascended elemental god, and he will not leave earth but teach all life how to ascend to the highest potential.

seeker orb. When an elemental is killed, as a last stand dying wish, that creature may send their orb to anyone they choose to. To use this ability, the dying elemental must sense the energy of the being they are trying to send their orb to.

shadow collectors: A cult of elementals on the shadow path who collect rare items and artifacts and save currency for Death's light-and-dark war.

shadow path. Creatures who follow the shadow gods.

Special Scouter Division. A collection of supercomputers that have the power to read power levels, orb levels, and essence of any elemental in the system's range.

"Summon your orb." An elemental can summon their orb into their palm. But if this orb is given away, that elemental dies.

twelve elemental keys. The twelve keys of the elemental gods that were used to imprison the shard energy god when he became overcome by god greed.

About the Author

Damian L. Johnson graduated from St. Phillips College but now attends South West Junior College. Damian is the author of several upcoming books such as the other six books of the *Elemental* series: *Project Cosmic Consciousness, Break the Chain (Urban),* and *Spirit Warriors.* Damian has a passion for writing and would love to write people who find joy in his books.

E-mail: damianljohnson25@gmail.com